Detective Jayne Moore
And The
Dangerous Game

Renée Perrault

Copyright © 2017 Renée Perrault

All rights reserved

No part of this publication may reproduced, stored in a retrieval system, or transmitted in any form or by any means, electronic, mechanical, photocopying, recording, scanning, or otherwise without signed permission from the author, except for the use of brief quotations for review purposes.

ISBN-10: 1545013799
ISBN-13: 978-1545013793

DEDICATION

This book is dedicated to my family and the friends that have become my family

Chapter 1

Being a cop can be challenging. Not the job, the dating pool. All the men I meet are either suspects or other cops, and believe me, I am not fishing off the company pier. I learned my lesson the hard way. So, never again. Too many female cops have caught their limit and became the brunt of a myriad of juvenile jokes. I refuse to become the next "Officer Tits" or "Officer Ass" unless it's "Officer Bad Ass."

Another issue. Why do I need to prove myself every single day? Nine years on the force and I've made some great busts. By the way, I'm sick of men looking at my boobs when I say, "great busts." Jeez, people, my eyes are up here. Two years ago I made Detective, so I just want to be known as Detective Jayne Moore, hardworking cop. Not a hardworking female cop, just cop. Oh, and forget about telling me any "dick" jokes. I've heard them all, courtesy of my fellow detectives who wanted to assure me they were big dicks. More like dickheads, which is another reason I don't date cops. That, and the fact the job is dangerous. And, in all honesty, I've already experienced one loss too many, and I'm not willing to go through it again.

So when my BFF calls me to go out for drinks, I reluctantly agree. Since my fiancé Matthew's death, Madison is making it her mission in life to push me back into the dating world. I'll never be over losing Matthew— it's been almost two years, and I'm still not ready. I'm too raw, and I'm still so angry. But, to appease Madison, I go home and change. We've been best friends since first grade, and she's not above ratting me out to my parents if I don't cooperate. She's been preaching that life goes on and Matthew would not want me to become a nun because of him.

I do want to be happy, but being happy is a lot harder than I thought and, frankly, too much work. The reality is, I'm too damaged to have a relationship. The thought of it sends me into a panic so intense, I can't breathe. I still have problems with PTSD from watching Matthew die. And that is a secret no one is going to learn, including my BFF.

Renée Perrault

***

Matthew and I met at the police academy. We were good friends, and after being on patrol for two years, we were recruited to join the bomb squad. Both of us would still be on patrol, but also on call for any situation that required a bomb tech. Training to be a tech is pretty intense. I got used to wearing a one hundred and twenty-five-pound bomb suit, and if you think your butt looks big in jeans, try a bomb suit. Something about that suit must have been a turn-on for Matthew because that's when it all started. At first, we joked that our relationship was "explosive," and since we both had "bombed" at prior relationships, we kept ours pretty hush-hush. Cops are prone to black humor; it deflects some of the sadness of the job, and keeps your feelings in check.

To say this relationship literally blew up would be entirely accurate. The sad thing is, Matthew wasn't even on a bomb-threat call. He was trying to diffuse a domestic situation. Neighbors called 911 with complaints of a loud fight going on next door. The husband had booby-trapped the house. When Matthew knocked at the door, the wife tried to open it, and a bomb went off. Matthew didn't stand a chance. The explosion sent the abusive husband straight to hell and blew a hole right through my heart.

So now, I'm still trying to pick up the pieces, no pun intended, and move on with my life. At the insistence of my BFF.

***

Madison always picks expensive, upscale venues for our girl's night out. Plus, she makes sure we dress up.

When I go out with the guys, we hit Delaney's, a well-known cop bar. Low key and the opposite of dressy, it's a place where most of the guys wear sweats after a long day on the job. Let's face it, for some of these guys, years in a patrol car and eating fast food have taken their toll. Sweats are the only thing that fit comfortably.

Not that I'm against them. If Madison hadn't begged for a girl's night, I would be home on my sofa in sweats with a cat on each side of me. Don't judge me, two cats does not make me a crazy cat lady. I'm a conscientious pet owner who works long hours and doesn't want my little Max to be lonely while I'm gone. He and his sister, Sofia, keep each other amused. With an auto-feeder and a litter box, I swear some days they don't care if I come home or not.

Like I said, it has been a long day, but then, they all are. I hurry home to change for my evening out with Madison. I pull my long blonde hair out of the tight bun I wear at work. I'm feeling very girlie, as I make up my eyes, and give myself a spritz of perfume. My little black dress is fire engine red, and if I can be a little vain, the spandex does some nice things for my curves. Rule one, you never want to put your little black dress on at the cop shop--the guys would razz me about it for days. Rule two, I never tell a man what I do for a living. It adds too many weird dynamics, and then they want me to tell "cop stories," which leads into some of the pain I'm trying to put behind me. I tell them I'm a librarian, and they never ask any questions.

I pick out a beaded evening purse from my closet and transfer my Glock 19--my other BFF--into it.

Walking into the Four Seasons, I automatically scan the lobby--cop habits are always in play, on duty or off. It appears some sort of computer gaming function is in progress. A large easel is outside one of the ballroom doors, displaying an agenda with speakers' names. The lobby is crowded, and I note that the people milling about look like gamers--various shapes and sizes, lots of facial hair on the men, and oh, make that a few of the women, too. Most of them are wearing sweats or the unisex uniform of jeans and T-shirts. Looks like this group doesn't need to dress for success.

The large expanse of marble floor is magnifying the voices, and the cacophony of sounds is setting my nerves on edge. I take a deep breath and shove the anxiety down deep inside where all of my secrets ferment.

One of my residual problems from the night Matthew was killed is loud noises. When I was forced to see the department shrink, he said it would not be uncommon for me to have some anxiety. I told him I was fine, but I did listen to his babble about how to "center" myself if it occurred. I take a deep breath and focus on each step as I make my way through the maze of people.

When I finally reach the cocktail lounge, I spot Madison at a table in the corner. Two men are sitting with her, and when I realize who they are, I groan. Michael Baker, a teacher at Madison's school, and his BFF, Sean Lindstrom. It looks like their butts are glued to the chairs and we're "stuck" with them. Michael has been trying to get close to Madison for months and has no qualms about inviting himself along. His friend Sean is a used-car salesman, and other than dressing normal, the rest of him is pure sleaze. He once asked if he could take me on a test drive and if I would recite the Dewey Decimal System, naked, in the backseat. As Jimmy Fallon would say, "Ewwww." I struggle to put a neutral look on my face.

As I approach the table, Madison stands up to give me a hug, a wide smile on her pretty face. We're both thirty-one, only somehow, Madison discovered the fountain of youth. She barely looks old enough to be in a cocktail lounge. It must be one of the benefits of not having a high-stress job with people shooting at you. Maybe I should become a pre-school teacher. As long as they still let me carry a gun--kids can be dangerous.

I whisper, "Why are they here?"

She gives me an extra squeeze and answers, "I thought it might be fun. You need to jump back into the dating pool."

Drowning sounds like a better choice than swimming in the dating pool with Michael or Sean. I can't believe she blindsided me like this. Madison gives me a slightly pathetic, I'm sorry look and shrugs her shoulders. I sigh and say hello to the two morons.

Sean is the first to speak. "Jayne, you're looking stunning as usual." His hazel eyes give me a slow once-over. "How's the library business?" The last bit was said with a smug little smile.

I ignore him to snag the first waiter I see and request a double Scotch.

The waiter must have sensed my mood and is quick to return with my Scotch. I sip on my drink and stare as Michael tries to charm Madison. It looks like she is buying it. She does several hair tosses. Her shoulder-length black hair bounces as she laughs at his lame attempts at humor. I can see amusement on her face when she looks over and sees Sean trying to talk to me.

I'm not sure what always sets me off about Sean. We've been thrown together three or four times, and other than some lame sexual innuendos, he's pretty quiet. His eyes constantly rove around the room like he's looking for prey. I don't trust him. I can't stand the smug, "I know something you don't know" look that takes over his face.

It's such a waste. He's not hard on the eyes; the man has some serious stuff going on. He's at least six foot four; his brown hair looks curly but is cut short, and his big square jaw is clean shaven. The whole package is appealing until he opens his mouth. If all of a sudden, he was struck mute, I could totally go for him but only for a quick one-night-stand-hot-sex kind of way. I am definitely not looking for more. And actually, after almost two years of celibacy, I can't decide if it would be worth the trouble.

I sneak a look at the time on my cell phone. Good God, has it only been thirty minutes? I pick up my drink and long to shoot it down. I figure I'll stick around for one drink and then make my escape to the comfort of my sofa and cats. I ignore Sean and check out the people in the lounge. Lots of women in skimpy little dresses and men in suits. Pretty much what's expected in the stately old hotel bar.

Cop eyes in play, I notice two men are sitting on the same side of the table, their backs against the wall. Their eyes dart around nervously, and then they check their watches. They're both wearing long coats on a warm summer evening.

Oh, damn, something's about to go down. The little hairs on my arms are tingly, and my female Spidey senses are going on full alert. I unzip my purse, and as I reach for my Glock, both men jump up and start firing automatic weapons. Damn. There goes my night.

I tell Madison and the men to duck for cover and pull my weapon out.

Chapter 2

Sean Lindstrom was starting to enjoy himself as Jayne squirmed under his steady gaze. Her distaste for him was obvious, and it amused him. He looked her over again. She was tall and lean and clearly in shape. Not an ounce of fat on her spectacular body and some nice curves in the right places. Her pale blue eyes were constantly in motion as she surveyed the room.

She kept looking back at a table with two men. At first, he was a little put off by her inattention, but something caught his eye when he looked over at them. He tried to peg their nationality--dark hair and eyes, and both were slightly built. He figured they were maybe Pakistani. Then he took in their long coats.

Sean glanced back at Jayne and saw her eyes narrow as she focused on the men. He was on full alert, as she pulled a gun from her purse when the two men jumped up and exposed the automatic weapons from under their coats.

Sean knew that automatic rifles have the capacity to fire thirty rounds in two point five seconds and only had time to think, "Oh, Christ, I hope she's a cop and not some crazy vigilante." He pulled out his Luger, pushed their table over for cover, and crouched down beside her. The two men fired bullets randomly into the crowd. White tablecloths quickly turned red and screams bounced off the oak-paneled walls as bullets ripped through the room.

"I'm FBI," Sean says.

"I'm a cop."

"Take the one on the left. I'll go right."

The perps paused for a moment and then aimed their guns at two waiters when Jayne and Sean both yelled. "Police - FBI. Drop your weapons."

Sean swore under his breath as the men turned their weapons on him and Jayne. He prayed she was a capable cop as he squeezed his 9mm Luger, hitting the guy on the right, bulls-eye to the heart, at the same time as Jayne's shot took out the guy on the left with a headshot.

Sean heard shots fired behind them, coming from the lobby area. Before he could react, Jayne yelled out to Madison to call 911, then she turned and ran out of the bar. He had no idea what she would be facing and silently cursed her for abandoning him at the scene. He jumped up on a table and yelled for everyone to stop talking. "People, I'm Special Agent Sean Lindstrom, FBI. I need to assist the officer who was here. This is former Marine Sargent Michael Baker, I'm putting him in charge. Under no circumstances is anyone to leave this room." Patrons huddled together, and some of the women were crying. Sean didn't have time to give any comfort.

Sean leaned over to Michael and told him to have Madison try and see about the injured and to do what she could to help.

"Michael, just stand at the door and hope the cops get here before the crowd decides to bolt."

Sean knew that at six foot five, and a muscled two hundred and forty pounds, the former Marine shouldn't have any challengers. At least he hoped not as he ran from the room to back up Jayne.

Chapter 3

I run toward where I assume the shots came from. I pause behind one of the large marble pillars that define the sitting area four steps above the lobby. Sofas and easy chairs are artfully placed in the area. An ornate coffee table in the center displays current newspapers and magazines. The large pillars give me an opportunity to look, undetected, down at the lobby. The doors to the auditorium are closed. I see two people crouched behind the large check-in desk, and a young man, one of the tee-shirt crowd, lying on the marble floor. I can see he is going into shock, his body is shaking violently and blood is puddling around him.

I stealthily make my way to him, kneel down, and whisper. "It's okay. I'm a cop. Did you see where the shooters went?"

"Pl-pl-please get me out of here. I was coming out for a quick vape break. They shot me as they ran into the auditorium."

I have no time to think about other shooters--I only know this kid can't lie here and bleed to death. The check-in desk is about twenty feet away, and the thick oak counter offers some protection. "I need to move you." I groan inwardly. He looks like a typical gamer, and by gamer, I mean couch potato. He must outweigh me by sixty pounds.

The young man stares at me and nods his head. At five foot eleven, I'm taller than a lot of the cops I work with, plus demanding physical standards keep me in shape, but this will still take a herculean effort. I half carry, half drag him to the backside of the counter where a male and female employee are huddled down. I lie him down and start looking for something to stanch the bleeding. The two clerks are wide-eyed with fear.

"I'm a cop. Call 911. Tell them shots fired, officer needs assistance, and to send multiple ambulances." They stare at me, unmoving. I grab the closest one and force him to look at me. I glance at his name tag and try again. My voice is urgent, but I'm trying to speak calmly. "David. Do you understand what I said?"

He slowly nods as I tell him again. "Do it now."

With shaking hands, he pulls out his cell phone and dials.

I turn to the other clerk. Her name tag identifies her as Mary Ellen. She seems to be in better shape than David. "Mary Ellen. Tell me what you witnessed."

Tears leak from her eyes as she responds. "Five men rushed the door, all dressed in black. They didn't even look our way. They carried big guns. You know, like the kind bad guys shoot in the movies. As they ran into the ballroom, I heard shots fired, and they shot this guy as he came out the door. We were so scared, we didn't know what to do."

My mind is racing. "I saw a gaming convention when I walked in earlier. Is that the group inside the auditorium?"

The girl pauses, and I can tell, despite the trauma of the last few minutes, she is trying to control her fear.

She finally replies. "Yes. It's a gaming convention. It's for people who want to make millions with their game or new app. The keynote speaker is Brian Edison. He was in the news about six months ago. He went from fast food worker to like a billionaire when his gaming company went public." She paused and her face lit up. "Wait. The agenda is on my I-Pad." Before I can stop her, she jumps up and reaches for her device. Her fingers fly across the screen. "Here it is. If they are on schedule, Brian Edison started speaking about ten minutes ago."

I pull out my cell phone and autodial my boss, Lieutenant Johns. "LT this is Moore. I'm at the Four Seasons. Shots have been fired, and a witness says there are five armed suspects in the auditorium, with approximately three hundred civilians. Two other suspects in the cocktail lounge have been neutralized, and we have an unknown number of people injured with GSWs. I'm not sure what's going on inside the ballroom. My best guess is a hostage situation. I'm looking at the itinerary. The keynote speaker, Brian Edison, is reported to be a billionaire. According to this, he would have been on stage doing his presentation when all hell broke loose."

I can hear my boss draw in a deep breath. "Okay, Moore, if it's a hostage situation, sounds like the Feds will be nosing in on this one. Stay low and keep your eyes open. I'll advise first responders that you're on the premises and armed."

Just as I hang up, Sean rushes in and crouches down next to me behind the counter.

"Damn it, you left me there to secure the scene and took off without backup. What's the status here?"

I look at him and recite the known information. "FBI and SWAT are on their way. My orders are to lay low until they arrive."

Sean frowns. I can tell he's trying to formulate a plan. His face looks as hard as a winter in Siberia. "Jayne, we need to be ready. If it's a kidnapping, they're going to try and get out of here quickly."

I turn to the check-in clerk. "Mary Ellen. How many exits in the ballroom?"

"There are six doors at the rear that open up into the lobby. There is a door on either side of the stage that leads to the back hall and into the kitchen."

Sean pulls up the floor plan on his phone. Handy. He studies it for a moment, types a quick note, and sends it with the floor plan attached.

"What's your plan, Sean?"

"I sent my team a text to cover the back alley. They will come through the kitchen and be ready at the two rear exits of the ballroom. I believe the suspects are going out the back exits because they're closer to the stage. If they grabbed Edison while he was on stage, it makes sense for them to take the shortest route. I'm going to circle around and hit the back exit. You stay here and wait for SWAT to arrive."

I raise an eyebrow and give him "the look." I don't like being sidelined. I start to protest, but I'm distracted by a van pulling up to the front doors. Before I can point it out to Sean, the ballroom doors burst open. We both jump up from behind the counter as two men drag a bound-and-gagged man, who I assume is Edison, through the lobby heading toward the entry. I have just enough time to say, "Sean, same as before."

We both yell, "Police, FBI. Drop your weapons."

The men push Edison to the floor and turn their guns on us. I line up my shot for the guy on the left. My shot hit as before, middle of the forehead, and I see the suspect fall backward from the impact.

Sean nails the guy on the right with his signature bullet to the heart. Looks like we're both creatures of habit. Brian Edison is still dazed as we grab him and haul him behind the counter.

There are no signs of injury to the man I assume is Edison. I start working on untying his restraints and getting the gag off him, but first I need to confirm his identity. "Are you Brian Edison?"

He nods.

"Hang in there, Mr. Edison. I'm Detective Moore, SPD, and this is Special Agent Lindstrom, FBI. We're not out of the woods yet." I turn to Sean, "The van out there is the getaway vehicle, and there are still three guys in the ballroom. Pick your battle."

"We can't go in with guns blazing. There are three hundred innocent people in the line of fire. My bet is they try and exit through the back to a second vehicle. That leaves the getaway vehicle for Edison and his party of two. Want to play dumb blonde and saunter out there?"

My head spins around, and green pea soup, ala Linda Blair in the *Exorcist,* almost shoots out of my mouth. "Are you kidding me? Even the dumbest blonde on earth isn't deaf. Shots have been fired." As I fume, I realize there is some logic to his plan and concede. "Surprise is always a factor."

I jump up and run toward the doors. From our vantage point behind the lobby desk, the view of the van was clear, but their view in is partially obstructed. I run toward the van, holding my gun behind my back, and scream like a girl. The passenger window is rolled down, and the two men are arguing. Criminals never cease to amaze me--now would be the time for them to be paying attention. Maybe they forgot their ADHD meds this morning. I stop the girl scream, reach into the window, grab the passenger by the ear, and put the muzzle of my gun to his head.

"Waiting for someone?" Out of the corner of my eye, I see Sean heading to the driver's side.

His dark eyes widen, and then he tries to grab his gun.

"Go ahead, try it. I broke a nail when I shot your buddies and now I'm in a rotten mood. I'm ready to shoot someone. Only fair, since I ruined my manicure."

Apparently, this guy doesn't have a sense of humor. Just as

I'm ready to yank him through the open window, blaring sirens announce the arrival of backup. Seconds later a deep voice on the other side yells, "Put your hands up and come out of the vehicle."

I open the car door, pull the suspect out, and throw him to the ground. As I wrestle one of his hands behind his back, my short little dress hikes up, but I don't have time to worry about it. A uniform rushes up and hands me his cuffs.

"Jeez, Moore, you sure live up to your name...as in showing more."

I give him a look. "Dobson put this guy in a car, and take him and his partner away. We need someone to process this van."

Dobson nods his head back toward the flashing lights. "Moore, the Feds, and our people are screaming out orders. But I'll do what you asked because none of them are wearing a tight dress hiked up far enough for vice to bust you." His eyes lock onto my personal region.

I look down and tug at my dress. "Dobson, my eyes are up here." Jeez, I get tired of saying that.

As I hand the suspect off to Dobson, Brian Edison is being led out by two FBI agents.

I turn to go back inside to check on Madison.

"Wait. Officer Moore. I want to thank you." Brian Edison's voice sounds urgent, and I turn back.

"I saw some of what you did tonight, and these agents filled me in on the rest. I'm very grateful you happened to be here when this all went down." He stops and gives me an appraising look from head to foot. "Looks like this little fiasco interrupted your evening out. Maybe I can make it up to you sometime?"

I'm caught a little off guard. I don't get a lot of people saying thank you for doing my job and hitting on me at the same time. I finally manage to stammer out, "It's Detective, and really, no thanks are necessary, it's all part of the job. If you'll excuse me, I need to check on my friends."

I could feel the heat rising to my face. It's times like this I hate being fair skinned. If I was ready to date anyone, Brian Edison's deep-set gray eyes and the movie star cleft in his chin could give my heart a jump start. His face reminds me of someone but the thought is totally derailed when I think about the adorable dimple Matthew had in the middle of his chin.

Chapter 4

Six hours later I'm sitting on my sofa in my "Hello Kitty" nightshirt with Max and Sofia. I suppose it is a little crazy cat ladyish. Madison gave me the nightshirt for my birthday as a joke. It fits more like a long t-shirt than a nightgown. I think it was made for a pre-teen girl, but whatever, I like it. It's bright pink, and the flannel is soft. After the episode tonight, I need some comfort, which is why I have a pint-sized Ben and Jerry's ice cream clutched in my hand like a lifeline thrown to a drowning woman. I'm relieved to see my hands aren't shaking as I shovel ice cream into my mouth. Progress.

The aftermath at the hotel was horrendous. Twenty people were shot in the attack in the bar. Three were in critical condition, four died at the scene, and two more on the way to the hospital. The rest were treated and released. Tears flow down my cheeks as I think of the slain couple on their honeymoon and an elderly couple celebrating their sixtieth wedding anniversary. Senseless killings like this make me want to go live in a cave, far away from the crazies.

It seemed like hundreds of cops and techs had descended on the scene. In reality, it was probably only about fifty. Most of them were interviewing the people attending the conference with Brian Edison. The uninjured people in the bar were interviewed and released pretty quickly. Among them, Madison and Michael, who, I believe, are going to comfort each other in private. Ewwww. Sean, like me, had to stay and be interviewed by Internal Affairs. Their job is to determine if the shootings in the bar, and lobby, were justified. The witnesses all backed up our story, but I'm on leave with pay until their official report.

Just as I finish off the last of the ice cream, I hear a knock at my front door. The thing about cats--they are lousy at letting you know someone is coming. I jump up, grab my weapon, and walk over to the door. A quick look out the peephole--I spot Sean on my porch. He looks exhausted, and I feel a smidgen of pity for him. I jerk the door open, not bothering to put my weapon back.

"What are you doing here?" I don't have to ask how he knew where I live. Damn FBI.

Sean looks at my hello kitty shirt and smirks. "Can't sleep and I figure you might be a little wired, too? I've been an agent for ten years. Whenever I fire in the line of duty, it takes a while for my adrenaline to settle down."

His admission shocks me. Not quite the macho a-hole he'd been before. "Yeah, I get it. But I'm fine. Shooting perps who are trying to kill innocent people won't have me losing any sleep." Now if I can just convince my subconscious.

"Then why are you still up at three in the morning eating ice cream?"

"How'd you know I was eating ice cream?"

"You have an ice cream mustache, right here." He leans over and brushes his thumb over the top of my lip.

My reaction to him surprises me. I feel a stirring deep inside and jerk away from him like I've been burned. Definitely not a guy I want to get involved with.

"So, can I come in?"

His question catches me off guard, and I stand to one side to let him in. As he brushes by me, I smell the fresh scent of soap. I showered too, just getting the smell of death off me helps to improve my mental state.

I walk behind him. "Sit down, I have another pint in the freezer." Instead of taking one of the two overstuffed chairs, he sits in the middle of the sofa. Of course, he's being a macho jerk and invading my space. I grab the ice cream and a spoon and go back into my living room.

Just as I am ready to sit in one of the chairs, I remember the night shirt barely covers my butt.

"I'll be right back."

I quickly grab a pair of yoga pants from my dirty clothes pile and put them on. As I walk back into my living room, I catch Sean gazing at nothing with a spoonful of ice cream halfway to his mouth. Okay, maybe this guy isn't quite the macho jerk I think he is.

I sit down in my overstuffed lounge chair and notice Sean checking out my yoga pants.

"I kind of liked what you were wearing before. What's wrong, Moore, are you nervous around me?"

Okay, still a jerk. "A man I don't know very well knocks on my door at three in the morning. It's not a booty call, so you don't need to see that much of me. A girl has to have a few secrets."

"Like being a cop?"

Darn. He has me there. "Since you're on the job, you know what it's like when people hear what you do. Probably not so bad for you, but a female cop tends to intimidate potential dates."

Sean smiles at me in a leering way. "So I was a potential date? That's why you said you were a librarian?"

Yeah, I think...until you opened your mouth. "It's just easier when I meet new people. And no, you were not a potential date. Who in their right mind would date someone like you?"

"Jeez, Jayne. I'm not so bad. I needed to maintain my cover. You should get to know the real me."

Before he has a chance to elaborate on all his virtues, both of our cell phones ring. I grab mine off the coffee table as Sean pulls his out. I glance down; the number is my Lieutenant.

I answer, "Moore,"

"Moore, we have a situation. Edison just received a death threat that references his narrow escape last night. The note also said there will be retribution for the deaths of their comrades. We're putting together a protection team. Edison requests, no, demands, that you be on it."

"Doesn't Internal Affairs have to clear me before I can come back to work?"

"Yeah, well, scratch that. This Edison guy has enough pull with the mayor that IA was rousted out of bed. You are cleared for duty. The deaths of the four perps were deemed necessary to save the civilians in the area."

"Yes, sir." I am scribbling furiously as Lieutenant Johns gives me the details. He makes one point perfectly clear: my life is on hold until this is solved. I'll be living with Edison until the threat is neutralized.

"Oh, and one more thing, Moore. The hotshot FBI guy Sean Lindstrom is also part of the team. We're trying to play nice with the

Feds."

Damn.

"Yes, sir. Anything else?"

"Stop by my office before you head to Edison's."

The phone line goes dead. I glance over at Sean. By the look on his face, I think he is getting the same piece of news. I rush into my bedroom and start pulling clothes off the hangers. I am packed, changed, and ready to go in eight minutes.

My neighbors, Ice and Sheri, have a key to my place. I'll text them later to look after the cats. Sean hangs up as I walk out of my bedroom. By the way he slams his phone back into the holder, I can tell the conversation hadn't gone well.

I raise my eyebrows and ask, "Problems?"

"I'm not a goddamned babysitter." His voice is controlled, but his anger is evident.

"What, and you think I am? I'm in the middle of a couple big cases, and now I'm pulled off to hold some billionaire's hand? It pisses me off, but that's why they call it a job. Don't know about you Feds, but cops do as we're told. I'm out of here, and so are you. See you at Edison's."

I push him out the door and lock up. I am damn mad, and my lieutenant will hear about it later. For now, I need to follow orders.

Chapter 5

Sean Lindstrom lived and breathed the FBI. Recruited after his second tour in Iraq, he spent ten years proving he was a resourceful, reliable agent. While excelling in his career, his personal life, other than his immediate family, was nonexistent. Sean had become the man of the family at age ten when his dad deserted him and his three little sisters. Ironically, his fierce love of family, and a desire for one of his own are what ended up breaking his heart eight years ago.

After his ex-girlfriend had screwed him physically, emotionally, and financially, he gave up on relationships. A one-night stand here and there was about all he wanted. That had worked for him until he had become intrigued by the tall lady librarian.

He seldom had regrets for any of his choices, but he kicked himself for adopting the "sleazy car salesman" persona in front of Jayne and her friend. He had done it spur of the moment when Michael introduced him to Madison and Jayne. At the time, he thought it would be funny to tease the preschool teacher and the librarian. He'd enjoyed watching Jayne's look of absolute disgust whenever he opened his mouth.

From the moment they'd met, her eyes had intrigued him. The aqua color reminded him of a tropical ocean, and they were always in motion. She would appraise an entire room, measuring the people and looking for the exits. He knew what she was doing because he did the exact same thing. He suspected the tall lean librarian was lying. He figured her for a cop, a crook, or a hooker. Every time he aggravated her, she glanced at her purse. He laughed inwardly, reading her mind that only a bullet would shut him up.

Seeing her in action was impressive. She never faltered and efficiently did what needed to be done. They worked well together, with a natural intuition of each other's moves. His attraction to her surprised him. It had been a long time since he had actually been more than sexually attracted to a woman. Jayne interested him, and he wanted to learn more about her.

Frustrated, he used his Bluetooth and dialed Michael. If he had to be up then, tough, Michael could wake up and talk to him.

"What the hell?" a groggy Michael asked. "Sean, why are you calling me at three-thirty in the morning?"

"The threat situation escalated. I'm going to be babysitting the billionaire who was the kidnapper's target."

"And you're waking me up to tell me this, why?"

"Because I'm guarding him with Madison's friend, Jayne. You know, the 'librarian.' Jeez, Mike, didn't I teach you how to gather intel better than this in Iraq? For God's sake, the woman now hates me. I need you to worm information out of Madison. Damn. I should have done a background check on her the first time we met."

A loud laugh answered his demand. "Looks like someone's got it bad for a woman you have no chance in hell with. Isn't a background check illegal without probable cause?"

"Yeah. Maybe being smoking hot is cause enough. Did you see the way she took down the shooter in the lounge? And you should have seen her in the lobby. Come on, buddy, help me out. Pump Madison and keep me posted."

Michael yawned. "No promises. You were an asshole to her. Even Madison was put off by your act. And right now, you sound like a thirteen-year-old girl with a big crush. Besides, Madison has told me more than once that Jayne refuses to date. I don't know the whole story, but her fiancé died and she hasn't dated since."

"Try to find out more. It's not like I want to marry the woman. I just want a couple dates. You know me…I don't do relationships."

Michael paused before he spoke. "Come on, Sean. It's been eight years since that bitch ripped you up. The baby wasn't even yours. You have to let it go."

"Buddy, you're starting to sound like my mom. I'm over it. I just don't need any complications. My job doesn't exactly make it easy to have a relationship. I'm just looking to spend a little horizontal time with the librarian." Sean winced as he said the lie. After everything went down, he had looked into her eyes and seen the pain. The same pain he saw in the mirror every day. He wanted to know what made Jayne Moore tick.

"Yeah, buddy. You just keep telling yourself that. I think you're finally starting to shed the big chip on your shoulder you have about women." Michael laughed, and before he hung up, added, "Hey, it's time to man up and move on. Stop being a jerk to her, and see how that works for you." Followed by more laughter.

    Sean wasn't laughing.

Chapter 6

I make a mental list of everything I need to do before I head to Edison's. I have notes on my current cases from yesterday and need to bring my partner up to speed. The clock on my dashboard shows four in the morning. My guilt button doesn't even tingle as I call his cell. Tom Kruze is not a morning person.

"For God's sake, Boomer, what's put your panties in a twist to wake me from my much-needed beauty sleep?" A yawn creeps through Tom's end of the phone. "So, what's up?"

Cops are notorious for nicknames. I became "Boom Boom" when I joined the bomb squad. They used to say, "Va Va Va Boom Boom," a cross between being sexist and funny, and also a mouthful. Nicknames come with the job, so I'm thankful that it morphed into Boomer and they dropped the Va Va Va Boom Boom part. My friend and mentor, Diane Davis, has been a cop for over twenty-five years. When she made detective, she became Dickless Tracey or DL for short. Some things aren't worth the energy to fight. Besides, getting cops to stop with nicknames is a losing battle.

"Someone tried to kidnap a local billionaire. I was out with Madison and got caught up in the middle of it. Now, I'm supposed to babysit the billionaire until SPD and the FBI get it resolved."

I hear Tom expel a breath in frustration. "Well damn. The timing couldn't be worse. We're right in the middle of a case."

I walk Tom through my notes from yesterday. Five days ago, we were assigned a murder case that appeared to be pretty cut and dried. The wife shot her husband four times in the chest. She claimed he'd abused her for years; however, the evidence didn't add up.

"I'm leaving all my notes on your desk. Call me if you have any questions. And keep me in the loop on this one. When women kill their husbands and try and use the get-out-of-jail-free card by claiming abuse, it really makes it hard for the women that are honestly being abused. It ticks me off."

"I know. You're right. The wife almost pulled me in with her act.

Glad you caught on and dug into her story." Tom yawns again, and I almost feel guilty for interrupting his sleep.

Tom's a straight shooter. I did a little internal happy dance when I was assigned as his partner. He's one of the few who recognize I'm not a minority quota fill but actually a good cop. Detective Tom Kruze is a solid guy. He and Lily have been married for ten years. Their three adorable little girls consider me their Auntie Jayne, and his wife and I are good friends as well. With four females and no males in his household, Tom has learned the secret of patience. In an interrogation room, he has a knack for cajoling suspects into spilling secrets like a dam opening for irrigation. I'm just lucky he hasn't zeroed in on mine.

His only downfall is his unconditional love of all things sports. When I told him my neighbor is a sports writer, he insisted on meeting him. Imagine his surprise when the "him" turned out to be Sheri McLellon, superstar sports reporter for *The Seattle Times*. From that moment on, Tom would bug me to invite him and Lily over to dinner, and invite Sheri and her fiancé, Jeffery "Ice" Zamboni. We've got a nice little five-some going now.

"I can't believe I got stuck with this." My voice still sounds a tad whiny.

"So you're going to be cozying up to a billionaire. Tough duty, Boomer."

"Yeah, think about how hard it will be keeping my mind on my work while I'm sitting in the lap of luxury. Oh, and did I forget to mention that I share the duty with an FBI agent who is about as sleazy as they come?"

"Sounds like someone is being a bit judgmental."

"If you ever meet Agent Lindstrom, you'll agree." I can't seem to keep the peevishness out of my voice.

"Jayne, are you talking about Sean Lindstrom?"

I swallow back a smart-ass reply. This good old boys network is too damn big. "You know him? Lindstrom is kind of a common name."

"Jesus. Must be the same guy. Six-four, brown hair, and what my wife would call 'hot.' We served together in Iraq, and all he talked about was joining the FBI when he got out. They recruited him before the ink dried on his discharge papers. Jayne, sorry you got off to a bad start with him, but he's a guy who will watch your back. I'd want him on my team."

I almost whine. "He's really slimy. When I met him, he told me he was a used-car salesman, and he acted like a jerk."

No one wants to listen to a grown man giggling.

"Moore. Did you tell that stupid librarian story again? He's sharp. He probably saw right through you."

Damn. Lily and I had too many margaritas one night, and I told her I never tell a man I'm a cop. When I told her my librarian story, she almost peed her pants she laughed so hard. Tom came in, and she broke the girl code of keeping secrets and told him. Then, I had to listen to both of them giggle like maniacs. I should have been offended, but they're so darn cute together, they make it impossible to be mad.

"Okay. So you served with him, and he's a good guy. He's still a jerk in my book." My voice doesn't sound as convincing as I want it to be. Damn. Sean Lindstrom is getting to me.

"Jayne, you don't need to like the guy. Just know he's got your back."

I have to admit, the guy had already proved that tactically--he's well trained. "Fine."

That gets a big belly laugh out of him. I wonder how he can be so chipper this early in the morning.

"I've been married long enough to know what 'fine' means. Keep me posted. And, be sure and tell Sean you're my partner. That ought to save you a little bit of grief."

With that parting comment, Tom hangs up on me. Well, fine. I continue my drive into the station. Parking my car at the loading dock, I walk through the back door, straight to the Ammo room to pick out some special accessories. I like to be prepared. After sweet-talking the officer in charge, and filling out a requisition form in triplicate, I take two armloads of gear back to my car. Then, I get the distinct displeasure of warming Lieutenant Johns' guest chair and getting briefed.

Lack of sleep makes me a whiner. "LT., I still don't understand why I'm stuck with this assignment. My caseload is full, and now I'm leaving my partner in the lurch."

"Taken care of. Listen, Moore, you don't need to understand why you're doing this. Edison is very connected, and this is coming from the mayor's office. Do what you always do, follow orders, and make my life easy."

"Yes, sir." I should learn to quit when I'm ahead. "Why does the FBI have to be in on this?"

"Gee, Moore. Let me think for a moment and explain this in a way you'll understand. Oh, yeah, the attempted kidnapping of a billionaire. We're not the only branch of law enforcement that frowns at that sort of thing. The Feds are wearing big frowny faces. Especially since it went down on their watch. And their frowny faces are more powerful than ours. In fact, you're lucky we're in this at all. Not often that the Feds play with the locals." He stares at me for a moment. "We're sending you in as the liaison between us and the FBI. You'll partner up with…" He stops and looks at his notes. "Special Agent Sean Lindstrom. You'll both be actively working the case with our task force as well as pacifying Edison. Got it?"

He doesn't wait for an answer as he wraps up our meeting "Now get the hell out of here. Edison is refusing to leave his house. Claims it is more secure there than any place else will be. Apparently, our new little billionaire lives in a gated community."

"Yes, sir." I'm relieved my voice isn't whiny. I leave his office and check out the billionaire's address. He lives in a neighborhood called Broadmoor. It's about as secure as a wet Band-Aid. What is the brass thinking letting this guy dictate where he'll be safe? This puts all of the cops watching him at risk. Got to love the good old boys, lots of back scratching going on, and all I'm getting is a pain in my ass.

***

I drive the four miles to Broadmoor. The rent-a-cop stops me at the gate. No gun on his hip, which is comforting based on how much his hands shake. The guy must be eighty, and the thick glasses do nothing to add to my comfort level.

"I'm Detective Moore, here to see Brian Edison."

"Let me check the list." He proceeds to painstakingly go down a long list of names.

It is now five-thirty in the morning. Operating on zero sleep does nothing for my patience or my mood. I think about pulling out my Glock and blasting a hole through his damn list. As I hold an internal debate, a car behind me honks.

"Miss, I need you to pull over, you're blocking our residents." The old guard's voice sounds as whiny as mine had been earlier.

"First of all, it is Detective Moore, not 'Miss.' I'm not pulling over. You can call Edison's house to verify or I can drive my car right through your little gate. Your choice. You have five seconds to decide."

The look on his face is priceless. His chest starts to swell, and he looks like he is going to make the mistake of trying to tell me what to do again. Instead, he opens his mouth and says sternly, "You know, young lady, you need to show a little respect. I was a cop before you were even a glimmer in your parents' eyes."

I stop myself from saying he was a cop before my grandparents had a glimmer in their eyes. This dude is so old, he probably has been retired longer than he had been a cop. Before I can reply, a car door opens behind me. I turn to see who is approaching, and a voice, smooth as oil, calls out.

"Is there a problem? I'm Special Agent Sean Lindstrom, FBI, and I need to get in."

When he hears Lindstrom's voice, he jumps to attention like a car battery has been attached to his ass.

"Yes, sir. Let me get this car out of the way. I'm still trying to reach Mr. Edison to verify she's on a list. A lot of women show up trying to meet Mr. Edison."

That's it. I jump out of my car and pick up the gold detective's badge hanging from around my neck and shove it in his face. "What the hell does this look like? You think because I'm a female I'm here for an early morning booty call? And this guy..." I gesture toward Lindstrom, "Gets to waltz right in, and you don't even check the list?"

I have enough steam coming out of my ears to work in a Chinese laundry.

Sean finally speaks up. "Detective Moore is part of our team. Open up the gate and let us through."

The elderly guard looks from Sean to me. If his hands were shaking before, they are positively vibrating after he looks at my face. "Sorry, Detective. You're so pretty I figured you were another one trying to visit Mr. Edison."

I refuse to be placated. "Next time, bother to take a look at the badge before you make assumptions." I get back in my vehicle and watch the gates finally swing open.

Sean is tailgating me so closely, I can see his face in my rearview mirror. The bastard is laughing.

***

Broadmoor was built in the 1920s for the Seattle elite. There are eight acres of homes, as well as a golf course. Brian Edison's house is very modest by today's McMansion standards. As I pull into the driveway, the garage door opens, and a big burly guy steps out. He's wearing a white polo shirt with the Linkz.com logo on the front. As he approaches my vehicle, he gestures for me to take the empty spot. I pull forward and pop the trunk button as I exit the car.

"You must be Detective Moore. I'm John Doe Smith. You can call me Alias. I'm Mr. Edison's personal assistant." A wide smile lights up what is otherwise a plain face.

"Alias?" I look up into deep brown eyes that remind me of my old German Shepherd. "John Doe Smith. Your parents must have a very warped sense of humor."

"Yeah. They were hippies in the sixties and thought the name John Smith would be easier to go off grid. Doe sticks with their hippy theme. My older sister is Fawn."

"So why not name you Buck?"

"Unfortunately, the day I was born, a doe wandered into our backyard. Dad is one-quarter Native American, and naming babies for the first thing you see after the birth is a tradition. It could have been worse. My sister swears the day I was born, there were two dogs going at it in the front yard. I could have been, John Two Dogs Screwing Smith."

I laugh. It must have been the lack of sleep because I laugh until an unladylike snort comes out. I'm sure he is pulling my leg, but a moment of levity feels good.

He takes my hand and gives it a medium shake. I appreciate the fact that he doesn't do the macho super squeeze. As he holds my hand, big brown eyes wander to my chest. Damn, not again. "John Doe Smith, my eyes are up here." Jeez.

Chapter 7

Sean watched Alias size him up as they shook hands. He decided to reserve judgment and see what the guy was all about. He didn't have to wait long, as Alias launched into his welcome speech.

"Agent Lindstrom and Detective Moore, I was briefed on what happened last night. Your quick reflexes saved Mr. Edison's life, which is why you are here now. I used our extensive resources to do a background check of my own on you both. Agent Lindstrom, thank you for your service in Iraq. You had several commendations during your two tours. You also distinguished yourself in the ten years you have been with the FBI. Detective Moore, you've been a cop for seven years and a detective for two years. Your file is also filled with commendations. Your record on the bomb squad was very impressive. I like that for the past five years, you have placed first in the National Police Shooting Championship. Good to know that Mr. Edison will be in such capable hands."

Sean let out a low whistle. "And last night, you hit both suspects dead center in the middle of their foreheads. Unless you're a sniper, we're trained to go for the larger body mass in a situation like that. What are you? Some kind of sharpshooting Annie Oakley?"

He watched Alias beam like a proud father. "Oh, she's better than Annie Oakley. As I'm sure you're aware, the National Police Shooting Championship is a big deal. She's come in first in a number of the sharpshooting competitions. I think there are some tidy whities that are in a twist because of Detective Moore." Alias was smiling, obviously pleased with his detective work.

Sean's own tidy whities began to twist. He knew all about the Championship. After witnessing her shooting skill in person, it's obvious she would be first. But being on the bomb squad? This chick has a serious set of cojones on her.

Sean snuck an appraising look at Jayne as she replied to Alias. "I've had extensive training in F.A.T.S. That's the Firearms Training Simulator. In a terrorist situation, or when a suspect is using an automatic weapon, you always go for a head shot. Otherwise, you stand a chance that his hands will recoil, and his gun will go off. That could result in the death of innocent civilians or the hostage."

Sean smiled at her. "Remind me to try and not piss you off anymore." He wasn't quite sure, but he thought she might have bit back a smile.

The moment was broken when Alias cleared his throat and said, "I've been instructed to show you two to your rooms. We were informed neither of you has had any shut-eye for over twenty-four hours. Mr. Edison went to bed a few minutes ago. He'll be asleep for at least five hours. Two SPD officers are here as well as two other FBI agents to guard him while you two sleep. Let me take you to your rooms. We'll go up the back staircase. I'll give you a tour of the home when you wake up, but here's a quick overview. The house was built in 1920, and Mr. Edison's grandparents were the first owners. It has been passed down for three generations. There are five bedrooms and four bathrooms. Mr. Edison, of course, is in the master bedroom with a private bath. The cook and I live in, and our bedrooms both include a private bath. The two remaining rooms are for guests, and the bath is shared. Will that be a problem? If so, I can change rooms with Detective Moore."

Sean wore his cool professional look. "No problem, unless you are going to leave a bunch of girly unmentionables lying around."

Jayne gave him a scathing look. "I'm sure we can manage just fine."

Sean's face creased into an innocent smile. "I forgot to pack my pajamas. Hope I don't open the wrong door when I'm using the bathroom."

Jayne smiled. "I sleep with a loaded weapon under my pillow. And, as Alias said, I never miss."

Sean winced as he realized he'd pissed her off again. He chuckled to himself and vowed he would try harder to not get under her skin. But why deny himself some fun?

Chapter 8

Using amazing self-control, I manage to not slam the door behind me as I walk into my room. I'm dying to get some sleep but first I have to unpack. My hasty job of packing is evident as I pull wrinkled pants and tops out of my duffle bag. Another reason why I always pack my little miracle steamer.

As I put things away, I feel like I'm in a time machine. The room is cozy in an old-fashioned way with rose-colored floral drapes and a matching bedspread. The double bed has an antique brass headboard and a mission oak dresser with an oval mirror attached to the back. The entire room looks like it is all original furnishings, which translates to really, really old. Luckily, I don't smell the musty odor that usually clings to old furniture.

Opening the door to the bathroom, I'm almost blinded by the white. The walls and floor are covered with immaculate one-inch white square tiles. When I turn and see the old-fashioned claw-foot tub, an involuntary sigh escapes. I can see myself relaxing with hot water, bubbles, and a glass of chardonnay, relieving the sore spots from the last twenty-four hours. As I stand there daydreaming, the door from the other side opens.

Sean walks in, and even though the bathroom is large, he seems to fill it up. I involuntarily step back, trying to regain some personal space.

"I'm finishing up. I'll be out of here in a second." I move toward the door. The large bathroom now seems cramped. Sean takes a step toward me, and I can smell a woodsy scent coming off him. It's pleasant, and I catch myself before I lean closer and start sniffing him like a sex-starved bloodhound. I look up into his eyes. I'm close enough to see that they're bloodshot, but there's something else I can't quite put my finger on. Usually, his hazel eyes are bright and lively when he's making fun of me or trying to yank my chain. Now, they're almost subdued. Not dull, but serious. I'm caught off guard as I realize, for some reason, this expression concerns me.

"You bring out the jerk in me," Sean said in a low voice.

I can't help but give him the stink-eye. "I honestly don't think I deserve all the credit. I'm sure you do fine on your own." His face turns red with embarrassment--another first.

But the man is not to be deterred. "You also bring out something else in me. Something I haven't stopped thinking about since I met you." I can feel him inching closer.

I know what he's hinting at and a shiver of excitement goes through me, which quickly turns to fear. "I could care less what you think about me."

For a quick second, Sean's face softens, and I swear I see regret on it. I can see hints of the real Sean and it scares me. He looks dead on his feet, and...vulnerable.

Without thinking I blurt out, "My partner is Tom Kruze. He says he did a tour in Iraq with you, and I should cut you some slack."

The tension breaks and a genuine smile lights up his face. "You're Tom's partner? I lost track of him. Funny, for a year we were together 24/7. We had each other's back. He's a good man. I can't believe ten years have gone by. What's he up to? Still married to Lily?"

"They are the happiest couple I know. Their three daughters are the cutest little girls you've ever seen." Proud auntie that I am, I reach into my pocket and pull out my phone. Thumbing through the pictures. I find a shot of the five of them. "Take a look at his beautiful family."

Sean looks down. "He looks great. They all look so happy."

I didn't miss the bit of wistfulness in his voice. "So, what about you? Anyone in your life?"

"No. Not for a long time. Besides, what did you call me? A sleaze? Who'd want to be with a sleaze like me?"

And he's back. Just when I think we might have a real conversation. "Hey, Sean, what can I say? When I'm right, I'm right" Disgusted, I turn to go back to my room. "I need to sleep. I'll catch up with you later."

I try not to stomp back to my room. My empty duffel bag has fallen to the floor. I think about Sean as I give it a good kick.

***

I hear a discreet knock on my bedroom door and force myself into wakefulness. I glance at the clock by the bed and realize I've slept for six hours. My clothes are rumpled and my teeth feel fuzzy. Alias' voice penetrates the door.

"Detective Moore, lunch is ready in fifteen minutes."

Before I can speak, my stomach rumbles. "Thanks, Alias. I'll be right down."

I open the bathroom door and lock the door on Sean's side. Lack of sleep has left me with bloodshot eyes and dark circles. I decide to break my no-makeup-at-work rule. Just one more little thing I do to blend in. Today, however, I'll make an exception. Not every day you are in close quarters with a good-looking billionaire, and the bags under my eyes need some help.

The doorknob rattles. Sean is up.

"I'm almost finished."

"Come on, Moore. I know you're in there primping for the billionaire. I need to pee."

Crap. Busted. "Agent Lindstrom, you're out of your mind. I'm putting toothpaste on my brush. You can wait two minutes."

I fire up my Sonicare and start brushing my teeth with one hand while finishing my face with the other. By the time my toothbrush stops, I have my makeup bag in my hand and throw the brush in as I open the door. "All yours."

Sean stands there, true to his word, in his boxers. I do a quick once-over. His body looks even better than I'd imagined, with six-pack abs and a broad chest. God help me, I can feel the heat radiating off him. I realize I'm staring and try to avert my eyes.

"Jeez, Jayne. My eyes are up here."

I scoop up everything on the counter and stomp into my bedroom--adding his hoots of laughter to my mental list of why Sean Lindstrom is a jerk.

***

Using the back stairs, I enter the kitchen just as Alias and a blonde woman disengage from an octopus-style embrace. From my viewpoint, it looks like he was giving her a courtesy tonsil examination.

"Detective. This isn't what it looks like. Mimi had something in her eye."

My eyebrows shoot into my hairline. "Oh, right." Really? I don't care if the help plays tonsil tennis or not. But I am wondering why he is so adamant with his little cover story.

Alias clears his throat. "Detective Moore, this is our chef, Mimi Jenkins. Mimi, Detective Jayne Moore, from the Seattle Police Department. She's the one that saved Mr. Edison's life last night."

Mimi walks toward me and extends her hand. She has long acrylic nails, with black nail polish, and lots of cleavage showing. The amount of thick makeup on her face would make a house painter proud, and the over bleached, brittle blonde hair completes the package.

While I'm still taking in the audacious Mimi Jenkins, she grabs my hand and does a macho hand squeeze. Ow...I was not expecting that.

"Hello, Mimi. My, quite a grip you have there. Bet you're good with a meat cleaver."

"Oh. Sorry, Detective."

She doesn't look very sorry. Not sure what her game is, but all of a sudden her face lights up and she steps past me. It doesn't take a mind-reader to know Sean just walked into the room.

"And who do we have here?" Mimi's voice changes to pure honey.

"Hello, I'm Special Agent Lindstrom." Sean smiles. I don't know why I take pleasure in the fact that it doesn't reach his eyes. Nevertheless, it is still a nice smile. His eyes seek mine, and I do a very slight shoulder shrug.

"I'm Mimi. *Your* cook."

Bitch. Now she's "his" cook? Wasn't she just having her tonsils checked out by Alias? I look over at Edison's personal assistant and detect a small frown line between his eyes. The rest of his face is carefully schooled with a neutral expression.

Thankfully, Sean gets right to the point. "I'm starved. What's for lunch?"

"I'm serving meatloaf, mashed potatoes, and green beans. I figure since you missed breakfast, lunch could be a little heavier." She glances over at me. "I didn't realize we would be having a female detective. You're probably one of those women who worry about their weight. I'll make you a salad."

My eyes widen in disbelief. Oh, no. She did not just say that to me. Now I have to prove myself and eat like a man? I guess the good news is, at least she's not staring at my boobs. "Meatloaf will be fine. Thank you." No way am I going to let her know it's my favorite food.

I'm relieved when Alias finally breaks up the conversation. "Mr. Edison is up and currently working in his office. He would like to meet with you at two o'clock."

"If you and Agent Lindstrom will follow me into the dining room, Mimi will bring the food out right away." He nods to her and takes us through double swinging doors that open to a large ornate dining room.

The floor-to-ceiling windows are covered with elegant draperies that pool on the oriental rug. They look like silk, and as in my bedroom, they are mauve. I can't believe a thirty-three-year-old guy can live with all this mauve. He either has a decorator who is into retro seventies, or the house is a shrine to his grandparents. I'm betting on the latter.

A mahogany table, large enough to seat twelve people, dominates the room. Built-in china closets, showing an expanse of dishes and crystal, anchor each side of the room. A huge picture window looks out to a private courtyard. The other end of the room has a sideboard table.

Mimi pushes through the doors and puts two platters of food in front of us. China plates with silverware wrapped in cloth napkins sit beside the food. A large basket of delicious smelling rolls calls my name as my stomach answers with a resounding growl.

Mimi sets her eyes on Sean. "I hope you enjoy your lunch." She manages to nod at me as she turns to leave. It makes me smirk when, as she walks away, her hips are moving so much, it looks like two pigs fighting in a blanket.

The minute she is gone, I make a beeline for the food. Sean stands beside me and whispers. "What is it about you that makes people act like jerks? What the hell did you do to her?"

I count to ten and hold my temper in check. Then, I see his good-natured smile and the teasing look back in his eyes, his earlier mood forgotten. "I walked in on her and Alias swapping spit. Alias claims he was getting something out of her eye. I have no idea why they are trying to conceal their relationship, but something's up with those two."

"Maybe your billionaire has a fraternization policy?"

"He's not my billionaire. Will you please knock it off?"

He's about to reply and then glances down. "Jeez, Moore. Are you going to eat all that?"

I look down at my plate heaped with food and smile like a Cheshire cat. "Yep."

He grimaces as he fills his plate with mashed potatoes and rolls. "Did you notice Mimi's acrylic nails? Those things are always so nasty looking. Wonder how much bacteria is stored under them? Isn't that how you mix meatloaf? Squishing it all together with your fingers? My mom makes it like that."

I look down at my meatloaf and think about those long fingernails. Damn.

Chapter 9

Sean felt like a jerk as Jayne stared down at her plate. "Hey. It's cooked. It should be fine. I'm sorry. I should have kept my mouth shut. Wait. I'll go dish up a piece. If I can eat bugs in Iraq, I can eat this."

He was rewarded with a smile.

"Don't force yourself on my account. I'm not all that squeamish."

He watched as Jayne shoveled a big bite into her mouth to prove her point. A few seconds later, he watched her mouth pucker up and was alarmed by the look of horror on her face as she forced herself to swallow the offending meatloaf.

She finally managed to say, "Something is not right here. The meatloaf is horrible and that's being kind. When we meet with Edison, we need to request the employee files on her and Alias. If she's a chef, then I'm a pole dancer."

Sean nodded. He'd gotten a bad vibe from Mimi Jenkins. "I agree. But I am enjoying the image of you as a pole dancer." He didn't leer but gave her a face-splitting grin.

Her laugh was easy on the ears. "I have two left feet."

Sean snickered and said, "I wouldn't be looking at your feet." As he expected, he got an exasperated sigh from Jayne.

The dining room door opened, and Mimi waltzed into the room. Sean looked up from his plate as her eyes locked on his like a heat-seeking missile.

He scrutinized Mimi. She was the type of woman that would only look hot at last call in a dimly lit bar, after at least eight shots of tequila, maybe more. He had picked up on her dislike of Jayne. Easy to understand. Jayne was naturally beautiful, and even wearing an outfit meant to disguise her body, and with her blonde hair captured in her prim librarian bun at the base of her neck, she still exuded a sexiness that Sean was very aware of. Mimi, with her skintight top and spackled-on makeup, was obviously jealous of Jayne.

"How's lunch? Anything I can get you, Agent Lindstrom?"

Before Sean could answer, she smiled coyly and said, "*Agent Lindstrom* is so formal. Since we'll be living together, for the foreseeable future, what's your first name?"

Without breaking a smile, he replied, "Agent."

Mimi stood there, a slight frown on her face until Sean broke the silence. "Mimi, great lunch." He gave her a smile to lessen the tension in the room. "Interesting meatloaf. Is it a family recipe?"

Mimi puffed out her chest so far, it looked like she was putting stress on her implants. Sean heard a soft snicker from Jayne and held in a laugh of his own. Sean looked into Mimi's overly made-up eyes and waited for her to reply.

Finally, her lips pursed together like an old school marm. "Yes. The meatloaf is an old family recipe. Sorry, Agent Lindstrom, I can't share it."

Sean saw Jayne do an eye-roll and cough a laugh into her hand. "Well, Mimi, it sure is different from my mother's. All I can say is wow. How did someone like you, with such a diverse culinary skill, end up working for Brian Edison?"

Mimi paused for a moment before she replied. "I move around a lot. I like to travel to new places, and I prefer to work smaller, more intimate venues, rather than restaurants."

"Nice that you could join the Brian Edison adventure on the ground floor." He leaned into her and said. "What a lucky break for you."

Mimi purred. "Let's say I was in the right place at the right time."

Sean's eyes kept cutting over to Jayne. He saw that her cop face was firmly in place, but he was positive he heard another suppressed snort of laughter. Jeez, brains, beauty, and a sense of humor.

***

Mimi walked out of the room, and Sean watched Jayne whip out her cell phone. She stood over the platter of meatloaf and snapped a picture.

Sean laughed, then whispered, "Are you trying to document

the deadly meatloaf?"

Jayne leaned over to him. "No," she whispered. "A clear thumbprint is on the rim. I'm sending it to my friend Diane in Forensics. Let's find out if our Mimi has a record. I'm willing to bet she's seen the inside of a woman's facility." He was close enough to read her note before she hit send.

Sean nodded. He liked the feeling of her whispering into his ear. "Great plan. If she doesn't turn up something, text it to me, and I'll try our sources."

"Diane is amazing. If anyone can find information, she can. She's been with the department for twenty-five years. Diane was a trailblazer. When I think of the crap I've been dished, I think of her. She had it way worse."

Sean gave her a weak smile. "You mean like the shit I kept saying to you?"

"No. Yours is just shit, not sexist shit. And for the record, most of the cops I work with are way past that sort of thing. There are a few holdouts. You're more like a nasty little fly that keeps buzzing around trying to get attention."

Sean stared at his plate of food. She had nailed it. He did want her attention. The more he was around her, the more he wanted. His eyes stared down at his uneaten lunch as he tried to figure out how he had gotten himself into this situation.

Sean looked up at Jayne as she smiled and said, "Hey, Sean, my eyes are up here."

Chapter 10

Thankfully, Alias breaks up our conversation when he walks into the dining room.

His expression is somber as he says, "If you two are ready, I'll give you a tour of the house."

We push our chairs back from the table like kids responding to the recess bell. I think both of us are relieved to get away from Mimi's food and our conversation.

"We'll start outside." Alias leads us down a hallway lined with a hardwood floor and busy oriental rugs. At the foyer, he throws open a massive six-paneled oak door and steps aside. Sean and I walk out onto the porch, and we have an unobstructed view of the street.

"Most of the yard is relatively clear of excessive landscaping. Except for the backyard, by the garage where you parked last night, which has overgrown shrubbery that I'll try and get taken care of this week." Alias pauses for a moment and then begins what sounds like a well-rehearsed tour. "The house was built in 1920, and most of it is still in its original condition. As I said, the Edison family are the original owners."

I walk off the porch, descend the six stair steps, and turn to stare at the house. It is massive, and I have to walk farther into the yard to take it all in. Sean follows me and turns at the same time to look back at the house.

I love old homes and, in freshman year, toyed with becoming an architect. "I took architecture in college. The square symmetrical shape and the decorative crown over the front door are classic Georgian Colonial."

Sean squints his eyes and says, "Looks like a big brick box to me."

I give him an elbow to the ribs and try to follow the long rambling history of the house that Alias is now going on and on about. I peer in each window as we pass, orientating myself to the house and the view each room has of the outside. I note the neighbors' roofs, trees, and any other object where a sniper or bad guy could be hiding. It's unsettling not knowing who we're dealing with.

After we circle the home, we come back in through the front door, and Alias launches into his inside tour. The stately foyer opens to a large living room on one side and a music room on the right. Next, a small parlor where I see two SPD officers sitting by the door.

I hear, "Detective Moore," as the older cop stands up with a big smile and extends his hand.

I grab his hand and hold it in both of mine. "Getting stuffy in your old age, Angus?" I am so happy to see a friendly face. "Special Agent Sean Lindstrom, meet Officer Angus Ferguson, the best training officer on the force. I spent all my rookie days with the toughest cop you'd ever want to meet."

Sean reaches out to shake Angus' hand, and I wait for the good-old-boy dance to begin.

Angus smiles at Sean and says, "I have to admit, when they saddled me with this female rookie, I wondered who I'd pissed off. An hour into the job, she saved my life. One hour! Can you believe it? Pushed me down to the ground when she spotted a guy coming out of a convenience store, his gun trained on me. I was so busy pontificating, I didn't even notice him. Jayne drew her weapon and yelled for him to drop his gun. When he didn't, she brought him down with one shot. Turns out the suspect had a rap sheet a mile long, and he wanted to add a couple cop-kills to it."

As Angus talks, I look over at the other officer. When I spot my nemesis, I keep my expression neutral and nod at him. "Officer Turner, we meet again."

I'm rewarded with his standard hate glare. I can smell dislike from him as if it's an aftershave called "Eau de Resentment." His eyes narrow, and he doesn't offer a handshake. Officer Spencer "Spike" Turner makes it obvious he is still pissed I made detective and he's still in uniform. He wears the chip on his shoulder like an epaulet of honor.

Turner has been a pain in my ass since I made detective. Rumor at the cop shop is he tried to file a lawsuit, claiming preferential treatment to women. Then Turner had the nerve to accuse me of sleeping with, not one, but all of my superiors. Jeez. And when would

I have had the time to do all that? When he found out his score had been the lowest of all the applicants, he finally shut up. It must drive him nuts that my score was near perfect, another reason for him to hate me.

I see him stand up straighter trying to negate the inch or so I have over him in height. I know it galls him to have to look up at me, which of course he avoids at all costs. I stare at him while Sean and Angus talk. He's got a cop swagger that is so at odds with his appearance. He's skinny with pale wispy brown hair that barely covers his oval head--to say he is follicle-challenged would be an understatement. His head looks like it was decorated with a few reddish-brown feathers, discarded when the hen laid his egghead. I watch his brown eyes dart and appraise Sean. Ignoring me, he turns to Sean, extends his hand and introduces himself.

I watch as Sean gives him the once-over and then shakes Turner's hand. It's obvious that Sean's body language is a classic blow-off, as he turns his back on Turner and faces Angus. He is enjoying the conversation with Angus and ignores Turner.

"Well, whatever you taught her as a rookie has stuck. She took out two perps last night in a matter of minutes. Then charged over to the getaway car and pulled the suspect out by his ear. She had him on the ground and handcuffed faster than a champion calf roper."

There. Sean has officially declared where his loyalties lie. Good for him. I feel my heart do a little pitter pat skippy thing. Damn.

The moment doesn't last long as Turner gives a derisive snort. "Yeah, everyone's talking about her big bust. No pun intended. Hey Boom Boom, you still wearing that red thong? It was the talk of the locker room last night. Bet your balls were hanging out."

I notice Sean's fists start to clench. I give a look that freezes him in place, and I put my hand on Angus' arm to stop him. "Spike, you had to have been there. I happened to be in the right place, at the right time. I wasn't planning on taking down a suspect. For those events, I find that granny panties are best to keep my balls tucked out of sight." I stop myself from going in for the kill. "Now, Spike, if you're done trying to bust my chops, Special Agent Lindstrom is in charge of this case. He wants to have a meeting to discuss how we're going to protect Mr. Edison. Alias, do you want to go check and make sure your boss is still good for our two o'clock meeting?"

"Sure, *Detective* Moore." Alias puts an emphasis on the word detective, and I inwardly smile at his show of support. I remind myself not to underestimate Alias. He was very smart at picking up on Turner's animosity.

Turner gives me a "this isn't over" look until I stare him down.

For the next thirty minutes, we listen to Sean talk about the property. His deep voice rings with authority as he says, "We have a team that is going to place cameras in the areas we've identified as vulnerable. For now, no one but us will know about them. I do not, repeat, do not want this discussed with the live-in help. At this point, we trust no one until we determine the real threat."

Sean pauses and looks at both men before he continues. "Last but not least is the accommodations. According to Mr. Edison's assistant, there is a two-bedroom apartment above the garage. You'll be staying there as well as the other agents. Any questions?"

Angus shakes his head no. I see Turner smirk, but it looks like he's still hoping Sean will man up and join his side, so he wisely keeps his mouth shut.

A quick rap at the door and Alias pokes his head in. "Agent Lindstrom, Detective Moore, Mr. Edison is ready to meet with you."

***

When Alias opens the door and announces Mr. Edison is ready for us, I feel like I'm being liberated from a prisoner-of-war camp. Thirty minutes of Turner's company has been twenty-nine minutes too long. I jump up from my chair and look at Sean. He looks as ready as I am to leave the room. To say Turner is a douche bag is putting it mildly. I know he will try and twist this entire situation, and yet again, I'll be the talk of the locker room.

Sean and I walk out the door and down the hallway, our footsteps muffled by the thick Oriental rug. Alias says he has things to attend to and leaves us outside Edison's door. As I raise my hand to knock on the door, Sean turns to me and, in a low voice, says, "I need to commend you. Turner is an asshole, and you managed to put him in his place without violence. I've seen his type before, all brawn and bragging. I really struggled with the urge to shoot him. It was hard, especially when he kept interrupting me during the meeting with his show of bravado on how he was going to guard Edison. What a jerk."

My partner is right. Sean Lindstrom is a guy you want to have your back. He proved it when he sang my praises in front of Turner. Demonstrating his confidence in me as a cop means more to me than I want to admit. Damn. I hate being wrong.

"You need to get in line. He doesn't just piss off the female cops, although we're his primary target. He's got a lot of cops pissed. No one wants to be his partner because he's too badge heavy. I'm not sure how we ended up with him on this detail." I have an idea, but I'm not ready to share it yet. Turner's wife has a relative on the Seattle City Council. I have heard Turner wants a high profile case to "prove himself." All he's going to prove is he's more of a liability than an asset. And if the rumors are true, Mimi will have her hands full. Turner's notorious for having a roving eye, and he's not all that choosy about who it lands on. That makes me chuckle, and Sean turns back to me with a quizzical look on his face.

"Is your girlish giggle in anticipation of meeting the billionaire?" Sean's teasing tone sounds forced.

Oh. My. God. Talk about a one-track mind. "Yes, it is. I'm so simple and shallow that the thought of being near a billionaire has my panties in a twist. In fact, I think they're falling to the floor right now." I give Sean a hard stare. "And quit looking down, my eyes are up here." Oh for the love of God, this is going to be a long assignment.

Dismissing the conversation, I knock lightly on the closed door and hear Brian Edison reply, "Enter."

I step in with Sean close at my heels. Brian Edison stands up, his hand extended, and walks around a very messy desk to shake my hand. "Detective Moore, it's a pleasure to see you again."

His left-hand joins the handshake to give what can only be described as a hand hug. I look down at my hand encapsulated in both of his. A second before it turns uncomfortable, he releases my hand and turns to Sean. "I'm sorry, Agent, can you refresh my memory?"

Sean's face tightens down into a cool unreadable look. It's like an eraser has been wiped over his features and no expression remains. Sean is now some serious, humorless man-in-black government agent. I tense up as he sticks his hand out. It looks like

Edison is in for one of those manly death grasps.

"I'm Special Agent Sean Lindstrom."

My mistake. Sean doesn't do the death grip, Edison does. The macho display surprises me. Edison is about four inches shorter than Sean and about forty pounds lighter. I am watching Sean's face and see his expression darken during the hand squeeze but he doesn't say anything.

Edison finishes his pissing contest and turns to address us both. "Please take a seat. I hope you enjoyed your lunch. I understand our Mimi is quite a cook. I know she makes an amazing peanut-butter-and-jelly sandwich."

I can't help myself. Peanut-butter-and-jelly sandwiches are so not my favorite, and I inadvertently blurt out, "Who over the age of ten would even consider eating a PB and J?"

Brian Edison's face clouds up for a split second and then a self-deprecating smile, that doesn't quite meet his eyes, surfaces. "That would be me. And if there is any threat of poison during this little terrorist siege, I'll make sure you are my food taster. I only eat peanut-butter–and-jelly sandwiches. Morning, noon, and night. Of course, the morning ones are toasted but the rest of the time, plain old PB and J."

I concentrate on not letting my jaw drop in shock. Glancing over at Sean, I see a ghost of a smile, and it looks like he's smothering a laugh.

Edison shrugs his shoulders. "I have ARFID."

At that, we both have blank looks.

"ARFID is avoidant/restrictive food intake disorder. It started when I was about three years old. I don't like most foods. I either gag on the texture or the look of the food." He shrugs his shoulders, clearly over the subject.

Damn. I am trying to think of how to apologize for making fun of him. I look Edison in the eyes and say, "I'm so sorry. That must be really difficult for you." His eyes are mesmerizing. Gray like rainclouds at dusk. I mentally slap myself. Rainclouds? Seriously? Where the hell did that come from?

He then gives me a look that screams, "Aren't I an adorable, quirky billionaire?"

I manage to hold back my smile, as I ask, "So a professional chef makes your PB and J?" The penny drops on how Mimi manages to keep her job with such questionable cooking skills. I look over at Sean and can tell he's coming to the same conclusion.

"Well, like I said. They're very good PB and J's. Mimi does a great job, and came highly recommended by Alias."

I don't want to raise his suspicions by focusing on Mimi. "Mr. Edison, we're going to need a complete list of your employees and their personnel files."

His mouth transforms with a flirtatious smile. "Please, call me Brian and I'll call you Jayne, and...." Belatedly he moves his glance over to include Sean. He pauses as he tries to recall his name, and finally, the lightbulb goes off, and he says, "Sean."

I hesitate and before I can reply, Sean jumps in.

"Mr. Edison, there is a crew of Seattle Police Officers and FBI agents here to help guard you until this threat is neutralized. While we will all be in close quarters, I would like to maintain professional boundaries, so morale will not be affected. I'm sure you understand." I notice a terseness in Sean's voice.

I release the breath I'm holding and try to maintain a neutral look on my face. I covertly observe Brian Edison, and he looks like he's thinking about a rebuttal but then abruptly changes course.

"As you like, Agent Lindstrom. Now, can you two tell me what the plan is to apprehend these terrorists or kidnappers?"

I take the lead back. "Both agencies are reviewing surveillance film from the hotel. We're checking into the identities of the four dead suspects and interrogating the men we apprehended."

Sean adds. "Our best forensics specialists are working on the case. We should identify the group responsible for this soon. Meanwhile, two agencies will be guarding you round the clock."

Edison nods, and then those gray eyes do a laser focus on me. "When is your shift, Detective?"

"Mr. Edison, I will be working with Agent Lindstrom to piece together the evidence and forensics so we can go after these guys. I'm overseeing the SPD officers, and Agent Lindstrom is in charge of the FBI agents. We will check in with you when we have something to report. I'm sure you've had time to replay this over and over in your mind since last night. Did you recognize any of the suspects? Have you received any threats or observed anything suspicious the last few days or weeks?"

Edison looks pensive for a moment. "This past year is a blur. Twelve months ago, I was working at a sub sandwich shop. Suddenly, three of my video games became mega hits, and now, I drive a Maserati. I sent my parents to live in the South of France, and went from living in the basement to owning the house." A smile crosses his face, flashing nice straight white teeth. "It all happened so fast, I haven't even had time to throw out the hideous mauve that my grandmother put in every room."

I can't help but let out a laugh. "Well, thank God for that. Of all my questions regarding this investigation, 'why mauve?' is at the top of my list."

Edison flashes me a look that almost does make my panties drop to the floor. "Ah, not only beautiful but a sense of humor, too."

Before he can continue, Sean cuts him off with another question. "So, while you were creating your video games, did you have the help of any investors? Did you piss off any employees?"

I appreciate that Sean is going for the hard questions, and I watch Edison carefully as he ponders his answer.

"Agent, I had three friends working with me. They invested in the beginning and also did some testing during development and design. Are they pissed off? I hardly think so, since they've been amply rewarded for their investment of time and money."

Before the two men start a macho hostility contest, I break in with a question. "Mr. Edison, what do you consider 'ample,' and is it possible they don't agree with your definition? Also, we need their names and contact information."

"Between the three of them, they managed to scrape together fifteen thousand dollars. When the stock went public six months ago, they each received one million dollars. I'd say it was a pretty good payback on their investment."

Sean's smile is cold. "So, you become a billionaire, and your only investors receive a cool million each? Seems a little lacking if you don't mind me saying so."

Edison stands up and leans forward, his hands on his desk as his eyes lock with Sean's. "I more than paid my dues, Agent. I spent over ten years developing the games. I lived in my parents' basement and worked a minimum wage job so I could devote every free moment to my company. Hell, it wasn't even a company then. It was me. That's it. Me. So no, I don't feel guilty because three guys chipped in a little money and spent some time playing video games. Last time I saw them, they were high-fiving me and pretty damn happy."

Something doesn't ring true. I try to diffuse the tension in the room by keeping my voice calm and a little apologetic. "You're right, that sounds like a good payback on their investment, but Agent Lindstrom asked a good question. Are you sure your friends don't have second thoughts about their compensation?"

Edison slumps back into his chair. "For the record, it isn't a billion dollars. The press grossly exaggerated my worth. I made two hundred and fifty million. Again, my friends were well rewarded for their investment. I'm tired of defending the money they received. I already asked my Admin, Sharon Gibbs, to send the information to you, as well as the contact info for Eric Ronds, Steve Zeas, and Billy McHendricks. You can talk to them yourselves. I guarantee they are happy." He pauses and glances at his computer monitor. "She just confirmed the envelope was picked up by a courier and is on its way." He ignores Sean and gives me a small smile. "Now, if you'll excuse me, I have a conference call to attend."

Our meeting is over. Sean stands and says, "Thank you for your time, Mr. Edison. We'll keep you informed." It almost sounds sincere, but I see the expression on Sean's face. He really has a dislike for Edison and doesn't work too hard to conceal it.

As we walk out the door, my phone buzzes on my hip. Checking the screen, I see a text message from my neighbor, Sheri McLellon. "Call me. Urgent."

"I'm sorry, I need to respond to this."

I dial Sheri the minute Edison's door closes behind us. She picks up on the first ring.

"Jayne, I'm so glad you called. You have a problem, but I think I fixed it."

"I'm in the middle of something here. Can you elaborate?"

Sheri draws in a breath before she says, "You know my goal is to ease out of sports and do more local reporting, right? We received a picture of you from the attack on Edison last night. The picture is great except for the fact that your dress is hiked up so far, the top of your red thong is showing. The creepy part is, it came with the message: 'Detective Jayne Moore showing the assets that got her promoted.' Looks like someone is pissed off. I received it right after a cell phone shot of you came through from the crime scene in the bar. It never ceases to amaze me that people can be in danger, and still think to whip out their cell phones. The shot is compelling and your thong is not showing. Obviously, we ran with the first photo. The article turned out well if I do say so myself."

"Sheri, I owe you. I have some thoughts on who sent the picture. Do me a favor, email it to Diane. I'll text an email address to you. She'll work her magic to figure out where it came from. I'll fill her in. Send me a copy, too."

"Will do. Hey, we're having a barbecue Saturday night. Tom and Lily are coming. Think you can break away from the case?"

"Saturday's only four days from now. I'll let you know. How are my babies?"

"They're fine, crazy cat lady. You know we'd never let anything happen to them. Especially since you're such a good shot!"

I laugh and disconnect the call. I hadn't realized Sean was behind me pretending not to listen.

He gives me a concerned look. "Everything okay?"

"Let's take a walk outside and I'll fill you in." Clearly, someone is trying to make me look like a bimbo cop, and the list of possible suspects is growing. Since this guy has already proved he's got my back, I want to hear his thoughts.

We walk out to the patio on the secluded side of the house. I fill Sean in on the phone call from Sheri.

Sean's eyes light up and his face has the teasing look I have come to recognize. "I'll need to look at the photo and see how much thong we're talking about."

I can't help but laugh. "Before I ever leave the house again, I'm putting on the granny panties...just in case."

Sean clears his throat. "All kidding aside, we need the photo to figure out where the photographer was standing. We can also take a look at the surveillance cameras in front of the hotel. Logic says it has to be a cop unless your natural charm has alienated someone else."

"Like any cop, I've put some bad people away. But there's also a short list of cops that were pissed off when I made detective. One in particular. It was Turner's third time taking the test, and he's been known to carry a grudge." I stop for a second, visualizing the scene outside the hotel. "Dobson was one of the first cops to arrive. We've never had a problem with each other, but I wouldn't mind having a little chat with him. Before we do that, our first priority is figuring out the whole Edison terrorist/kidnapping plot. I'm not that worried about the picture, DL is working on it."

"Who's DL?"

"My friend and mentor Diane Davis. She earned the cop moniker, Dickless Tracy, over twenty-five years ago when she made detective. She's amazing. There is no piece of information she can't ferret out on her computer. She'll know if it's a cop and what computer or phone it was sent from. Being called 'Boomer' is pretty tame after all the harassment she went through."

Sean chuckles. "Is Boomer a variation of what Turner called you earlier?"

My turn for a big red blush. "He's an ass. The guys on the bomb squad thought they were funny and called me 'Va Va Va Boom Boom' when I started. It was half funny, half sexist, and of course, the name stuck. I was called some variation of that the entire time I was with the squad. When I became a detective, the name followed me, but, thankfully, now it's just Boomer. The cops that don't like me, use Boom Boom."

"Yeah, I picked up on that when Turner called you Boom Boom and made it sound like a stripper's name. You're right, the guy's an ass."

I am spared more commentary when my cell phone rings. I look at the number. It's Lieutenant Johns.

I glance at Sean as I answer. "LT. what's up?"

"Moore, you and the FBI guy need to come in for a meeting. We've got some preliminary forensics back, and we've identified the suspects. Need you here in half an hour."

"On my way." I hang up as Sean's phone rings.

His conversation is short, and as he disconnects, he asks me, "I assume you got the same summons to downtown?"

"Yeah, your car or mine?"

His eyes crinkle. "Let's take your car, so I can watch you harass the gate guard."

We walk back through the house and alert everyone we will be downtown for a meeting. As we exit through the kitchen, Alias approaches with a sealed package.

"This is from Sharon Gibbs, Mr. Edison's Admin. I was told to deliver it to you personally."

"Thanks, Alias. Agent Lindstrom and I are going to a meeting downtown." I notice beads of sweat on his forehead as I grab the package. There are damp marks on the envelope from his clammy hands. Darn. Much as I like him, this guy has my suspect meter pegging out.

Sean and I walk into the garage where he stops and does a low whistle.

"Nice Maserati. Decent ride for our little billionaire. Oh, sorry, a quarter of a billionaire. These things start at a hundred grand. Guess that's a drop in the bucket to him now."

I pause before I speak. Sean is cooking up a big recipe of dislike for the person that we are supposed to be protecting. Trying to keep it light, I ask, "What's the first thing you'd buy if money was no object?"

A faraway look clouds his eyes. "Peace. I would buy world peace."

Well, knock me over with a feather. Damn. He really does have some depth.

"Then a strip club with pole dancers." This time, his eyes dance with merriment as he waits for my reaction.

This guy is definitely keeping me on my toes.

Chapter 11

Sean sat back and enjoyed Jayne's driving. She was aggressive and kept a running commentary going as she berated drivers for their slowness. Since she was driving her personal vehicle, there were no lights or sirens to open the way. Technically, it wasn't an emergency situation, and Sean was enjoying the time away from the mauve prison.

He opened the envelope Alias had given Jayne. Pulling out the list, he was relieved there were only five names. "Looks like the boy billionaire's company is still small. We ought to be able to run these names down pretty fast. She's also included contact information for Edison's three investors."

"Good. Did you feel the bad vibe when he was talking about his friends? I got the feeling that he was holding back. And just a guess, I bet they weren't happy with their investment return."

Sean beamed. "Yeah, I caught that too. Glad we're on the same page. I'm anxious to read the information on those three. We also need to check out the five employees as well as any hired services he's used."

"Sean. This is not my first rodeo. But I do agree with you."

Traffic was light, and when they pulled into the parking garage, Sean looked at Jayne, exclaiming, "Jeez, you made it downtown in seven minutes. You should consider a job with NASCAR. You'd probably make more money than pole dancing."

Jayne chuckled. "Your buddy, Tom Kruze, says my driving scares him. At least you managed not to slam your foot on the floor looking for the extra brake."

As she spotted an open space in the next aisle and sped up to get to it, Sean's big body fell to the driver's side, landing on Jayne's shoulder. She pulled in before the car approaching from the opposite side beat her to it.

He appreciated her quick responses as he righted himself in his seat. "Good job. Really, NASCAR could be a great second career for you."

He loved listening to her laugh as she answered. "Nah. I like catching crooks. And by the way, I still say Mimi Jenkins is no chef. I can't wait to dig up the dirt on her. Also, as nice as Alias is, my gut says there is a story on him too."

"I agree. We've got a lot of information to give to the task force. We can start on the list after the meeting."

The two of them got out and started walking through the garage to the elevator. The elevator doors opened, and Tom Kruze started to walk out. He stopped so suddenly, the uniformed cop behind him smacked into his backside.

Before Jayne could say hello to her partner, Sean's face lit up with a big smile "Tom Kruze. Brother, it has been too long."

"Lindy. Is that really you in that FBI *Men in Black* uniform?" A hearty laugh followed as Tom stuck out his hand, and when Sean took hold, they did the new version of the man hug.

"Hey, Boomer. This guy treating you all right?" Tom gave her a hopeful smile.

"He's making more of an effort than I thought he would. And he did willingly eat poison for me this morning, so I can't complain."

"Poison? What the hell are you talking about?" Tom's eyebrows were barely south of his hairline.

Sean laughed. "There is an alleged cook working for the Quarter Pounder. She needs to be checked out. As your partner says, 'if she's a cook, then I'm a pole dancer.'"

Both Tom and Jayne said in unison. "Quarter Pounder?"

Sean shrugged his shoulders. "Guess the guy isn't all he's cracked up to be. Word on the street is he made a billion off his video games. It was only a quarter of a billion. Poor guy. Gonna be hard to attract babes with that paltry sum."

Sean saw Jayne trying to control a smile and finally lose it with her characteristic snort of laughter.

She looked at Tom. "He's right. It is only a quarter of a billion, but lucky for him, he's got a pretty face so that should help him with the 'babes.' Me thinks someone might be a tad judgmental about our victim."

Sean knew he was being an ass, and Jayne was probably right

about being judgmental, but he wasn't ready to let it go. Before he could speak, Jayne looked at her partner and said, "We've got to get going. Keep me up-to-date on our cases. I'll check in with you later." And then she proceeded to the elevator.

Sean said a quick goodbye to Tom and stepped into the elevator. He turned to face the doors as he glanced down at Jayne. "All kidding aside, something about this guy doesn't add up. You feel it, too."

Before Jayne could answer, his phone rang. Sean looked at the caller I.D.

He quickly answered. "Hey, Mom. What's up? Everything okay with you and the girls?"

The stainless steel box quickly ascended to the twentieth floor. When the doors opened, Sean stepped away from Jayne to finish his call.

"No problem. No. Mom. Really. Send me an email with the bid attached, and I'll look it over. It needs to be done. I swear the roof was old before Dad left, and that's been over twenty years. I'm on a case now and ready to go into a meeting. I'll try and call you tomorrow. Are the girls okay?" Sean paused, and let out a laugh as he listened. "Sounds like them. Mom, I've got to go. Love you."

Sean disconnected the call and frowned at the phone for a moment. Then he walked back to where Jayne was standing.

"Everything all right? You look worried."

"Everything is good. That was my mom. She needs some help with a contractor she's getting bids from."

Jayne drew in a breath and blurted out. "You know, I have a thing about always being right. So far, I've mostly been wrong about you. You aren't a total jerk."

Sean lowered his voice and gave her a sexy grin. "Not being a total jerk is a huge step up from being a sleaze. I'll take it." Then in his FBI voice, he said, "Showtime."

***

Sean and Jayne shoved the glass doors to the conference room open, noting that the long table had each agency on opposing sides. Lieutenant Johns motioned to the two chairs at the head of the table. Jayne and Sean sat down and waited for the meeting to begin.

Chief Inspector Hennessey sat at the opposite end, next to an SPD official. Sean noted several familiar faces among the FBI sitting together on one side of the table.

Hennessey stood and called for everyone's attention. Hennessey was in his mid-fifties. His full head of gray hair was cut stylishly. His face was relatively unlined with the exception of the frown wrinkle in between his eyes. "People, let's get started. First, I'm going to introduce FBI Agent Sean Lindstrom and SPD Detective Jayne Moore. I understand you two interviewed Brian Edison this morning. Give us an update."

Sean took the lead. "Brian Edison reportedly made a billion dollars on his video games. The media didn't get it right, it was only a quarter of a billion but still worth kidnapping him for. He lived in his parent's basement for ten years and worked minimum wage jobs while developing his games. His parents paid all his bills, and he also had three investors."

Jayne interjected. "When Edison got his big payoff, he gave each of his three investors one million dollars. He assured us they were happy with that amount, but something is not ringing true. Agent Lindstrom and I feel there is more to the story. We have their contact info as well as the H.R. files on his five employees. We'll be paying them a visit once we review their information."

Sean waited for her to finish and then spoke. "Brian Edison has a cook and a personal assistant who live with him. The two appear to be pretty recent hires. Looks like the minute he got his parents out of the house, he hired a replacement mommy and daddy."

Jayne added to Sean's assessment. "I have to agree with Agent Lindstrom. The cook made our lunch today. A stomach pump should be standard equipment in that house. Apparently, Brian Edison has an eating disorder and only eats peanut-butter-and-jelly sandwiches. Morning. Noon. And night. So he is in no position to judge her cooking. John Doe Smith, a.k.a., Alias, is the personal assistant and got her hired. They have a relationship. He's about thirty-five. She's at least ten years older, and the extra years look like they were hard ones."

Hennessey nodded, and Lieutenant Johns cleared his throat. "You said you've got the employee list. We'll have both agencies run it to make sure we don't miss anything. Meanwhile, the SPD geek looked into Edison's games. Sargent Davis, give us the rundown."

Diane Davis stood up, punched a couple keys on her laptop, and addressed the group while images appeared on a screen in the room. "I started looking at the amount of money his games were making on the internet. Basically, Edison has zeroed in on the free app or the pay ninety-nine cents gaming arena. Don't be misled by the word free. Let me throw out some numbers. There are games and apps available on your phone that would shock you at their marketability. Example, Pet Hotel has an estimated revenue of fifty million dollars and over sixty million downloads. The developers make their money by add-ons during the game. With Pet Hotel, the player stocks their hotel with exotic pets and breeds them. Sounds crazy, right? People are so hooked, pretty soon, they're buying exotic pets to add to their stock. Ka-ching. Ka-ching."

Diane paused to glance around the room to gauge the reaction of her audience and continued. "A Genie game has earned forty-five million dollars with over thirty million downloads. The premise is the player thinks of a character, and the genie will tell them who they're thinking of. Get this--it can be a real person, fictional, living, or dead. People will download and play until the novelty wears off, but still, forty-five million is nothing to sneeze at."

Chief Inspector Hennessey let out a scornful laugh. "What is wrong with these kids? It explains so much about this generation that they can be so entertained by such nonsense."

Diane nodded her head. "Yes, sir. It gets worse. Another game is 'God Island,' where you can literally control primitive islanders and decide if they live or die. Think of all the vengeance in the bible if you want a hint at the violence level. There are hundreds, if not thousands, of games out there. We've all heard of the shoot 'em up and video game violence, but it seems like our little quarter of a billionaire added a new wrinkle to one of his games. He's taken on ISIS and is thumbing his nose at them. It's like 'God Island' joined forces with Hitler and Attila the Hun. His game is a war between ISIS and, as the game describes them, true Americans. Very bloody and extremely violent."

Diane paused and took a sip of water. "A quick overview of ISIS. They believe they are fighting for all Muslims, which is untrue. The Quran specifically prohibits the killing of innocent civilians. ISIS bastardized a religion that's followed by over 1 billion people. Edison's game pits Americans against ISIS. All of the violence ISIS unleashed on the world is a focal point of the game. Including beheadings, floggings, crucifixions, people buried alive, and slavery. You can download the game for free. The game comes with basic weapons. Both sides are equipped with artillery, Stinger Missiles, tanks, Humvees, and anti-aircraft guns, but there are other weapons the player needs to buy. Because ISIS uses swords, daggers, crucifixions, and chemical weapons, players also need to purchase those items. It's a very dangerous game."

Diane switched to a screen with statistics on gamers. "On an interesting side note, I found that a large percentage of women gamers are playing it. Comments online indicate they are taking up the fight for all the women who have been kidnapped, raped, and killed. There are more levels to be explored, but that's the basic premise. Even the name is graphic, 'Heads in a Basket.' I forgot to mention that every time you kill a member of ISIS, you get a head in a basket. The more baskets, the higher your score. There are some people on this site with some very high scores."

Hennessey quipped, "Quick, let's get them on a plane to kick some ISIS butt. Especially the angry women. I'd love to see ISIS taken down by a bunch of women with PMS."

The occupants in the room, including Jayne and Diane, erupted into laughter.

Jayne looked at Diane. "I did not see that coming. I haven't seen anything that would indicate that Brian Edison holds any strong political views. When we interviewed him, he was at a loss as to who was after him. My way of thinking, if you offend a large volatile segment of society, they would be at the top of your list of possible suspects. This guy is either incredibly naive or stupid."

Sean fake-coughed into his hand, saying, "Stupid."

"I'm sorry Special Agent Lindstrom, did you say something?" Jayne turned to Sean.

Sean shook his head no, and Diane cleared her throat and

continued. "Detective Moore, there are many studies about how violent games affect children and adolescents. Oxford Press published a paper detailing the increase of aggression in teens who play these games. It has also been linked to school shootings. These kids don't realize that in the real world, dead is dead. But we're getting off topic. Mr. Edison's game is like throwing a red cape in front of a bull. The FBI will be giving the specifics of the four men killed last night. I'll give you a spoiler alert: from our preliminary review of their social media presence, they all had ties to ISIS."

Lieutenant Johns gave a rare smile. "Well, the plot thickens. Moore and Lindstrom, get with Davis and run the list of names. Let's hope something shakes out." He turned to Hennessey. "What do you know about the dead guys?"

"As Sargent Davis mentioned, we've tied the two guys in the bar to ISIS from their social media pages. Johnson, pass out the fact sheets on this cluster-fuck."

For the next hour, the two agencies discussed the four dead suspects and their known associates. The two suspects from the bar both had over fifteen hundred Facebook "friends." The two kidnappers were illegal aliens who had attended the University of Washington. Both had been expelled the year before and then disappeared, rather than face deportation.

Hennessey cleared his throat and scanned his notes as he told the group, "The men in the van are still being interrogated, but so far, they have not given up any useable information. We know they are brothers and are also attending the UW. We have a team at the UW that is interviewing all of their friends and associates. It hasn't gone unnoticed that these guys all came in on student visas and ended up in some sort of terrorist cell. Their uncle, Mohammed Azzanni, is paying for their tuition. We are looking into him now."

Hennessey paused and looked around the room. "We need to step carefully. We do not want to cause a mass panic and create a witch hunt in our Muslim community. We have a lot of law-abiding Muslims that are assets to our community."

Jayne raised her hand to interject and Hennessey nodded at her. "Sargent Davis and I volunteer at a Multi-cultural community center in South Seattle for at-risk youth. We work with many great

Muslims who also volunteer their time. I'm concerned when the press gets wind of this, they are going to create a panic that has people categorizing all Muslims as terrorists. The last thing we need is some racist vigilante group targeting Muslims."

"I agree, Detective. We will be very careful with our interaction with the press. We'll meet again tomorrow. Get cracking, people."

Chapter 12

We leave the conference room and follow Diane to her office. Sean walks next to Diane and I keep pace behind them, where I can listen to snippets of his conversation with her.

"Nice to meet you, Diane. Jayne told me you're brilliant at finding information. Glad you're on our team."

Diane throws him an appraising look. I smile, knowing if Diane detects any bullshit, Sean will be called out on it.

"Jayne's a good cop. And usually a good read of character." Diane turns around and faces me. "You two have had a long day, and I didn't miss the remark about the cook's food. Give me the list, and go grab a bite to eat. It shouldn't take me more than an hour to pull up what you need. Jayne, you look like you could use a break."

"What the hell, DL? I'm fine. Let's get to it."

Diane refuses to budge. "No. I want to run the names and take a few minutes to look at them. I know you. You'll be pulling the stuff off the printer and be halfway out the door before I get a word in. Now go. Lindstrom, not sure how familiar you are with Seattle, but there's a great deli down the block. Meatloaf sandwiches to die for."

At the mention of meatloaf, I turn a little green. But I know Diane, and there is no sense fighting her. She has something up her sleeve. "Come on, Sean. No use arguing. Besides, I could really use some decent food. Mimi's wasn't fit for human consumption. We should have put it in an evidence bag and arrested her for attempted murder."

My little joke is rewarded with laughter from Sean and DL.

Ten minutes later, we are sitting at the deli. I watch Sean study the menu. Despite being on the go with only a few hours sleep, he looks refreshed and energized.

"So, what's your beef with Edison?" I say.

"You have to ask?" He looks peeved. "The guy is a jerk. He lived in his parent's basement for ten years. He's what? Thirty-three? The first thing he buys is a Maserati and ships his parents off to

France. It doesn't smell right. I'm looking forward to meeting the three investors. I'll bet you anything they're no longer friends."

The waitress brings our orders. I look longingly at my sandwich. It will have to wait. "I don't disagree. But I'm wondering why you can't give Edison the benefit of the doubt. He's the victim here, remember?"

"The guy is so easy to read. He's a spoiled brat who expects everyone to agree with him. His entire demeanor changed when you challenged him on his relationship with his investors. And let's not overlook the fact he was hitting on you."

I take a big bite of my ham-and-cheese sandwich, thinking of my response as I chew. I can't resist--he deserves it for being a jackass. "I know. I'm so lucky to be working with someone like Brian Edison. He's so in charge, and did you see his beautiful gray eyes? What a hot-looking guy."

Sean's mouth drops open, then snaps shut. "Jeez, Moore. Didn't realize you are so easily impressed. Of course, there are a quarter of a billion reasons to like the guy."

Oh damn. He has to go there again. My little joke has totally backfired, and now the old Sean is rearing his ugly head. "Relax, Lindstrom. I promise not to jump his bones until the case is solved. Besides, I'm wearing my granny panties, and they're not the best underwear to wear when you're trying to impress a guy." Okay, buddy, put that in your pipe and smoke it.

The new Sean closes down and reverts in front of my eyes. It's kind of cool. Almost like a sci-fi movie or maybe watching Sally Field play *Sybil*. Wow, this guy is good at burying his feelings. I'd hate to see him with a bone. I continue to eat as I study his face.

Sean finishes his sandwich with a few quick bites.

"Come on, Moore. Let's find out if your friend has worked her magic." Sean stands and heads to the trash can.

I swallow the last of my sandwich, wad my wrapper up, and take a shot at the trash can from the table. "Oh look, Lindstrom, I scored. Maybe it's the start of a winning streak."

The look on his face is totally worth it. I don't get mad, I get even.

***

We walk back to the station in total silence. I find myself already missing the new Sean, and I am pretty pissed the old one has shown up.

When we walk into Diane's office, she has a smug look on her face. First, I think it's because she has some good info, but I catch the look in her eye and realize she is playing matchmaker. Damn.

Diane's office is small, and awards, testifying to her years of service, are all over the walls. A credenza behind her displays pictures of her husband and son. A number one mom trophy holds a position of honor.

I give her my "I'm on to you" look, and ask, "Hey DL, what have you found?"

"Boomer, I have goodies like you wouldn't believe. First of all, let's start with Brian Edison. He's been working a lot of minimum wage jobs which you already knew. He's basically pretty clean, no juvie record. Credit card charges were pretty high but paid off monthly. Based on his minimum wage job, I'd say mommy and daddy were chipping in."

At that, Sean does a little snort of laughter. I turn and glare at him, but it looks like he's already immune to it. Damn. I catch DL watching me, barely able to contain her smile.

Sean manages to control himself and turns to Diane. "DL, sorry, I mean Diane..."

"No worries, everyone calls me DL, which is really so much better than people yelling 'Hey Dickless' Go ahead."

"Okay, thanks. What kind of minimum wage jobs did he hold?"

"Nothing really significant. Mainly restaurant jobs as busboy or dishwasher. One short stint at Dick's Sporting Goods. They sell guns, so someone needs to check if he used his employee discount for any fun little items."

Sean and I look at each other and nod. A working truce has been called.

DL continues. "His friends are pretty interesting. Interesting, as in losers. Truly, big losers. He went to high school with Steve Zeas, Billy McHendricks, and Eric Ronds. None of them, except for Edison, have a strong academic record. They had steady jobs, but not challenging jobs. Zeas was in construction. Ronds was a janitor in a machine shop, and McHendricks was a bartender. Their jobs were flexible enough to enable them to spend endless hours playing Edison's game. I managed to look into their S.A.T.'s. As you would expect, Brian Edison aced the tests, and the other three were below average. The brain of the entire operation is--no big surprise--Brian Edison. It is reinforced when you look at how each of them spent their million dollars. They all went on spending sprees, adding to their considerable amount of credit card debt.

"To say these guys aren't the sharpest knives in the drawer would be insulting to the dull knives. None of them paid off their credit cards. They continue to pay the minimum payment every month and, of course, pay huge interest charges. Tell me, when you have a million dollars, why do that? These guys are living like frat boys, buying big TV's, stereo equipment. Funny, no new clothes or furniture. Of course, they all bought new cars, and their bar bills are astronomical. We can't track their marijuana purchases since that is a cash only transaction. However we looked at their cash withdrawals at an ATM by their neighborhood pot store, and it adds up to a sizeable hunk of change. I think you've got the total picture. Unbelievable that three grown men are, essentially, living the dream of a fifteen-year-old boy. These guys are what, thirty-three? Oh, and their low-end jobs are a thing of the past. They all quit the day they got their million dollar checks."

I stare at Diane. "I feel like we're about to step into *Wayne's World*. Anything else you can tell us before we interview them?"

Before she can reply, Sean asks. "DL, what kind of cars did they buy?"

Diane taps some keys and stairs at her monitor. "The boys all flew down to Reno for a Barrett Jackson car auction. McHendricks bought a classic 1969 Camaro for $148,000. Ronds bought a 1969 Mustang for $169,000, and Zeas bought a 1962 corvette for $220,000. Looks like these boys like the classics."

Sean finishes putting notes into his phone. "And Quarter Pounder bought a Maserati."

Diane guffaws. "I knew I liked you. Quarter Pounder. I like it. Just looking at his picture makes me think we should stuff one into his skinny body."

"Oh no, DL," Sean says. "Our little Quarter Pounder only eats peanut-butter-and-jelly sandwiches. He suffers from a weird eating disorder." Sean's obvious pleasure at yet another put-down of Brian Edison is pissing me off, and DL's laughter is not helping matters.

I look at the two of them bonding. It is not making me happy. DL is laughing so hard, she has tears coming down her cheeks. If Sean had not reverted back to being an asshole, I would enjoy the moment. DL catches my look and stops mid-laugh.

"Okay, I've had enough fun. You two run along, and I'll start doing some research on the employees. Sounds like I should start with the cook and personal assistant. Sean, your FBI crew is working on it, too. Between our two agencies, we ought to find out all the dirt there is to uncover in a few hours. But call me competitive, I want to be the first one to find it all."

I stand up. "Thanks, DL. You're amazing, as usual. I'll keep in touch. Come on, Lindstrom. Let's head out. If you're nice, I'll let you sing 'Bohemian Rhapsody' on our way to *Wayne's World*." I was rewarded with an actual smile.

"Okay. But no singing. I sound like two cats fighting at midnight when I sing."

I laugh. I sang Karaoke one night at the cop bar. I think those were the exact words they used to describe my voice. Damn.

***

"Bohemian Rhapsody" is stuck in my head. I am about to burst into song when Sean stops me cold.

"Why do you like Brian Edison so much?"

I can tell he is trying to keep his voice neutral. "I think a better question is, why do you dislike him so much?"

"Oh no, you don't," Sean said. "I asked the question, and besides, I've already told you what I think of him. Tell me what you find so great about him. And don't do the B.S. you've been throwing out about his money. You're not like that."

Damn. He picks now to be perceptive? I think for a moment and decide to go with a version of the truth. "Well, he is nice looking.

And he took the time to thank me for saving his life. Best part, he's as far removed from the cop world as a person can get. I'm tired of living and breathing the job."

Sean exhales. "I was worried you were going to say your insides get all gushy when you're around him."

"Gushy?" I try not to laugh. "Seriously, gushy? Where on earth did you come up with that word?"

"Three little sisters. I heard about every single crush they ever had. Gushy seemed to be a theme."

I tap the steering wheel as I drive. "Well. For your information, I'm not gushy about Edison. As usual, being a cop is always in my head, and even if I was 'gushy' about him, there are still alarm bells ringing. Some things aren't adding up. And until they do, the granny panties stay on."

Sean leans back in his seat. "Well, so far, the only thing he's been right about is you. Brains, beauty, and a sense of humor. Killer combination."

Oh. My. God. Shut the front door. Did I just receive a compliment from former pain-in-the-ass, Lindstrom? Maybe this day isn't a total loss. Before I can reply, GPS announces we are nine hundred feet from our destination. First stop, Billy McHendricks'.

Sean points down the street. "Looks like we've hit the millionaire trifecta. There's a classic Mustang and Corvette out front, and a Camaro in the carport. Jeez. This neighborhood looks kind of slummy for a brand new millionaire."

I look at the house with the Camaro in the carport. It's a two-story home with two dormer windows upstairs and badly in need of a coat of paint. The yard is overgrown, and if there had ever been flowerbeds or landscaping, it is long gone. The sidewalk has cracks with weeds sticking out. "Looks like it's the gardener's decade off."

Sean looks around the yard and then takes in the house. "I can't wait to see if the inside is as impressive as the exterior. Let's get to it."

As we approach the house, music starts blaring. We both look at each other. I shout over to Sean. "Maybe some new sort of burglar alarm?"

He raises his hand up and bangs on the door.

Within five seconds, it jerks open and a short man glares at us. His brown hair is either purposely spiked or he has a serious case of bedhead. His eyes lock on Sean as his hand comes up, holding a black object. I have my hand on my gun when he points the object behind him and the music stops. I look past him to where two men stand frozen in classic air-guitar poses.

"Who the hell are you, and what do you want? Like I've told the hundreds of people before you, I'm not handing money out. I'm not some sort of philant...philant...you know, the guys who give away money."

I manage not to roll my eyes. "Mr. McHendricks, are you trying to say, philanthropist?"

He gives me a long slow once-over. I can feel Sean tensing up beside me. Time to pull out some hardware. I pick up the badge hanging from my neck and flash it at him. "Mr. McHendricks, I'm Detective Moore from the Seattle Police Department. The gentleman next to me is Special Agent Sean Lindstrom, FBI. We'd like to ask you a few questions."

"Sure, sweetheart. Come on in. Can you leave him outside? I'd really like to play with you and your handcuffs, if you know what I mean." He raises his eyebrows and licks his lips.

Short little guy is pretty brave or really stupid. I am at least three inches taller, and Sean towers over him. "Let's get this straight, Mr. McHendricks. I will be happy to show you my handcuffs when I haul your ass downtown for impeding this investigation. Now, I suggest you take seriously the fact that officers, from two agencies, are on your front porch. We need to ask you a few questions."

As he mulls it over, I study his face. He looks closer to his mid-twenties rather than thirty-three. His nose is elongated, pointed at the end with a slight turn up. It reminds me of a fox. His eyes are close together. Jeez, this guy is like going to the zoo and seeing all the animals in one. His eyes look like pig eyes. His odd features give him a predatory appearance. His scheming look doesn't escape my notice.

He opens the door wider and steps to the side. "Do I need my lawyer?"

I stare at him. "Mr. McHendricks, you don't even know why

we're here. Why do you think you need a lawyer?"

"Seems like now that I have money, everyone wants a piece of it. Old girlfriends are crawling out of the woodwork trying to get some. And when I say some, they're looking to reconnect with old Billy here."

The leering look on his face makes me want to smack him. "We're only going to take a few minutes of your time. So grateful you can work us into your schedule." My sarcasm is lost on the idiot.

"No problem. Me and the guys are in the middle of practicing our air-guitar routine. Some dudes on *America's Got Talent* played air guitars on the show. We figure we could go on the road with our act."

I look to see if he is kidding me. No such luck. Seriously? Air guitars? I look at Sean and notice his jaw clenching as he bites back laughter.

"Are these two, Steve Zeas and Eric Ronds?" The pair stand, still frozen in their air-guitar poses, waiting for instructions from McHendricks.

"Yeah. In the flesh."

Sean walks in first. "We need to talk to all three of you."

The living room is in shambles. Beer bottles and bongs cover most of the coffee table.

Sean glances around the room. "Must have been some party."

McHendricks has a confused look on his face. "Party? Nah, dude. We've just been hanging out and enjoying life. It's all legal."

Sean's voice is affable. "Sure, dude. Why don't you introduce us to your two friends, and then we can all sit down and chat."

McHendricks points to the guy with long scraggly blond hair, his Nordic ancestry firmly imprinted on his face. His blue eyes are so glazed over, it's like Viking meets Cheech and Chong. "This is Eric Ronds. The other dude is Steve Zeas."

Steve Zeas also sports the blank stoner look. His dishwater blond hair has corkscrews of curls sticking out and hangs almost to his shoulders. With his blond hair and big blue eyes, he looks like an aging Goldilocks. He barely glances at me or Sean. Instead, his eyes flick back and forth, from Billy to the bong on the table. This guy looks like a lap dog waiting for his master to give him a treat. It doesn't take a genius to figure out who calls the shots here.

Sean starts the good cop act. "So, air guitar? My guys and I used to play when we were in Iraq. We didn't see a lot of entertainers, so we made up our own." He purposely glances at the table. "Looks like you boys are having a good time. Probably been too busy to watch the news or read the newspaper today?"

As I expect, McHendricks speaks for the group. "Nothin' in the world we can change, so why bother watching the news? We just want to party and enjoy life."

Sean continues. "So I guess you didn't hear about the attempted kidnapping last night of your buddy, Brian Edison?"

Zeas and Ronds look shocked. I carefully study McHendricks' face. I don't see shock. For a brief moment, I think I witness a look of glee, but it is hard to read those little pig eyes.

Sean picks up on it and looks at McHendricks. "You don't seem surprised."

"Hey, man. The guy is worth like a billion dollars. Who wouldn't want a piece of it?" His voice is borderline petulant. "Besides, his game probably pissed off some of the wrong people. It's a dangerous game."

Obviously, he isn't aware Edison's worth has been grossly exaggerated.

Again Sean takes the lead. "Actually, he only has a quarter of a billion. You can do the math, right? That means he only has two hundred and fifty million, not a thousand million."

Steve Zeas chimes in. "Still a lot of dough considering we helped, and hardly got nuthin' for ten years of work."

His whiny voice irritates me. Time for bad cop. "Really? From what I heard, you guys only played the game. It's not like you wrote the program or contributed anything more than if chimpanzees had been testing it." Ka boom. First shot fired. My mood starts to improve. I used to hate playing bad cop, but I'm enjoying the expression on McHendricks's face.

McHendricks raises himself up to his full five foot eight. I love that he has to look up to meet my eyes. "You don't know shit about what's gone on for the last ten years. You only know what Baby Brian told you."

"Baby Brian?" Sean and I say at the same time.

"Oh hell, yes. The guy can't sneeze without mommy wiping his nose. She picks up after all of his messes. His parents paid all his bills. He worked a minimum wage job, so his mind could be free to 'develop ideas.'"

His fingers do air-quotes when he says, "develop ideas." Old Billy boy has some serious anger issues. Time to poke the little piggy.

"So you feel you didn't get your fair share? That's what you're claiming? What did you guys expect on your tiny investment of five thousand dollars each? Seems to me you made out pretty well. Nice cars and unlimited party time, and you don't have to punch a time clock. What else did you expect to happen?"

"We were supposed to be equal partners. Brian promised. When the game went viral with seventy-million downloads, we thought we'd hit the mother lode. We didn't expect him to hand us a check for a million bucks and then cut us off."

Billy boy is so worked up, he has spittle flying out of his mouth. The other two have frowns on their faces.

Eric Ronds's stoner eyes travel from me to Sean. He must have decided Sean would be more sympathetic because he ignores me and addresses him. "Man, we've been friends since high school. When guys picked on Brian cuz he was a geek, the three of us would kick their asses. We looked out for him, and he trusted us. We trusted him too. We didn't need no contract. Brian said so. I think he would have fixed it for us, but then his parents butted in. They're the ones that screwed everything up. They screwed us over."

Steve Zeas shows his crooked teeth with a smug smile. "Yeah, but they'll be sorry. We got a lawyer. We're suing his ass, and his parents, for alienation of affection."

I manage to cut my snort of laughter off, but still, an unladylike noise escapes. "Alienation of affection? How did you come up with that?" More importantly, I'm wondering what kind of lawyer these guys have hired.

McHendricks puffs up. "You know the dude that advertises on TV? He's always on the sci-fi channel, usually after midnight. He's gonna help us get our money."

Sean and I raise our eyebrows. The sci-fi channel? What decent lawyer advertises on the sci-fi channel? I can't resist. "So what's this lawyer's name? Is he human or an alien?"

"Go ahead and laugh. Myron 'My' Champion is a great lawyer. He's gonna get us our fair share." Billy's eyes bore into me.

"Really? His name is My Champion?" With all three of them nodding at the same time, it is like watching bobbleheads. We spend the next half hour getting information from them.

It all checks out to what DL has already told us. I stand up from the sofa and pray there isn't grass on my ass or a big old beer stain.

Sean tells the three to carry on, and we will be back if we have any more questions.

We walk out to the car. Thankfully it's out of sight from the living room windows. Any tension we had before is gone. We laugh until I snort, and then we laugh some more. After five minutes, we wipe our eyes and at the same time say, "Dude. DL is going to love this."

That sets us off again. This time, I don't mind the man giggles.

Chapter 13

Billy McHendricks watched the two cops walk to their car. He thought about all the things he'd like to do to the lady detective, but then took another look at her partner. The man was the size of a small building and had towered over Billy during the interview. He had always hated his lack of height. He thought again of the tall lady cop and how he wanted to climb her tree.

He said to Zeas and Ronds, "As soon as I get the money, women like her will be flocking to me. All of the bitches will want ole Billy."

Eric looked at Billy. His eyes were so glassy, they didn't look real. "Dude, should we be worried the cops came here? Why would they come? Man, we haven't even seen Edison in months."

Steve looked from Eric to Billy. "Maybe we should call Brian. I mean, what happens to us if someone kidnaps him?"

Billy shrieked like a girl. "Keep your mouths shut about Brian. The guy screwed us over, and now you're worried about him? Fuck him. Too bad they didn't kill him. We wouldn't have to deal with his lyin' ass. We could sue his parents. Probably be easier to get the money out of them, cuz they'd have all of his money. Thirty million would be nothing to them."

Billy stood over Eric and Steve. "Yell if the cops come back. I gotta do something."

Billy headed upstairs to his bedroom. He noticed a rank smell when he walked in and kicked a path through the piles of dirty clothes on the floor to get to his bed. He reached under the flimsy mattress and pulled out a burner phone. He punched in the phone number and waited. Three rings and finally a voice said only one word: "Message."

Billy knew the rules. Leave a short message and hang up immediately.

"FBI guy and a hot lady detective came by to ask questions. Wanted to know about the financial deal with Brian." Billy paused, the brief summary taxed his brain. He tried to think if he should say anything else. "Ah, I guess that's all."

Billy hung up and stuffed the phone back under his mattress. He would receive instructions within eight hours. He knew he was now a puppet in some dangerous game involving his former friend, but a strong moral code was not in his DNA.

No matter what it took, he was going to get the money Brian owed him. Hell, he'd even take Zeas and Ronds shares, too. He was going to have enough money to move to a country with lots of pot and willing underage hookers. Billy McHendricks was looking forward to living like a king.

Chapter 14

Sean hadn't laughed so hard in years. Every time he thought he was through, a new image would hit him. "And what about when they all shook their heads up and down like bobbleheads?" More laughter.

Jayne wiped her eyes. "Damn...I bet I have mascara running down my face."

Sean turned in his seat. "No. You're beautiful."

"Watch it, Lindstrom. You're turning human on me, and it is pretty scary."

Sean was about to answer when Jayne's phone rang. Tim McGraw's "Live Like You Were Dying" lyrics filled the car. He started humming along to, "...and all of a sudden going fishing wasn't such an imposition."

He saw Jayne push the accept button on her dashboard hands-free, and she said, "Yes, sir."

"Jayne, is this a bad time?" a deep male voice inquired.

"No, sir."

Hoots of laughter filled the car. "It must be a bad time. When in your life have you ever called me sir?"

Jayne's face turned bright red. Sean was beginning to think she had a boyfriend on the line and wondered who the hell else his competition was.

"I'm busted. Hi, Dad. What's going on? Everything okay?"

Sean felt relief like a punch to the gut.

"Where are you? I went fishing today and limited out. Your mom is going to cook up a batch. Come home for dinner."

Glancing over at Sean, Jayne replied, "No can do. I'm on a case and riding with an FBI agent."

"I saw your picture in the paper today. Sounds like an interesting case. So does the FBI guy eat food? Are you planning on eating dinner on the road at some fast food place rather than eat your mother's cooking? Wait for a minute while I tell her."

Jayne cried out in mock exasperation. "You are a horrible

man. All right. You win. Hold on. Let me ask if the man-in-black eats fish. Trout or salmon, Dad?"

"Salmon."

"Oh God, the fish whisperer has done it again. You caught your limit? I'd better come home before half the neighborhood gets there and you run out. Hold on."

Sean's mouth was already watering. Jayne looked over at him. "Well, you heard the man. It's after five. If we go straight back to Edison's, chances are Mimi will try and force us to eat her cooking. I can drop you off there, or you can come with me."

Sean couldn't say yes fast enough. "Are you trying to kill me? I can't do two of Mimi's meals in one day. I'm in. Thanks."

"You heard him, Dad. Two for dinner. We're on our way. Remember, we're working, so we can't stay long." Jayne hit the disconnect button on the dash and said, "My dad is a bit overprotective. I make a point of picking up his calls if I'm not in the middle of something. Otherwise he worries. I hope you're hungry, as the house is only about fifteen minutes from here."

***

A few minutes later, Jayne pulled the car over to the curb in front of an older home with a well-maintained yard. "This is the place. You'd better be on your best behavior. You don't have to worry about my parents--they know you're a work associate. But my little sisters are here." Jayne chuckled. "Hey FBI man, you're in for it now."

As they walked up the steps, the front door flew open. A tall man stepped out of the front door with his arms wide open. "Here's my girl." He enveloped her in a gigantic hug. Jayne hugged him hard and let go.

Sean surreptitiously studied the two as they hugged. Jayne's dad was tall, a couple inches shorter than him. His gray hair was thinning a bit. His blue eyes were identical to Jayne's, and the smile on his face was one of pure love. Sean liked what he saw.

"I see the girls are here. Oh, wait, let me introduce Special Agent Sean Lindstrom. You can call him Sean. This is my dad, Jerry Johnson."

Sean made a mental note of the different last names as he extended his hand, and Jerry shook it with hands as big as oven mitts. "Nice to meet you, Sean. You can call me Jerry or Jer. Your choice."

"Thanks, Jerry. I appreciate getting to come for dinner. You may have saved two lives."

Jayne jumped in. "Sean, don't scare my Dad. He's referring to the cook at our victim's house. If she cooked for convicts, it would be considered cruel and unusual punishment."

Jerry and Sean both laughed. Sean added, "She's not exaggerating."

Jayne asked her dad, "Usually you invite half the neighborhood when you limit out. Who else is coming?"

Jerry looked abashed. "I invited Madison, but she said she had--and I quote--'a hot date.' So it's just us, Mom, and the girls."

Jayne chuckled, and Sean laughed, too.

"She must be going out with Michael," Jayne said. "Never thought I'd say this, but he's a good guy. That's twice I've been wrong lately. Hope it doesn't become a habit."

Sean gave her shoulder a quick squeeze. "Thanks. He's a really good guy. I'm glad you're giving him...well, maybe both of us...a second chance."

Sean saw Jerry out of the corner of his eye and didn't miss the smile on his face.

Jerry asked Sean. "So how does this two agency thing work? Do you share duties?"

Sean paused and chose his words carefully. "Interagency partnerships are always awkward, but Jayne's been easy to work with. She's a hell of a cop. I got lucky."

Jayne smiled and said, "Thanks. So far you've proven you have my back and I appreciate it."

Jer's eyebrows raised up. "Jayne, tell me what's going on before we go inside. You know how worried your mom gets. Everything okay? The newspapers were kind of vague. Great shot of you by the way."

"There was a kidnapping attempt on a local guy who's made a quarter of a billion with some internet games." She gave Sean an amused look. "We're trying to find the group responsible. SPD and the FBI are working on it together, so Sean here, is my new, temporary, partner."

Jerry scratched his head for a moment. "Did you say a quarter of a billion for video games? That's insane."

Sean's face split open with a wide grin. "Yes sir, it is."

A woman's voice called out. "Are you all going to stand on the porch all night? Jer, send our girl in here. I can hug and cook at the same time."

Jayne made a beeline for her mom, and the two women shared a big hug. Sean smiled. He liked seeing Jayne in her element.

She introduced Sean to her mom, Terra, and then Jayne took her hand. In a stage whisper, she said, "Where are my demon sisters?"

"We can hear you!" The footfalls on the stairs sounded like wild horses galloping through the prairie.

"Girls! Stop running in the house!" Her smile belied her stern warning. "They will never grow up!"

Two tall blondes came into the kitchen. Sean looked at the three women. The family resemblance was strong. Seeing the petite Terra, he concluded the height was obviously from Jerry's side of the family.

Emily zeroed in on Sean. "Jaynie, who is this?"

Jayne looked at her younger sister. "Ems, this is a colleague. Special Agent Sean Lindstrom, FBI. We're working a case together. So, do me a favor and behave yourself."

Emily gave Jayne a fake pout. "Agent Lindstrom, nice to meet you."

Right behind her, Amy waited for her introduction.

After introductions were completed, Jayne tugged on Sean's sleeve. "Sean, I've got that picture I told you about. Let's take a look at it here, I'd rather not discuss it at Edison's." She looked over at her dad. "Dad, we need the office for a few minutes."

"Sure, baby girl. I'm going to put the fish on the barbecue. Dinner in twenty minutes. Will that work?"

"Yeah, Dad. Thanks." Jayne turned to Sean. "Come on."

The office was good sized with a partner desk in the middle. Sean looked at the neatly labeled filing cabinets lining the wall and the in/out box on the corner of the desk. One side was meticulous, and the other side was littered with paper and a few fishing brochures.

"My parents share the office. You can probably guess which side is my dad's." Jayne laughed as she fished around on the computer for the port, finally saying, "Got it," as she connected her phone to a USB port, and the picture appeared on the large monitor.

"Sheri McLellon received this at *The Seattle Times* with the message, 'Jayne Moore, showing the assets that got her promoted.' Fortunately, Sheri McLellon also happens to be my neighbor and friend. Obviously, it didn't make it into the paper."

They stood side by side and stared down at the monitor. "That's Officer Dobson on the right. I borrowed his cuffs. We can eliminate him."

Sean studied the photograph. "From this angle, the hotel's security camera should be able to give us a shot of who took the photo."

Jayne paused. "We can check later. I'm sure the film has already been pulled by the FBI or SPD. Diane can probably check it and, while she's at it, look into the IP address. But this is not a priority. This situation is a personal problem. It has nothing to do with Edison's attempted kidnapping. We can't waste time with this until we solve the Edison case."

"Jayne. You need to realize this attack on your character could be just the beginning. Someone is trying to discredit you. It failed this time, but it doesn't mean they won't try again."

"I have some ideas of who it could be. Turner has a beat in Ballard. It would be like him to answer a call out of his area if it sounded high profile. He's always looking to be in on something 'worthy of his experience.' The guy is an egomaniac. His wife is connected to the City Council. I'm sure she pulled some strings to get him assigned to this case."

"Yeah, but he's nothing more than a glorified mall cop guarding Edison. How can that work for him?"

Jayne stared up at Sean. "He'll figure out a way to discredit me. I never thought I'd say this, but it feels good that you have my back."

The moment was getting too serious. Sean gave her a leering

look. "Hey, Moore. Nice thong."

"Dude. My eyes are up here." And then she laughed. "And now, for that comment, I'm going to sic my sisters on you."

"Bring it on, Moore. Did you not listen when I told you about my three younger sisters? There was so much hormonal stuff going on at my house, I'm surprised I didn't have a period too."

"Oh. My. God. I did not hear you say that." She was about to say more, when Amy and Emily came down the hall.

Sean looked the two girls over. They reminded him of his sisters and that spelled trouble.

"They don't bite, Sean. Emily and Amy just started their freshman year at the UW."

"Twins?" Sean looked back and forth between the girls.

"We're fraternal twins," the girls said in unison.

"Double the trouble. You remind me of my sisters. So how do you like the UW?" Sean watched an odd look come over the girls' faces.

Emily took point on the question. "The UW is okay. We're getting used to being in a dorm, and we've met lots of new people."

Sean made a mental note that she said new people and not new friends. "Sometimes new schools and new people are hard to get used to. My sister, Julie, left for college when I was in Iraq. She hated it. Julie said the kids only cared about partying. And she didn't like the whole sorority and fraternity atmosphere."

This time, Amy spoke. "They try and make you feel like you're not cool if you don't join. And there's this boy I like. He's in a fraternity and his 'brothers' said he couldn't date me unless I pledged a sorority. That's not my thing. They seem to exclude anyone who doesn't conform to their standards."

"Here's what I told my sister Julie when she got the cold shoulder. Stand firm on what you want and believe in yourself. If this boy isn't strong enough to stand on his own, then in the long run, he's not worth it. There are a lot of good guys on that campus that aren't involved in Greek row. Join some clubs that interest you, and you'll meet new friends. And if all else fails, tell them your sister's a cop and carries a gun."

Sean's moment of levity broke the tension. Both girls smiled and then burst into giggles. "We'll tell them that only as a last resort."

Amy looked up at Sean. "Did your sister finally like college?"

"Yes, she did. The next year my sister Anna was a freshman, and then the following year, my sister Jackie started. They had a lot of friends. We skyped almost every day when I was in Iraq."

Amy asked, "What are your sisters doing now?"

Sean looked sheepish and glanced at Jayne. "Julie is a librarian. Anna is a legal assistant, and Jackie is a high-school math teacher."

Jayne's dad yelled for everyone to come for dinner and the girls scampered off.

Jayne's look was incredulous. "Seriously? A librarian?"

"Yeah. I could tell you really weren't one. My sister quizzes everyone on what books they like to read and what's new to read. When you didn't talk about books, I was thinking you were a criminal, a hooker, or a cop. I was really relieved you weren't one of the first two."

Jayne's face was unreadable, so he kept talking. "I know I was rude to you and kept saying weird things. I was trying to figure out who you really were. I'm sorry."

"Rude doesn't even begin to describe you! There were times I was tempted to shoot you." Jayne paused and begrudgingly added, "Sounds like you're a pretty good big brother. And thanks for talking to my sisters."

Sean shrugged his shoulders. "Our dad left when Jackie was still in diapers, so I guess I've kind of spoiled them. God, I hate to admit this. Whenever I'm home, they make me go with them for pedicures. To say they've got me wrapped around their little fingers is an understatement. Your sisters seem like pretty level-headed girls."

"They are. Sometimes people need the unbiased opinion of a stranger instead of confiding in family." Jayne pulled out her phone and checked the time. "Come on. We need to eat and head back to Edison's." Jayne turned and walked down the hall toward the kitchen.

He heard a muffled snort of laughter, and her shoulders shook a little. Sean was surprised at the relief that flooded through him.

Sean had to admit, Edison was right. She had beauty, brains, and most importantly, a sense of humor.

***

"Dad, you're not going to be offended when we eat and run, right? We need to get back to Edison's house." Jayne glanced at Sean.

"Yeah, Jerry. I wish we didn't have to go but duty calls." Sean was disappointed to have the evening end. The dinner had gone well. Jayne's parents were easy to be around.

Sean took his last bite of dessert and let out a contented sigh. When he looked up, he caught Jayne watching him. He smiled at her, and saw a blush creep up her face. He looked away to minimize her embarrassment and saw her parents exchange a smile and a private look. He felt like he'd just passed an important test and smiled to himself.

Chapter 15

Sean is uncharacteristically quiet on the ride back to Edison's. I glance over at him as he turns toward me.

"How come you're Moore and the rest of your family is Johnson? Do you have a husband stashed in an attic somewhere?"

"No. My parents died in a car wreck when I was four. Jerry is my mom's little brother, and he took me in. He was twenty-one, unmarried, and had to fight like hell to get custody of me. He was the only relative willing to raise me. He always likes to say that I helped raise him because he went from being a wild-and-crazy single guy to being a dad. When I was eight, he married Terra. She's amazing. So, I got a new set of parents. And I have two sisters."

"Losing your parents must have been really tough."

"I was so young, I only have a few blurry memories. But you know what my new dad taught me. Sometimes life sucks. Not all the time, but sometimes bad things happen to good people. But it's important how you handle the problem. It doesn't have to make you hard as nails, but it does make you stronger. Life isn't perfect. You don't win every race, or every competition. You do your best, and every day you get up and start all over again."

"Wow. Sounds like a lot of wisdom to try and give a four-year-old."

I smile. "He didn't try and make me a wise four-year-old. He has given me his wisdom and love every day of my life. I am so lucky to have him. When he met Terra, he wouldn't propose to her until he knew the three of us would be okay together. It was a pretty big gamble to take, considering I knew I had him wrapped around my little finger. He didn't spoil me with things, he just made me the center of his universe. I wasn't sure I could share him. Then I met Terra, and it was love at first sight. I hadn't realized how much I missed having a mom until she came along. I still went fishing with Dad, but now, with Terra, all the girly things came my way. And talk about unconditional love, Terra has always been my biggest champion."

Sean flashes his killer smile. "I knew I liked your dad when I met him. Your mom, too. But why are you Moore, and they're Johnson?"

"Like I said, my memories of my parents are kind of blurry, but I have one very clear memory. I remember sitting at the kitchen table with my parents, and they were teaching me how to write my name. It was just before they were killed. It's the only thing I have left of them. When Jerry adopted me and said I would be a Johnson, I started crying and said I had to stay a Moore. I don't know why at four years old I dug my heels in, but I had to. I told him my daddy had taught me how to write my name, and I didn't want to learn a new one."

I pause, change lanes, and head toward the gate, praying I wouldn't encounter the same guard as last night. "Jerry understood. He has always tried to keep my parents alive for me. He likes to tell stories about my mom when they were kids, or talk about what a great guy my dad was. He's been my dad almost my entire life, and one of the things I love the most is that he takes the time to keep them in my memory."

Sean's voice is soft. "I'm really glad to have met your family tonight. They're great." Then his smile widens and his voice is normal. "That salmon dinner really makes up for drawing the short straw and getting you as a partner."

I can't help but laugh. Sean has a way of diffusing serious moments. I pull the car up to the gate. Another white-haired rent-a-cop is manning the booth. I roll down my window and flash my badge. "I'm Detective Moore. We're going to Brian Edison's."

"Yes, ma'am. You're on the list." As he speaks, the gates open.

I turn to Sean. "Now this is how it's supposed to go. One less battle to fight tonight."

"You're expecting battles tonight? With whom?"

"I'm sure Turner will have some choice words. He needs to assert his authority at all times, and it just kills him to realize he doesn't have any over me."

"Turner's an ass. His kind of cop is part of a dying breed. You're a good cop, Jayne. We'll keep an eye on him together. I'd actually like to catch him at something. He makes my fist itch."

I chuckle. "An itchy fist, huh? I'm sure Turner will give you a chance to scratch that itch."

I pull the car into the garage. Last night, Alias gave me a garage door opener, and I park next to Edison's car. We walk into the back door, through the mudroom, and into the kitchen. First thing I see is Turner. He's leaning over onto the kitchen counter, giving Mimi Jenkins a broad smile, and it looks like he's in the middle of telling a joke. The minute he sees me and Sean, he stops mid-sentence and stands up straight.

"Nice of you two to join us."

His whiny voice sends me into bitch mode. "Last time I checked, Officer Turner, I don't report to you."

His mouth turns surly, but before he can respond, Sean asks him. "Turner, anything to report? What's going on with Edison right now?"

"Ferguson and one of your FBI guys are watching him. He's in the basement working out in his home gym. I'm on dinner break. Mimi was just about to dish up some of her delicious-looking stew." Turner's voice is cool and professional.

I watch Turner still trying to win Sean over. Shows the man is as dumb as a post. He just can't read body language.

Mimi is staring at Sean. "Special Agent Lindstrom, can I get you a plate of stew? It's my specialty."

I stifle a laugh at the way she emphasizes "specialty."

Sean shakes his head. "Thanks, Mimi, but no. Detective Moore and I have eaten."

Mimi's eyes flick over to me. It is obvious she hadn't even thought about offering me a meal. The bitch. I smile sweetly. "Gosh, Mimi, if your special stew is as good as your special meatloaf, Martha Stewart better watch out."

God, another person in the room dumb as a post. She actually preens.

***

When I enter my bedroom, I can tell someone has been in it. My pillow is positioned a little off from the bed. I'm a precision bed maker and would not have left it like that. I had filled one drawer with my makeup bag and toothbrush. I can tell it has been opened, and it appears the contents have been rifled through.

I send Sean a text asking him if anyone had gone through his room.

His reply is short. *Not that I can tell. What's up?*

Next thing I know, Sean is knocking softly on the connecting door from the bathroom. I open it up and step aside for him to enter.

"What's going on? Someone was in your room?" I can hear anger in his muted tone.

"Some of my things have been moved. I can either think we had room service or go with the idea that someone was in snooping. I would guess it's the latter. I'm putting my money on Turner or Mimi."

Sean glances around the room. "Anything missing?"

"I don't think so. Maybe I should count my granny panties. If any are missing, it would point directly to Turner. He's the type that would get off on that."

Sean suppresses a laugh, keeping his voice low. "Hey, don't count me out on that. I'm sure no matter what you wear, it would look sexy. Even granny panties."

I can feel my face heating up. I really need to go underwear shopping for something that is in the middle range, between a thong and granny panties. This is getting embarrassing. Before I can think of a reply, we hear someone walking down the hall and freeze.

Sean stands close to me and whispers into my ear, "I'll go skulk around and see if there's any movement from room to room. I'll check with Olsen and Hopps to see if they noticed any unusual activity."

Sean's body radiates heat, and it feels like I've been transported to the Sahara Desert after two years in Antarctica. I struggle to maintain a neutral look on my face but find myself leaning into his warmth.

I hear a soft laugh. He knows exactly how he's affecting me. "Oh, and great day, partner. Thanks." He steps away and my body temperature drops.

Sean silently walks back through the bathroom, and I hear him open his bedroom door to the hallway.

A whoosh of breath escapes me. I don't know what just happened, but I'm flustered and feeling like an awkward teenager. And wouldn't you know, it's a hormonal, sex-crazed teenager. My libido has picked a hell of a time to reappear. Damn.

Chapter 16

Sean walked back into his room. He had placed his weapon on his pillow but put it back into his shoulder holster. He quietly opened the door and closed it softly behind him. The thin Oriental rug in the hallway was on hardwood, forcing Sean to walk lightly to suppress the sound of his footsteps. He and Jayne were in the "guest wing" of the home. Mimi's and Alias's rooms were down the hall, closer to Edison's master suite.

He turned the corner and saw two agents sitting at the end of the hallway with a clear view of Edison's door as well as Alias' and Mimi's rooms.

"Hey guys, how's it going?" Sean's voice was low.

Tom Hopps spoke. "On a scale of boring, one to ten, this is definitely a twenty. Edison went in about an hour ago. This is going to be a long night."

Dick Olsen looked at Sean. "At least you got out of here today. Detective Moore is pretty easy on the eyes. How's it going?"

Sean was about to get defensive but realized Dick was just saying the truth. Jayne was definitely easy on the eyes. "She's a good cop. You heard how she took down the two guys at the scene. I trust her."

Dick nodded. "Lucky you didn't get saddled with Turner. He's borderline psycho. I don't trust him. I've got a friend at SPD. Turner's got a pretty bad reputation. He's burned quite a few cops. He was sure bad-mouthing Detective Moore. Claims she slept her way into the Detective job. And by the way, my friend says Moore's reputation and job performance are stellar."

Sean's fist clenched. He tried to compose himself before he spoke. "Turner's trying to discredit Jayne. He's got a real hard-on over the fact that she made detective, and he didn't. This guy is going to try something to make himself look good and sink her."

They were still discussing the problem in low voices when Mimi Jenkins walked out into the hall, wearing very revealing sleepwear. The startled look on her face was obviously faked. Her coy voice was directed to them all, but her eyes were on Sean. "Oh, gentlemen, I didn't know you were out here. Does anyone need anything before I call it a night?"

All three men shook their heads. When Mimi went back into her room, the agents tried to muffle their laughter. Dick was the first to speak. "That woman is a piece of work. She looks like she was rode hard and put away wet. She's got so much paint on her face, she looks like Tammy Faye Bakker's twin sister."

Sean looked blank.

Olsen sighed. "Okay, that was a dated reference to a defrocked minister and his overly made-up wife. Happened in the eighties. God, I'm getting old."

Sean chuckled and changed the subject. "How was the stew?"

Hopps and Olsen groaned.

Olsen patted his ample belly and said, "With her cooking, this is the toughest case I've ever been assigned. I see some weight loss in my future if I have to eat her food."

"You didn't have to eat her meatloaf. That old family recipe was straight out of the Addams family." Sean groaned for effect. "Okay, let's get back on track. Moore says someone was in her room today. Did you see anything unusual? My money's on Turner or Mimi. On a side note, we suspect something's up with her and Alias."

Hopps nodded. "I haven't seen anything unusual. Turner and Ferguson were with Edison up until an hour ago. That gives Turner time to be the snooper."

Olsen chimed in. "Mimi and Alias have a weird interaction. Looks like they're a couple, but she kind of puts it out there like she's fishing for something better. She and Turner have their flirt on. I hear he's married, but he doesn't act like it."

Sean clapped Olsen on the shoulder. "Meanwhile, we're running background checks on Mimi and Alias. I'll let you know what we find out. Keep an eye on Turner. Moore personally vouches for Ferguson. And that, gentlemen, is the score as I know it."

Sean took a step down the hall and stopped, turned back and said, "If the food gets too bad, I have some candy bars stashed in my nightstand."

***

Sean decided to take a quick walk around the house and outside grounds. He knew Ferguson was outside. He was walking by the back patio when he saw Turner standing by the flagpole talking on his cell phone. He paused and took advantage of the shadow of the house.

"Hey, baby. Do you miss me?" Turner's voice was as slick as oil. "What are you wearing?"

He paused as he listened. Sean could see a leering smile on his face. "Oh, baby, that sounds so good."

Just as Sean was ready to lose his dinner, Turner said, "Oh, fuck. Gotta go. The ball-and-chain is calling. See you soon, sweet lips." Turner disconnected the call and curtly said, "I told you not to call me when I'm working. What do you want?"

Sean couldn't make out the words, but the tone was unmistakably shrill, and he almost laughed as he saw Turner deflate and try to placate his wife.

"Okay, okay. I'm sorry. I didn't mean to snap. I'm on a case, and it's one that's gonna get me noticed." Turner's whiny voice stopped as he listened for a moment. "I said I was sorry. You don't need to go tattle to your dad. Jeez, Marianna, calm down. There aren't any women here unless you count some dyke detective. Are you going to punish me forever for one little mistake? You know I love you. Can't we talk about something else for a change? Wasn't today your Weight Watchers day? How'd it go, honey?"

This time Sean could hear her from fifteen feet away, as Turner held the phone away from his ear. "Quit harping on my weight, you asshole. You just love using it as an excuse to cheat on me."

Turner sighed and for a nanosecond, Sean almost mustered up a little pity, but he quickly got over it when he heard him say. "Honey, I've gotta hang up. That dyke detective is heading this way. Looks like she's pissed about something. I'll call you later." Turner disconnected the call and exclaimed, "Fucking bitch."

Sean was about to make his presence known when Ferguson tapped his shoulder.

"Follow me," Ferguson whispered, as he turned on his heel and headed to the other side of the house, away from Turner who was already making another phone call.

Sean followed Ferguson.

Ferguson wasted no time. "That guy's an ass, and he's a blight on all the hard-working cops. I know you're ready to defend Jayne, especially after hearing the crap he was telling his wife. The thing is, you've got to back off. If you run to her defense, he'll use it against her. I'm keeping an eye on him, and he's getting just enough rope to hang himself. There are some things he's into that are going to bite him in the butt. Plus, he's doing his best to undermine Jayne's credibility. Talk about male ego. The thing is, he refuses to believe that Jayne is a good detective. She and her partner have the highest percentage of solved cases in the department. I keep track of my rookie, and trust me, Turner will not be messing with her or her reputation. Not on my watch. So young fella, you and Jayne get these jerks that have it in for Edison, and get us out of mauve hell. I'll watch Turner."

Sean pushed his anger against Turner to the bottom of his list. "Angus, you're a good cop. You're right. Turner is an ass. He's starting to get close to Mimi Jenkins and that can't be good. We think she and John Doe, a.k.a., Alias, are up to something. Probably not the terrorist kidnapping plot, but my gut says there is something going on. Jayne's gut feels it too. Plus, Jayne says someone was snooping around her room today."

Angus paused a moment, digesting the theory. "I'm sure you and Jayne are running checks on the staff. Alias has a tattoo on his arm that looks like a prison tat to me. It will be interesting to see what comes up. I was with Turner all day, but that's not to say he couldn't have gone into Jayne's room. I'll keep a better eye on him."

"Thanks. My gut says it's Turner, but we also have Alias and Mimi in the mix. Yeah, we've got both the FBI and SPD running the lists of employees as well as Edison's friends. We should have something by tomorrow." Sean stopped, thought for a moment, and then asked, "What's your take on Edison? Have you had a chance to talk to him?"

Angus chuckled. "That kid has all the money anyone would ever need, and he eats peanut-butter-and- jelly sandwiches three times a day? Unbelievable. He should use some of his money to get a shrink to fix his problem." Angus patted his belly. "I'd sure know how to spend it. I'd go to the finest restaurants in the world."

Sean slapped Angus on the back. "That's because you are a man of class and distinction. I'm really not sure what we have with Edison. Jayne and I asked him if he could think of a reason why he would be targeted and he drew a blank. Then we find out he's just released a violent video game that pits Americans against ISIS. Is he that naïve to not see the connection?"

Angus smiled. "My sister's kid, same deal. He's been coddled so much by my sister and her husband that he's never assumed a role as an adult. That's what I see in Edison. And that guy, Alias, he's like a daddy figure for him, always directing him on what to do. Now, we can't exactly call the cook a mommy figure, but you should see how she cuts the crusts off his sandwiches. It's classic mom stuff. Kind of creepy when she's doing that, and at the same time making sure he gets a look down her top when she bends over his desk. I'm not sure what to make of her, but I get the feeling that her favorite movie is *The Graduate.*"

"The what? Oh, wait, I remember. My mom used to talk about that movie. Older woman seduces a younger man? I don't think that's going to happen. He's got his eye on Jayne." Sean spoke the last words with a dose of irritation.

The older cop's voice was stern. "Sean, Jayne's a smart woman. She's not dazzled easily, and if you imply to her that she'd go after someone strictly based on the fact they have money, you're going to piss her off and believe me, that would be a wrong move. The woman can shoot the ass off an ant at fifty feet."

Sean knew he was coming off like a jealous teenager and mentally gave himself a slap. "You're right. Thanks. Okay, I'm turning in. You stay on Turner, and I've got Jayne's back."

Angus stood up straight and had to look up to meet Sean's eyes. "You make sure you do. I'd put nothing past Turner and his ambition. And by the way, there isn't anyone I'd trust more to have mine. I'm pretty attached to my rookie. She's a hell of a cop."

Sean looked down at Angus. "I'm counting on it."

Chapter 17

With forty-eight hours of only minimal sleep, I not only hit the wall, I think it reciprocated and fell on top of me. I'm so beat, it's all I can do to check my weapon and place it on the pillow next to me. I hate not sleeping in my own bed. When I napped on the bed this morning, I had been too tired to feel all the lumps. Now, I keep squirming around trying to find a comfortable spot.

Also, I can't keep Sean out of my thoughts. He has turned out to be so different from what I expected. And how had Sean managed to sucker me with the used-car salesman story? I must be losing my edge. I guess, in the interest of fairness, I did lie about the librarian thing. God, how embarrassing. He saw right through me, and I bought his jerk routine, hook, line, and sinker. It's hard admitting I was wrong, and there's way more to Sean Lindstrom than meets the eye.

The clock beside my bed shows 11:30. I need to clear my head, but the day's events keep replaying over and over. Too many things aren't passing the smell test. This whole thing with Edison failing to mention the content of his video game sends a red flag. Could he be so incredibly naive? Is Edison some giant kid disguised as an adult? That little pig Billy McHendricks might be on to something with Alias and Mimi filling the new mommy-daddy roles. It seems pretty far-fetched with Mimi, but Alias definitely holds some power in this household. His dubious choice of cooks is another red flag. What is their story? Pieces start to fall together in my mind, only to be lost when, finally, sleep takes me faraway.

I hear my bedroom door open and someone walks in, the sound almost swallowed by the thick carpet. I reach for my gun as the intruder opens the connecting door to the bathroom. I can see the silhouette of a man. I jump off the bed, take two steps, and place my gun firmly to the back of his head.

"Freeze."

"Jesus, Jayne. What the hell? You locked my side of the bathroom door, and I need to pee." Sean's voice sounds both amused and annoyed.

"What are you doing sneaking around?" I am pissed and can still feel the adrenaline coursing through my body. I flip on the light and glare at him. "Why didn't you just text me or call me. Or better yet, here's a novel idea, maybe knock on my door and ask me to unlock the other side. What in holy hell made you think sneaking through my bedroom would be a good idea?"

"Jayne. We've both had only about five hours sleep in the last forty-eight hours. I didn't want to bother you. How am I supposed to know you're some sort of ninja sleeper?" Sean pauses as his eyes wander from my face to check out my pajamas. "Nice jammies, but I prefer the Hello Kitty nightshirt. It's more you."

He laughs as he walks into the bathroom. I can hear the sound of him peeing. And speaking of jammies, he wasn't kidding about sleeping in his boxers. The image of him shirtless in boxers will take a little time to download from my memory. Ah, never mind. I'll leave it there.

***

My alarm goes off at six. I am surprised how easily I fell back to sleep after Sean's little stunt. I grab my toothbrush and open the bathroom door. I put my ear to Sean's door and listen to the sound of soft snoring from the other side. Great. With any luck, I'll be out of here before he wakes up. I lock the door on his side and quickly shower. For a nanosecond, I think about skipping the make-up, but vanity gets the best of me and I hit my lashes with some mascara and the cheeks get a bit of blush. This time, I realize I'm not doing it for Edison, but maybe, just maybe, for Sean Lindstrom. An image of him in his boxers hits me, and a little sigh escapes. My fantasy is interrupted when Sean tries to open his door.

"Hold your horses, Lindstrom. I'll unlock it and go to my room."

I click the door lock to open. Instead of waiting, Sean opens the door and peeks his head around, keeping the rest of his body hidden.

He whispers, "Are you going to eat breakfast? Want to go to an I-Hop or Denny's to discuss the case and avoid the chance of ptomaine poisoning? Besides, we need to go in and talk to DL."

I try to lean away from him. Antarctica is a safer place for me, but I can still feel heat from him. I mentally shake myself back to reality and listen to his words. Relief at not trying to eat Mimi's food floods through me. "I agree. However, I need coffee. I'll head downstairs and nose around a bit."

Sean puts a mock serious face on and says, "Be careful. Right now, the kitchen is the most lethal room in the house. But I spotted a Keurig, so at least the coffee will be safe."

I smile and go back into my room. I step into the hallway and notice no agents are sitting in front of Edison's bedroom door. He must be up. I use the front stairs and come out at the entryway. Edison's office is to the left.

As I approach, the two FBI agents look in my direction and smile. Dick Olsen stands up and gives me a cheery smile.

"Detective Moore, you're up bright and early."

I can't resist. "Yeah. I want to make sure I get some of Mimi's yummy breakfast before you guys gobble it all up."

The look on his face is priceless. He went from incredulous to jaw-dropping stunned. Then he let loose with a huge belly laugh. "Good one."

Hopps chuckles, too. "Detective, you're in luck. Mimi came downstairs a few minutes after Edison went into his office. She's already brought him his toasted peanut-butter-and-jelly sandwich. She headed back to bed and told us we are on our own. Good news for my digestive track."

I like these two. So far, the FBI guys and Angus are making this almost pleasant. "What time do Angus and Turner come on duty?"

"In five minutes, thank God," Hopps said.

"Agent Lindstrom and I are expected downtown at eleven. We plan on re-interviewing Edison before we go, but first I need some coffee."

I turn and head to the kitchen. Mimi, as expected, is not in residence. I open cupboard doors until I find two cups and stand in front of the Keurig checking out the coffee pods. The rack holds at least ten varieties.

I hear footsteps behind me and turn to see Sean. His hair, still wet from his shower, is sticking up in little spikes. He has a teasing smile on his face, and I feel my body flush again. Good God...a crush at my age? What's next, pimples?

I watch as he pretends to look in the pantry for Mimi, waggling his eyebrows like Groucho Marx, and then looks under the kitchen table. We are both laughing, and it feels good to enjoy a lighthearted moment. But then reality hits and I stop giggling. The fun will have to wait. I really want to wrap this case up.

He looks at me, and I know he's on the same page. Sean gives my hand a quick squeeze and says, "We need to re-interview Edison. Nothing is adding up."

I take a sip of coffee. "I know. And shockingly, I agree. There's a slight fishy smell to his story. Either the three stooges have dirt on him, or he is dumb as a post. Do you think they had more input to the game than Edison is admitting? He's geeky enough that I bought into the boy genius thing, but he didn't strike me as the type to screw over his friends. Maybe the bobbleheads are right, and he's totally controlled by his parents. If so, then why did they leave him to his own devices? Let's suck down a cup of coffee and hit him again. We'll do good-cop-bad-cop. Keep your role as bad cop but with a slight change. If we don't get anywhere, you fake a phone call and leave me alone with him. Deal?"

I see a flicker of doubt cross his face, but then he looks at me and simply says, "Okay."

He surprises me by agreeing so quickly, and for a moment, my suspicious mind starts to question his motives. Then I realize this guy trusts me as a partner. I manage to stop myself before a goofy grin blossoms on my face. The ring of my cell phone derails my unwanted side trip to Crushville. I look down and see my lieutenant's name on the screen.

"Good Morning, LT."

"Moore. What's going on there? Did you two make any headway with the people on the list?" His voice is agitated.

"Sir, we interviewed his three friends. We are about to re-interview Edison. As we mentioned yesterday, his friends each invested five thousand dollars in his game development, and claim they spent ten years testing the game with Edison. Looks like they feel their efforts deserve more than a million dollars each. They brought up a lot of points that need to be followed up on with Edison."

I hear Lieutenant Johns sigh. His voice sounds exhausted, as he replies, "Boomer, I don't need to remind you to take it easy on Edison. His family is well connected to the mayor's office. But more importantly, remember he is the victim here."

"I realize he is, but there are quite a few things that aren't adding up. He's not being forthright with important information. We'll take another run at him." I pause and add, "A gentle non-confrontational run at him."

"Okay. Remember what I said. Don't ruffle any feathers. I do not, I repeat, do not want a call from the mayor with any fallout. Got it?"

"Yes. It shouldn't be a problem. I'll have a report for you when we meet at eleven o'clock."

He disconnects the call. My turn to sigh.

Sean has been behind me, getting his coffee, and obviously eavesdropping.

"Problem, Boomer?"

Awww. Now he's using my nickname. "No. Just my lieutenant telling me to 'be gentle' with our Mr. Edison."

Sean's phone buzzes. He looks at the number and says, "Bet you ten bucks I'm about to hear the same lecture." He frowns as he answers and walks out of the kitchen.

I need a quick bite before meeting with Edison. I open the refrigerator and look at the stacks of plastic cartons of jelly. For God's sake...all raspberry. Not only does our Edison restrict himself to just peanut-butter-and-jelly sandwiches, he only uses one kind of jelly. This is getting weirder by the minute. Oh hell, when in Rome. I grab bread, jelly, and peanut butter, and start assembling.

Sean walks back into the kitchen. "Just got the same instructions from my boss. I'd sure like to know who these people are connected to."

The four-slice toaster spits out the bread. "I made toast for you. Do you want a brain sandwich or just toast?"

"Brain sandwich? Where are we? Zombie Land?"

"Funny. I figure since Edison eats nothing but toasted PBJ's, and he has a quarter of a billion dollars, it must be brain food."

Sean's laugh is genuine. "Okay, give me the brain food. God knows I could use a boost."

We are both slathering peanut butter and jelly on the toasted bread when Angus and Turner walk in. Angus gives me a big smile and turns toward the coffee machine. Turner surveys the scene, and his face gets an unflattering pinched look.

"Isn't this a touching little domestic scene? Well, Boom Boom, looks like you and your new partner are getting along well." He smirks and makes the mistake of looking over at Sean.

Sean's face is glacial. He looks ready to scratch his fist itch. Angus grabs Turner's shoulder, gives him a push toward the door, and says, "Come on, Spike. Time for our shift."

Turner shrugs and struts out of the kitchen. Angus pats my shoulder as he walks by with his coffee.

I watch him and Sean make eye contact and do a slight nod to each other. As Angus walks out, I turn on Sean. "What was that about?"

He actually looks confused. "What? What was what about?"

"You and Angus did the 'bro nod.' I want to know what's going on."

"Turner has it in for you. We both know it, and he does nothing to disguise it. He keeps it under wraps when I'm around, and that just makes him a sneaky little snake. Angus and I are both keeping an eye on him. We're pretty sure he's the one who went into your room. I don't trust him at all."

I sigh. "He's a throwback from the caveman days. I'd like to hit him with a club and drag him around by his hair."

Sean, for some reason, finds my comment hysterically funny. "Will you be wearing a leopard-skin cavewoman outfit when this all goes down? It's got to be better than those uni-sex pajamas you were wearing last night."

"Agent Lindstrom, it may have escaped your notice, but we are working. This is a job. I am not on vacation. We're here to figure out who's trying to kill the Quarter Pounder." I paused for a second and realize I've used Sean's nickname for Edison. "Come on. Let's eat breakfast and then interview Edison." I take a big bite out of my toasted peanut-butter-and-jelly sandwich. I have to admit--not as bad as I remember. Still, eating them three times a day is just plain crazy. Why would anyone want to be involved with a guy who only eats PBJ's? Yeah, this is a real deal breaker.

Sean rinses his dish in the sink and sighs as he says, "Let's get it done." He looks over at me and then leans in. "You have jelly on your face."

He puts his thumb on my chin and wipes it off. A buzz, like an electrical current, shoots through me. I can tell he feels it, too. I see his eyes widen and then a look of wonderment comes over his face. It's like the gauntlet has been thrown down. I try to mask my feelings and fail. I'm praying I'm not sporting a silly grin. I force myself into cop mode and put on my best poker face.

Sean gives my hand a squeeze. His smile is blinding, and then it's gone and we are back to business. He shoots me his cool professional look, and says, "Now, let's go round two with Edison."

"Okay. Make sure you remember the plan."

Sean grimaces. "You got it."

***

We walk out of the kitchen and down the hall to Edison's office. Turner and Angus are outside the door, sitting in two hard straight-back chairs from the dining room. They look uncomfortable as hell, but at least it will keep them from falling asleep.

I knock twice and walk in before Edison acknowledges it.

"Good morning, Mr. Edison. Agent Lindstrom and I need to bother you with a few follow-up questions. Hopefully, it won't take too long."

"I need to be on a conference call in twenty minutes." He gives me his killer smile, and I realize I'm immune.

Sean immediately starts his bad-cop routine. "Okay. We'll try and be brief." Sean sits down and pulls his chair as close to Edison's desk as he can get. "Detective Moore and I were a little surprised to find out your video game, let me add, your bestselling game is about a war with ISIS. I haven't personally played it, but I understand it's pretty violent, and based on our intel, you've ruffled some feathers. Surely you're aware of how ISIS deals with perceived insults from Western culture. Why did you fail to mention this when we interviewed you yesterday?"

Detective Jayne and the Dangerous Game

I'm observing Edison's body language. He is clearly on the defensive and a light sheen of sweat is glistening at his hairline. I decide to chime in. "Mr. Edison. We're very concerned about your safety. The two shooters in the bar have definite ISIS connections. They had been on social media declaring their support for ISIS."

Edison turns to me. "I didn't see the men in the bar. I barely saw the guys who were trying to pull me out to the van. It all happened so fast."

Sean jumps back in. "You didn't notice the men were foreign?"

"Agent Lindstrom, in my world, there are people of all nationalities that come to this area. Microsoft hires many people from India. There are plenty of other software companies who also hire from abroad. I don't pay attention to color, or nationality."

I was ready to give Sean a signal to leave when the sound of his phone buzzing assaults the room. He reaches into his breast pocket, pulls out the phone, looks at the screen, and frowns. "I've got to take this. Detective Moore, please finish up the interview."

I'm a little pissed at the look of relief on Edison's face. So, he doesn't think I'll be as tough? Damn. He's right. I'm going to stay with my current strategy.

Sean shuts the door behind him, and I give Edison a sincere look. "Now that Agent Lindstrom is gone, and it's just you and me, I need some answers, Brian. As I said, I'm very concerned about your safety. Let's start at the beginning. You're saying you had no idea your game 'Heads in a Basket' infuriated ISIS?"

"All games have a certain amount of smack talk that goes on. For the most part, players brag about scores or the number of weapons they've stockpiled in their arsenal. The game does appeal to certain segments of society. On one side, the die-hard Americans who think the scenarios in the game are the exact reason we should have the right to bear arms and buy assault rifles. They feel like they are defending their country by putting heads in a basket."

Edison paused and looked at me, trying to gage my reaction. Then continued, "The game doesn't target the Koran or their actual religious beliefs. It's basically two opposing cultures at war. A game depicting World War II and Hitler would probably be more brutal. He believed in the genocide of an entire race of people. ISIS at least gives people the opportunity to convert and save their lives. Not that I'm a proponent of their beliefs. I'm just trying to explain there shouldn't be anything ISIS would find insulting in my game."

I want to reach across the desk and shake him until his teeth rattle loose. I take a moment to compose myself. "When's the last time you played the game?"

He looks sheepish. "About thirty minutes ago. I like to keep track of what's going on."

"What do you mean?"

"You know. Stats on how many players are online. I also check on the high scores. Sometimes I go into the chat room and talk a little smack to keep people excited about the game."

I look at his face. He looks so proud of himself, and he was waiting for me to comment. "What kind of 'smack' are you talking about?"

"Nothing serious. I like challenging some of the players to a game. Sometimes we fight to the death. Or they'll use up some of their weapons and need to buy more. It's just a game."

I will myself to remain calm. Like many people with high IQ's, he is book smart, but dumb as a post when it comes to real life. "Let's talk about the chat rooms. Do you go in often? Are there people you chat with frequently?" An idea was forming, and I wanted to see if he would pick up on it.

"I chat with some of the die-hard Americans. People like Johnny Rebel, Southern Comfort, Abe Lincoln, Captain America, Red Neck Power, and Get Even."

He pauses and takes a bite out of his toasted PBJ that is, by now, stone cold. I recognize a stall when I see one. "What about the opposing players? What names do they use?" I'm scribbling down the names he had mentioned and then stop, ready for the next batch.

"I haven't paid much attention to them. It's always something with the name Mohammed in it."

I make a note to have DL sign into the site and then switch tactics. "I'm sure this has been very stressful for you, Brian. It must be hard not having your family here. Do you have any siblings?"

"No. I'm an only child. My parents said I was such a perfect baby, they knew they'd never be that lucky again."

I work hard to control my inner-gag reflex. "You must miss them."

Brian Edison makes a face and, for a moment, looks like a twelve-year-old. "I have lived with my parents my entire life. Most people move out during or after college, but my mom wouldn't let me."

My eyebrows shoot up.

Edison continues. "I know it sounds funny but it's true. She was so supportive of my gaming projects. She was the only one who truly believed in me. My dad kept telling me to grow up and get a real job, and she would always defend me. I couldn't have done this without her. My mom has always been there for me. She is my champion. She would take on the teachers at school when they didn't give me the grade I deserved. She helped pay my bills for years. You know, it is impossible to have a decent life on minimum wage."

I manage not to scream DUH. I paste a smile on my face and ask the question that has been spinning around in my head. "Did your mom like your friends?"

He looks chagrined. "Billy, Eric, and Steve were my best friends in middle school and high school. I was a skinny little kid and pretty geeky. For some reason, they always stood up for me. If anyone picked on me, they'd beat them up. My mom didn't especially like them--they didn't live up to her standards--but she was happy they looked out for me. She says they're destined to always be losers and told me I gave them way more than they deserved. Which is kind of funny."

Hmmm. This is getting interesting. "Why is it funny? How much were you going to give them?"

"I was going to give them ten million each. It seemed fair. They spent a lot of time here and had some good ideas. My mom said it was way too much, and they'd be dead in six months with that amount of money."

"Why would your mom think that?"

"They tend to smoke a lot of marijuana. They quit their jobs the minute they got the money. So now, all they do is smoke and play air guitars. They're obsessed with a band from the seventies, The Doobie Brothers. They've been this way as long as I've known them."

Well, not surprising. Talk about a case of arrested

development. "Do you keep in contact with them?"

"No. Billy thinks they got screwed and stopped talking to me. Steve and Eric do whatever Billy says, so they won't talk to me either."

I'm thinking no big loss, but his mournful little puppy dog look is getting to me. "So now you have a quarter of a billion dollars and no friends. I'm sure you could rectify it if you wanted to."

"I was going to try, but when Billy got so ugly about the entire situation, I decided not to. My mom said it will all work out, and she's usually right."

I can feel my lips starting to purse in disbelief. I mentally slap myself and put a smile back on my face, but I can't help but think how looks can be so deceiving. This is one big momma's boy. "It must be very hard for you with your mother so far away."

He has the audacity to laugh. "Are you kidding me? I feel like the chains have been lifted, and I have been liberated." His smile is wide, like a kid on the first day of summer vacation. "I finally get to do what I want. I'm going to hire a professional decorator and change the entire house. I hope I never see the color mauve again."

To me the answer is simple. "Why not move?"

"No. This house has been in my family for three generations. I can't sell it."

Good God, this guy is sheltered and stupid. "Well, if I were you, I'd give it back to your parents and let them deal with it, and go buy a McMansion on Lake Washington."

I can see he is getting overloaded with my revolutionary thinking, but I still have some mommy questions. "Can I ask how much money you gave your parents? You mentioned yesterday you bought them a house in the south of France."

"Fifty million. It seemed like a good repayment for everything they have done, or at least my mom has done."

The lightbulb flips on. I realize he never mentions his dad. Hmmm. "Your mom sounds so supportive. You're lucky. What's your dad like?"

Brian pauses. He licks his lips nervously before he replies. "We're not very close. Never have been. I was close with my grandfather and did a lot with him as a kid. My dad's pretty athletic. Golf and tennis are his life. Sports never interested me, so there wasn't much we could do together. He hates computer games and was pretty angry when my mom let me live in the basement for the last ten years. He said I'd never amount to anything."

"Maybe your dad has a difficult time admitting he's wrong. I'm sure it was very hard for your mom to leave you on your own and go halfway across the world." Boom...let the fishing begin.

"Oh, she didn't leave me entirely on my own. I have Alias. He's my mom's cousin's son. She didn't want me to be without any family. Alias has taken over where my mom left off." He lets out a nervous laugh. "Except for the nagging. Alias is pretty good about not nagging me. Well, at least not as much as my mom did. He's been great. I never have to bother with any of the mundane details of running the house. He pays all the bills and takes care of scheduling house cleaners and the gardeners."

Interesting. I'm ready to high-five myself. Now, for the million- -or maybe billion- dollar question. "And he hired the cook?"

"Yes. She came highly recommended. Alias did a lot of research and sorted through almost one hundred resumes before selecting Mimi. We're lucky to have her. Apparently, she was scheduled to go to France and work in Paris."

Oh. My. God. I'd love to see what kind of work she would do in Paris. "Yes. Lucky describes it best. She has a very unusual cuisine. It's a shame you haven't tasted any of it."

"I'm glad you're enjoying her food. Her PBJ's are quite good, too." He looked me in the eye and paused for a second. "You've been asking a lot of questions, and now I have one for you. Would you ever consider leaving the force and working private security? I will pay you five times what you make now. I've seen you in action. I can't imagine being in safer hands."

The way he says "safer hands" has my creep meter pegging out. When did this happen? How did the very attractive quarter of a billionaire turn into a wimpy momma's boy? And a job offer? Seriously? Working in this nuthouse with Mimi and Alias? I need to wrap this up and head downtown. "That's a very tempting offer. I'm going to sleep on it. Let's keep this to ourselves, I don't want the other agents and officers to hear about it."

"You got it. Although I have to tell you, Officer Turner

presented a pretty good case for being hired on as my head of security. In fact, if he hadn't asked me for a job, I wouldn't have come up with the idea to hire you."

Oh, snap. "Well, it certainly would behoove you to take a look at his credentials. They're quite impressive."

"See, you're smart, beautiful, funny, and generous. You've got such great qualities. I want you to think about the job offer."

"I will. I think I have all I need for now. Thanks for your time, Mr. Edison. Agent Lindstrom and I will be heading downtown. I'll keep you posted."

"Now we're back to mister and detective?"

"I think it's for the best until we get this all sorted out." I give him a smile. Then I notice where his eyes are. Jeez. "Mr. Edison, my eyes are up here."

Chapter 18

Sean was pacing in the kitchen when Jayne resurfaced from Edison's office. She gave him a nod, and he followed her out the door. Jayne headed for the passenger side of his car. "You drive this time. I have to write up some notes."

Sean got behind the wheel and the minute they hit the street, Jayne started talking. "This is getting crazier by the minute. I'm going to try and give you the abbreviated version while I add to my notes. Then I'll go back and fill in the details."

Jayne spent the next fifteen minutes telling Sean about Edison's controlling mother, inattentive father, his job offer, Turner soliciting for a job, and how Edison wanted to give his three friends ten million each but his mother nixed it.

Sean's kept his eyes on the road but listened intently, interjecting questions as Jayne told him new details. "So Edison is controlled by his mommy? And Alias is her second cousin? He offered you a job? What'd you tell him?"

Jayne laughed. "I told him I'd sleep on it. Good God. Can you imagine being stuck inside that house every day with Mimi?"

"So, that's a no?" Sean tensed, waiting for her to confirm it.

"Sean. What do you think? I love what I do. There is no amount of money that would pull me from actually making a difference in this crazy world to working for Edison."

"I'm glad. You're a good cop, Jayne. I think you do make a difference, and Edison is a spoiled brat with obvious mommy issues. Working for him would be like being a babysitter. And think of eating Mimi's food or PBJ's every day."

Jayne winced. "You make an excellent point. Edison couldn't pay me enough money to eat Mimi's food on a daily basis. Hurry up, you drive like an old lady. I want to see what DL has dug up before the briefing starts."

Sean floored it and put on his blue lights and siren. "Yes, ma'am."

***

Jayne and Sean were in the hallway on their way to DL's office when they heard a scream, followed by, "Die, you asshole."

Weapons drawn, they rushed down the hall and threw open the door to DL's office. She was sitting in front of a large computer monitor. A joy stick was being maneuvered by her right hand, and her left hand periodically slapped the desk.

Sean watched in fascination as DL screamed in agony and, then, in triumph. "Got the bastards."

DL turned in her chair. "Whew. That was intense."

"Do you want to explain? You seem to be pretty worked up." Jayne's tone was bemused.

"Okay. I was telling my husband and son about this game last night. We are a multi-computer household, so between the three of us, we managed to get into the game, get into a chat room, rack up some pretty impressive points, and piss off some people. I'd call it a successful night. I was just playing the game this morning so I can build credibility. Everyone in the chat rooms has pretty high scores. They're not going to tell me anything if they don't think I'm worthy."

Sean was looking at DL with nothing less than a little hero worship. He smiled and said, "DL, that's pretty darn impressive. Who'd you chat with?"

"Well, Agent, that's the interesting part. There are more than a couple chat rooms. One is basically people talking trash about their mad gaming skills. My husband, Steve, was engaged in a conversation with someone called Big Mac. Seems like this person likes to brag that he or she helped invent the game, and I quote, 'All the fucking cool stuff wuz my ideas.' Based on what you told me yesterday, I'd say it has to be one of Edison's initial investors/friends. Steve jotted down all the notes. This guy is alternately argumentative, boastful, or taunting. He's always looking to challenge other players to try and beat him. Steve labeled him as a narcissus…and a terrible speller."

DL paused and took a sip of her coffee before continuing. "In one chat room, there's a guy called, believe it or not, the Avenger, who likes to spout some pretty crazy ideology. Seems like he's always looking for a fight. The mix of people seem to be divided between Americans and Europeans. There are some definite ISIS supporters that jump in. The frightening part, based again on their syntax, is that they are either Americans or Brits. The Avenger seems to be concentrating on Edison."

Jayne said, "How so?"

Diane pulled out a notebook and flipped through it. "Basically, the Avenger is angry that Edison made a reported billion dollars from his attack on ISIS and their beliefs. He is calling for supporters to kill Edison."

"Whoa. He just flat out called for Edison to be killed? On a public forum?" Jayne's tone was incredulous. "Can we track him?"

DL put her coffee cup down. "The thing about chat rooms, they're impossible to monitor. You can't get a trace on where these people are. That's why most FBI sting operations try to get the person in a chat room out for a meeting where they can then be grabbed. If we could find them, I'm sure all government agencies would be knocking on the offenders' doors as we speak."

Before Sean could answer, Diane looked at her watch. "We have only ten minutes before the briefing. Tell me about meeting Edison's friends."

Sean and Jayne alternated giving details about "the Bobbleheads." The three of them were laughing so hard, people were sticking their heads in the door and telling them to keep it down.

"You're serious? Air guitars? Oh. My. God. Who on earth does that?" Diane wiped a tear from her face. "This job gets way too serious sometimes. It's good to have a little comic relief."

Jayne wiped the tears from her eyes. "You're telling me! Honestly, it was like we walked through some time warp and hit the eighties."

Diane nodded and then switched back to business mode. "Hey, I got some dirt on Mimi Jenkins and John Doe Smith. Darn, look at the time. I guess you'll hear it at the briefing. Let's head out."

Before she exited her office, she paused and pulled off a perfect air-guitar pose. "Oh man. This case is going to be a trip down memory lane."

***

Sean surveyed the room. It was the same cast of characters from yesterday. He laughed to himself as he saw people jockey for the same chairs they sat in the day before. That's why criminals are in jail--when you're a creature of habit, eventually you get caught. Sean and Jayne headed for the only two seats left, the ones they had sat in the day before.

For the next hour, the information from the day before was rehashed. There was still a lot in the works. The final days of the four dead men were being pieced together. Keeping a neutral expression on his face, Sean willed himself to stop thinking about Jayne. He'd sworn off relationships eight years ago after a colossal burn by his ex-fiancé. Besides, being an agent and taking care of his mom and sisters was all he had time for. He forced his attention back to the meeting.

He watched the screen Diane was again using to present her information. She must be some sort of PowerPoint guru. He looked at Alias' picture. It was a mug shot from five years ago. Diane looked like she was in her element.

DL held everyone's attention. "John Doe Smith, a.k.a., Alias, is the second-cousin of Brian Edison's mother. She is first cousins with Smith's mother who apparently begged her to give Smith a chance. Smith was arrested five years ago for stalking his ex-girlfriend. He had done a number of things to her. He hacked her Facebook account, alienated her boss, which resulted in her getting fired, and messed up her credit. He followed her relentlessly and, finally, the coup de grace, tried to kidnap her, and landed in the slammer with a sentence of seven years. He was out in five years. We can thank prison overcrowding and the fact that he was a nonviolent offender since no weapon was involved. He had been doing low-paying jobs and living with mom until this gig with Edison."

Jayne was the first to speak. "So, let me get this straight. Smith tried to kidnap his girlfriend, went to prison and now, as an ex-con, is babysitting our victim? So, how does Mimi Jenkins fit into all this?"

DL looked like the cat that just swallowed the canary. "Mimi Jenkins was a prison guard at Washington State Penitentiary in Walla Walla."

When she posted a picture of Mimi next to Alias, the room

erupted into snickers and guffaws.

DL continued. "There is nothing to indicate that Smith or Jenkins have any plot against Edison. Well, let me amend that statement. Let's just say that there is no evidence that they're linked with the terrorists. If they have a plot, and I do say *if*, it's just two terribly unqualified people making an astronomical salary for doing next to nothing. Jenkins salary is a cool $150,000 a year. She was a corrections officer Level Three in Walla Walla. Her salary was $47,000. Nice increase. Smith is making $300,000. I need a calculator to determine what percentage of increase that is over his prior minimum wage jobs. Based on the money these two are pulling in, I doubt that they would want to kill the goose and his golden egg. We are currently looking into their banking statements to make sure that they're not pulling some sort of embezzlement scheme. Mimi Jenkins has a history of living higher than her income. She's filed bankruptcy three different times. I wouldn't be surprised if she isn't upgrading from Walmart to Nordstrom right now."

Jayne snickered. "Only if Nordstrom has opened a Frederick's of Hollywood department."

That brought a round of chuckles from the group.

When it got quiet, Jayne spoke again. "Seriously, is an ex-con the best person to have control over all the household finances? Alias seems to be okay on the surface, but there's something up with him. He has sweaty palms and he's obviously got something going on with Mimi he doesn't want Edison to know about. I caught them playing tonsil tennis in the kitchen. Jenkins appears to be looking to trade Alias for any upgrade that comes along. I don't trust either of them."

Lieutenant Johns spoke up. "I agree with you, Jayne, but right now, they're not the primary suspects. I'd say that whatever they're up to goes on the back burner until we catch the group that is making the threats." Heads around the table nodded in agreement.

The next forty-five minutes was spent presenting possible ISIS supporters and discussing a "Heads in a Basket" chat-room strategy. The chat room was being monitored 24/7 by DL and her FBI counterparts. They were setting up several online personas in order to draw out any ISIS sympathizers.

The meeting ended and Jayne nudged Sean.

Sean frowned and said, "I've been sitting here trying to process everything that has been discussed. I'm telling you, Jayne, I did three tours in Iraq. I've seen how these people are with a grudge. They're not done with Edison. It's just a matter of time before they either try to kidnap him again or try to blow him up. There is no middle ground with this group."

Jayne said tersely, "Dealing with terrorists is a crap shoot. It's hard to get into the head of someone that actually wants to die for their cause. There's no rational."

He looked at Jayne and said, "I know. Trust me, dealing with people that don't care if they die makes my balls shrivel up and hide."

Jayne looked at him and arched her eyebrow.

Sean let out a nervous laugh. "Sorry. That was probably too much information. Let's go interview the Admin assistant and the other two employees, and then head back to Edison's."

"Okay, but first let's check back in with DL."

***

Next to DL's office was a small conference room. Three people were crowded around a monitor as she gave them an overview of the game and instructions on what to do in the chat rooms.

When DL was finished, she joined Sean and Jayne in her office.

"Okay, we've got some more FBI guys on board with our little chat-room operation. What are you two going to do?"

Sean spoke first. "We're going to check out his employees. His Admin is Sharon Gibbs. We want to talk to her and see what else Edison is holding back on."

Jayne nodded. "I'd like to see if Sharon is another substitute mommy for our little Quarter Pounder. It's clear that he may be a gaming genius and very smart, but the man couldn't last a day on his own."

Sean managed not to smile when he said, "She's right. Plus, with all that money, he can't seem to leave his childhood home."

DL addressed Jayne. "Looks like you've changed your opinion of Edison."

Jayne got a sheepish look on her face. "DL, he seems to be a very nice person, but I have never met a bigger momma's boy. I have to tell you, his mom sounds like a piece of work. I'm surprised Brian Edison can blow his own nose."

Sean's face sprouted a big grin. "Based on the interview notes Jayne shared with me, she's right in her assessment. Jayne, can we tell her about the offer?"

"Yeah." She leaned over toward DL and lowered her voice. "Turner has been trying to sell himself to Edison to become his head of security. All that did was give Edison the idea of asking me to be his head of security, at five times my annual pay." Jayne laughed and continued. "Can you imagine what Turner would do if I actually took the job? Which, by the way, you know I would never do."

DL tone turned serious. "If there is a God in heaven, please let Edison hire Turner and get him off our backs."

Jayne grabbed DL's hand and raised it in the air. "Amen, Sister. Amen."

Chapter 19

Sharon Gibbs turns out to be a surprise. I must look like an Amazon warrior as I stand next to her diminutive frame. A small woman in her early thirties, her thick glasses make her eyes look large compared to her finely featured face. When she puts her small hand in mine, it almost feels like I'm shaking a toddler's hand. Her voice fits the rest of the small package.

Out of the corner of my eye, I see Sean trying to fold himself in half to get close enough to hear her soft voice. Sean smiles at her and gently asks, "Ms. Gibbs, is there a room available for a private chat with you?" We both observe her eyes go wide with shock.

"Is Brian okay? I've been so worried." Her tone is urgent as waves of concern wash over her small frame.

I jump in to reassure her. "He's fine, Ms. Gibbs. Not enjoying being stuck in his house with a bunch of strangers, but he's doing fine."

We follow her into a small conference room. Linkz's offices are in a loft on Western Avenue, north of the Pike Place Market. Floor-to-ceiling windows frame an impressive view of Puget Sound and the Olympic Mountains. I look out the windows as two Washington State ferries pass each other, one heading to nearby Bainbridge Island, the other ready to dock in Seattle. It will be hard to concentrate on the interview with this spectacular view as a distraction.

"What an amazing view." Sean stood at the window, taking in the sights.

Ms. Gibbs settles into a chair, her back to the view. "Yes, I guess it is. I'm usually too busy to appreciate it."

Sean gets right to it. "How long have you known Brian Edison?"

Ms. Gibbs blushes to the roots of her hair. "We went to the same high school, although we didn't hang out or anything, but we knew each other. Even back then, you could tell Brian was someone special and would do great things."

I interject. Nothing like a little double teaming. "Did you keep in touch after high school?"

She shakes her head no.

"How did you become reacquainted?" I'm trying to keep my voice soft and non-threatening.

"At Geek Wire Start Up Day. It's where all the gaming people meet and try to get investors or sell their game. I worked for a little start up, and he stopped by our booth." The smile that lights up her face speaks volumes.

Sean and I share a look. We are traveling toward Crushville, and I can tell Sean doesn't want his ticket stamped. He abruptly stands up and pulls his phone out. "I just received a text message and I need to respond. Detective Moore, please carry on." Sean slithers out and closes the door behind him.

Normally I resent being delegated to the girly role, but I realize his strategy makes sense. Ms. Gibbs appears to be shy, and a man as large as Sean can seem intimidating.

"So Sharon. I can call you Sharon, right?" She nods and I continue. "Sharon, did Brian recognize you when you met up at the Start Up Day?"

"Not at first and I almost didn't recognize him either. In high school, he was kind of on the small side, which is why I liked him." She pauses remembering the moment, her eyes welling up. "Then Brian started staring at me, and he gave me a big smile. He said he was happy to see me again and offered me a job on the spot."

"No resume or anything?" It doesn't surprise me, as with all things Edison, he needs the security blanket of family or friends around him. Mimi being the only exception.

"He talked about how smart I was in high school. I was smart, but I never knew he noticed, we barely even spoke in class." Her face flushes again, and I look through her coke-bottle glasses into beautiful green eyes that glisten with unshed tears.

Sharon continues. "Just like in high school, his friends were with him at Geek Wire. They always traveled in a pack at school. Funny, they look the same, and still act the same." Sharon Gibb's face pinches up into a prim little grimace.

I enjoy the look of distaste on her face when she talks about the bobbleheads. "Yes, we've met his friends, or I guess we should say his initial investors. Sounds like they parted badly."

Her eyebrows rise to her hairline. "Badly? Detective, that's an understatement. For months we received phone calls from Billy McHendricks. He wouldn't let up. Constantly harassing Brian and telling him that he'd be sorry. Talk about stressful! I know Brian wanted to make things better, but then his mother forbade any more contact. Mrs. Edison demanded I screen his calls and block any contact from Billy."

Oh, snap. "Mrs. Edison gives orders at her son's business?" I'm glad Sean walked away from this conversation. We are about to get our girl snark on. "Is she as scary as she sounds?" I like my new little friend Sharon--she actually shudders before she answers.

"This is just between us, right?"

Her pleading look has me nodding, but then my conscience kicks in. "Your information will be kept confidential. No one in the Edison family, including Brian, will know what we discuss here. However, I will be sharing it with other law enforcement agencies if anything you tell me is pertinent to the case or will help keep Brian Edison safe."

She looks relieved and continues. "She's a witch. She used to swoop in here on her broomstick and stick her nose into every aspect of the business. Talk about demoralizing. We're a small staff, and her presence was very disruptive. Plus, she ordered us all around like she owned the company."

"From what I gather, and you just confirmed it, she sounds like a control freak. I'm surprised she and Brian's dad moved to France. How did that happen?" I'm pumping this little well for all it's worth.

A smug look comes over her face. "One day I asked her about Europe. I told her I was planning a vacation and wanted ideas. Mrs. Edison talked on and on about France and how beautiful St. Tropez is and all the fabulous people that go there. Then, of course, she ruined the moment by telling me I probably couldn't afford to go and that it was a playground for the rich and famous, not someone like me." Sharon's face reflects a flash of anger and her owlish eyes go hard. "It gave me an idea. I researched villas in St. Tropez and found the perfect one. I told Brian about his mother's love of all things French and suggested that this would be the perfect Christmas gift. I hate to say it because Brian's such a sweet person, but he's pretty easy to manipulate. He bought the villa and sent them off to France. At first, his mother was reluctant, but then she hired her cousin's son to be the faux babysitter."

My jaw almost hits the desk, and I do a serious re-evaluation of our little Ms. Gibbs. "Wow, Sharon. Way to slay the dragon."

A self-satisfied smile contorts her face. "My mother always said being small doesn't mean being weak, you just have to find an alternative way to get what you want."

"Your mother sounds like a wise woman. How did you find out Alias is her cousin?"

"Oh, that was easy. There was no way that Mrs. Edison was going to have a stranger overseeing the house and paying the bills. When John Doe Smith came in for me to do the paperwork, I chatted with him. With his date of birth and social security number, I was able to run a check on him. I have a great search engine that not only gave me his criminal history, I was able to track the family connection." Sharon Gibbs looks very proud of herself.

"Good job, Sharon. If you ever want to change jobs, you would be great in law enforcement."

"Sorry Detective. I've got big plans of my own. I've been working on a project in my spare time that just might have a big payoff." Her voice puffs up with self-importance.

"Good for you Sharon. One more question, did anyone else besides Billy McHendricks threaten Brian?"

"Yes. But Billy McHendricks is the only one that we actually know. All the other threats have come from the game chat room for 'Heads in a Basket.' Brian just laughs them off and says it's good for business."

"What kind of threats?" I want to see if she repeats what Edison had told me about people talking smack.

"Kind of what you would expect from a macho site like that. A few were more descriptive." Sharon pauses, and I see her face light up with glee. "Wait. I have a file of screen-prints." Sharon jumps up and heads to her office. In seconds she comes back with a file folder about two inches thick.

I grab the file and start thumbing through it. "Sharon Gibbs, you are seriously my new best friend. This is invaluable. Honest. This may help us figure out who is responsible for the attempted kidnapping." I can't wait to dive into the file, but try to tamp my enthusiasm down a notch in case our little Ms. Gibbs has more bombshells to drop.

"I made notes on some of the pages. As an example, you can always tell when Billy McHendricks is on. He calls himself 'Big Mac' and likes to brag about how he basically invented the entire game. The one that scares me is the Avenger. He started chatting about three months ago. He talks a lot of religion and calls all the players American infidels. I know I don't have all of his chats, but I can tell you this--I believe the Avenger is in the United States." Sharon turned her big owl eyes onto me and waited for my reaction.

"Why do you say that?" I am intrigued.

"I'm guessing but it's a time zone thing. I track the activity on our gaming sites. We do a lot of studies on what age group is playing, what time of day is the heaviest traffic, et cetera. I do it so we can maximize our advertisers. Anyway, I keep track of the Avenger, and he usually plays between 6 pm and 8 pm. He stops for a half hour and starts again, 8:30 to midnight. That tells me he's obviously employed or he would be on during the day. He stops for one half hour every night, without fail. I think he's doing his evening prayers. If he were in another country, the timing would not work. Or, if it did, he would be playing in the middle of the night." A look comes over her face, like someone popped her balloon. "I guess it's possible he's playing from another country. It sounded so logical."

I take an abrupt detour when a thought occurs to me. "Sharon, what's Brian's dad like?"

Her brow furrows, and she looks out into space for a second.

"Detective Moore, I only saw Mr. Edison once. I drove Brian home one day when his car was in for service. When we got to his house, Brian's parents were having a very heated argument. Mrs. Edison was screaming about him going off to play tennis. He had his tennis whites on and his racket in his hand. I swear, by the look on his face, he was ready to beat her to death with the racket, but, instead, he got into his car and roared off. If looks could kill, Mrs. E. would be six feet under!"

"So Brian's parents don't get along?" I need to fill in this family picture.

Sharon's voice cracks a little and sadness dulls her features. "Brian told me some things and is always vocal about not ending up like his parents. He says he'll never get married."

"I'm sure he's just overreacting." I can't stand to see sadness snuff out her personality.

"That's what I thought, but he said that what I witnessed was a mild exchange, and it had always been that way as long as he could remember. He claims his parents hate each other and only stay married because of his grandfather."

"Her father?" The pieces are starting to drop into place. "Hasn't he been dead for over ten years?"

"Yes. Brian said if his parents ever got divorced, she would lose her inheritance. They can't take the risk. I guess the grandfather has some ironclad will. And Mr. Edison doesn't actually have a job. From what Brian told me, his life is tennis, golf, and fighting with his wife."

I start running possibilities in my head. I look her in the eye and smile. "Sharon, you have given me a lot of things to follow up on. Good things. Great job." I'm anxious to go back to the Quarter Pounder and probe a little more about life in the mauve prison.

I see Sharon puff up with pride and give me a big smile.

***

Thankfully, Sean interviewed the other two employees while Sharon and I talked. We exchange information as he drives us back downtown. We're both anxious to review the screen-prints with DL.

"So, our little Ms. Gibbs has the hots for the Quarter Pounder?" Sean makes no effort to disguise the glee in his voice.

I give up. I'm through defending Edison and all his mommy issues. "Poor girl. I bet she's had a thing for him for years. I do love how she got Mrs. Edison out of the picture. Speaking of Mrs. Edison...am I the only one that finds it odd she hasn't come rushing to her son's side?" Once the thought hits me, I can't get it out of my head.

Sean thinks for a moment, and replies, "Yeah, good call. You should ask him tonight. If I ask, I won't be able to keep the smirk off my face."

"I admit Mrs. Edison sounds like a piece of work, but don't you think a mother would come rushing back if her child's life was in danger?" I'm curious to hear his response.

"My mom would do anything for me and my sisters. She also understands there are things she can't do. She couldn't protect me when I was in Iraq, she can't protect me when I'm doing my job with the FBI, and she accepts that. If anything ever happens to me, she'll be on the first plane, train, or automobile to be at my side. That's her, being a mom. In my everyday life, I make my own decisions, and there is no interference, only support, and of course, unconditional love. From what you said about Edison's mom, she's all about control."

I look at him and try to keep from laughing. "That's some speech. I guess you have some strong thoughts on the subject?"

He laughs for a second and then is serious again. "My dad just up and walked out one day. My mom had to take on a lot to raise four kids by herself. We all came through it okay. You'll like my mom and sisters."

Whoa. He slipped that in without missing a beat. We haven't even had a first date and he's bringing up his mom and sisters. I am trying to decide how I feel about it when he pulls into the parking garage and we are back to cop mode.

I look over and see him staring at me. He knows he has freaked me out. He smiles and pushes his hand across the front seat and gives my hand a quick squeeze.

As he gets out of the car, he leans back and says, "Jayne, we've been together for 48 hours. One cop hour is like twenty-four civilian hours. Plus, I met you a few times when you were the librarian. I just feel like I've known you a lot longer. Don't get all panicky, I won't drag out my mom unless it's an emergency."

Damn.

**

We get out of the car and head to DL's office. I push open her office door, and exclaim, "Hey, DL. We come bearing gifts." I pull the folder out of my handbag. "Turns out, Quarter Pounder's Admin, Sharon Gibbs, keeps track of the chat room comments. But before I forget, I need you to do a total background check on Edison's parents."

DL scribbles a note on her "to do" list. "Any particular reason?"

"If anyone asks, we're just running some leads. Maybe Mrs. Edison ran her mouth off to the wrong people in San Tropez. Anyone could be trying to get a bite of the Quarter Pounder." Another thought occurs to me. "Plus, am I the only one who finds it strange the house hasn't been updated for at least thirty years? Wasn't Mrs. Edison's dad some rich, influential pillar of Seattle society? Rich people redecorate. I want to know how that trait slipped by them."

DL nods in agreement. "What do you think, Sean?"

He chuckles as he says, "Seriously. It's straight out of the seventies. I'm no decorating expert but the last time I saw that kind of decor, it was at my grandma's house, thirty years ago. But back to business, you're right. Mrs. Edison could have said something to the wrong person. And there are a lot of people in the South of France who could be the eyes and ears for ISIS."

***

We spend the next few minutes sharing the information from our interview with Sharon Gibbs and Edison's other employees.

DL shuffles through Sharon's file. "This is great. She's made some notes. I'll look through everything in the morning."

"Oh, one more thing. She has an interesting theory that the Avenger is in the United States." I give DL Sharon's time-zones theory.

Sean looks at us and asks, "What's the last screen-print you have for the Avenger?"

DL shuffles through the stack. "Here's a screen-print from two days ago, and I saw him in a chat room last night." She stops for a moment and reads out loud, "Your time is limited. We will avenge the death of our comrades, the true believers, Mohammed's chosen. You will pay for your disrespect with your life. You and those close to you." She looks up and says, "Sounds like a threat to me."

Sean's smile is grim. "Well, we all agree on that. I'm wondering what he's planning on for his next move. If this Avenger guy is the mastermind, I'm sure he has minions that do his bidding. Suicide missions don't detour them. We've got to figure this out quickly."

I pipe up. "I think we need to relocate Edison. It's no secret where he lives, and the so-called 'gated' community is a joke. Anyone can get in there."

"You're right," Sean replies. "Problem is, we need the buy-in from both of our bosses. Plus, the Quarter Pounder doesn't want to go anywhere."

DL pauses and then says firmly. "Call your bosses. Feed them the idea. With two agencies in the mix, nothing is going to be resolved in a day, but maybe you can convince them in the meeting tomorrow. Go back to Edison's house, and we'll pray that the Avenger is just blowing smoke."

I think through our options. "If the suits don't let us move him, I say we kidnap the attempted kidnap victim."

I look at Sean and DL. They both silently nod in agreement.

Chapter 20

We are both quiet as Sean drives us back to Edison's, deep in thought about the facts from today's interviews. At least that's what I'm telling myself. I keep thinking about when he touched my face in the kitchen. It was sensual and sweet at the same time. The kind of touch that I've missed for so long, but something I'm not ready to think about right now. Hunger makes itself known when my stomach growls and the sound reverberates around the car.

I sneak a look at Sean. "Oh my God. Sorry. That was embarrassing." I pull out my cell phone and hit speed-dial.

Sean asks, "Who are you calling? Please tell me you're ordering food."

"I'm saving our lives," I reply with a smirk.

"Pizza?"

Oh jeez. This guy really gets me. "Yeah. You look kind of like a sausage, pepperoni, and olives guy to me. Does that work for you?"

Sean answers with a wide smile. "Perfect. Can you add mushrooms, too? And let's buy enough for the entire crew. No sense in letting Mimi do the terrorist's job for them."

"You forget the Quarter Pounder won't eat pizza and is still at Mimi's mercy," I reply, with an evil grin.

"True. More for us," Sean says, as he licks his lips.

I finish ordering the four extra-large loaded pizzas and put my phone back in my pocket as Sean pulls up to the gate.

The same guard I dealt with on the first night steps out of the shack. He looks down into the car and makes a point of saying, "Hello *Detective*," stretching the word detective into six pissy-sounding syllables. His tone is not polite. I ignore him, but Sean apparently enjoys making small talk.

"So, how's your evening going? Very busy?" Sean sounds tired but at least he makes an effort to let the old guy feel important. Good. I guess.

The retired cop puffs up. "I've been keeping an eye on things.

Nothing out of the ordinary to report. I just let a truck in with two gardeners about five minutes ago. Other than that, it has been pretty quiet."

Oh, no. It is pitch black outside, and this bozo let in some gardeners? Sean and I both look at each other. I yell, "Punch it." And we speed off to Edison's house.

I scan the street by the house. No truck. Maybe this is legit, and the gardeners are at some other house, but I can't shake my gut feeling. We drive up the driveway, and both of us have our weapons drawn when we exit the car. As we rush to the back entrance, we spot Turner handcuffed to the flagpole by the patio, wearing a vest with what looks like enough sticks of dynamite to blow up the block. Oh. Crap. Make that double crap. I throw my keys to Sean. "Quick, I need the black duffle bag out of my trunk. Hurry." I feel panic climbing up my nerves like an invasive vine.

Sean pauses, and then his partner mentality kicks in. "Don't do anything stupid before I get back."

Okay. Let's say that most of his partner mentality kicked in. I'm standing twenty-five feet from Turner. He looks dazed and blood is streaming from a gash in his head. I try to steady my hands as I push another speed-dial number on my phone. I make it brief. "It's Moore. Suicide vest strapped on an officer. There are at least twelve sticks of dynamite and a timer." I give them the address, hang up, and focus my attention on Turner.

"Turner, what happened?" I keep my voice calm and low. "Where's Angus and Edison?"

As I ask the question, Turner's eyes roll into the back of his head. I can't approach him without the duffel bag. As I stand there contemplating my next move and trying to tamp down my panic attack, he comes around again.

"Moore, get me some help." Turner's voice is raspy and, as usual, irritated.

"Spike, just hang in there for a minute. We're getting help. Can you tell me what happened?" My voice belies my internal struggle.

His face grimaces. I can't tell if it's from physical pain or maybe I'm the pain.

"I came out to use the phone. Next thing I know, I get whacked on the head. I didn't see anyone."

I do a cautious turn around the flagpole. I have a clear view of the timer--one minute, fifty-nine seconds, and counting. They obviously left enough time for their escape before the blast. Doesn't sound like crazy suicide bombers, but I'll ponder that later.

Sean approaches at a run with my bag. "What's the situation?" He sets the bag at my feet, his weapon in his other hand.

I drop to a crouch and start to quickly pull out what I need. "If the guard let them in five minutes ago, I don't think anyone in the house is aware of the situation. Sean, you need to verify they haven't snatched Edison and clear the area. Now." When I look at his face, my heart wrenches seeing the concern, and then resignation contorts his handsome features. The sound of sirens approaching pierces the quiet neighborhood.

"Looks like the cavalry is on its way." His lame attempt at a joke falls flat.

"Sean, you need to check on Edison and the team. The squad will work on the immediate area." The thing I like about Sean is he doesn't ask dumb questions. He nods his head, gives my shoulder a reassuring squeeze, and jogs toward the house.

Okay. I have a Kevlar vest and my tools. I would love to see the "makes my butt look big" bomb suit, but no such luck. I don't have the luxury of time. I am pissed that I'm risking my life for a jerk like Turner, but that's the luck of the draw. I put on my vest and grab my tools. A warm breeze hits me and for a moment I feel calm and peaceful. I think of Matthew and can almost feel him at my side. I swallow the acid in the back of my throat and get ready to do my job.

"Spike, I'm going to diffuse the bomb, and I need you to stay calm." I take slow steps toward him. Turner's eyes are wide, and for once, he keeps his mouth shut. Maybe this will work.

I approach, looking at the vest and how the dynamite is connected. All righty. Nothing I haven't seen before. People always think diffusing a bomb is so intricate. It can be, but most of the time, it all comes down to a simple item you'd find at a hardware store and, oh yeah, making sure you cut the correct wire. I have the wire cutters in my hand and gingerly walk around Turner. The timer shows forty-five seconds and counting. Crap.

I kneel down and do a close inspection of the wires. Sweat beads up on my forehead and moisture drips down my back. I take a deep breath and try to push thoughts of Matthew out of my head. I release my breath and take another deep breath and hold it. My wire cutters are poised and ready. I stare at the wiring and methodically trace each wire. I force myself not to think about Matthew. I'm sure I have it, but the thing about bombs, sometimes they're booby-trapped. Sometimes, you are forced to just clip and pray. I raise my hand and will myself to stay calm. My hands are steady enough. Not perfect but better than I expected. I take one more look at Turner, hoping he isn't the last person I see on this earth. That would truly be a lousy ending. The timer is still counting down, and I need to make my move. The bomb squad has arrived, but there is no time for them to intervene. It's up to me. I take another breath and hold it. Sweat is pouring down my face, and I pray it stays out of my eyes. My hands reach out. Snip. I release a long woosh of air. Oh. My. God.

Before I have time to realize I'm still alive, I wrinkle my nose in distaste as the smell of urine permeates the air. I look down at Turner. He has tears streaming down his face and a big wet spot in his crotch.

"Unlock me, Moore."

Something snaps in me. "Really? No please or even a thank you for saving your life? You can sit here until your partner gets here with a key. I don't have one on me." Okay, sue me. Sometimes I'm bitchy.

Sean rushes out of the house with Angus.

I look right into his eyes and try to get him into mind-reading mode. "Sean. What we discussed earlier. We've got to do it. Give my keys to Angus." He nods and hands them over. I need to be brief, I have no idea who we can trust. I walk up to Angus and whisper. "Edison. Trout. Carpet."

Angus and I have our own shorthand way of communicating, and I can see the comprehension in his eyes as he nods his assent. He even manages a brief smile.

Sean jumps in and says in a low voice. "We need to move him out now, while there's some confusion going on, in case the suspects that planted the bomb are watching."

You never have to tell Angus anything twice. He turns on his heel, pauses, throws a set of handcuff keys to Sean, and hurries into the house.

Sean winks at me. "Should I wait until everyone sees him in his glory?"

I look over at Turner. The defeated look on his face doesn't tweak my heartstrings, but I realize no cop wants to be seen in a weakened condition. "Nah, go ahead."

Captain Tom Thompson, leader of the Bomb Squad is approaching. "I need to talk to the Captain." My stomach does another epic growl. "This mess better not hold up our pizza."

Captain Thompson walks up to me. "Hey, Boomer. How are you doing?"

Talk about a man of few words. Tom Thompson, at forty-two, has been in charge of the bomb squad for the last ten years. He'd been on the force eight years when his National Guard status stamped his ticket for Afghanistan and he became a bomb expert. One of the few people on the squad who knew about me and Matthew, his question isn't an idle greeting.

I smile and say, "I'm good, Captain." It's nice to actually mean it.

"Squad's not the same without you. Glad you were here for this little fiasco. Want to give me a run down?"

I look over to the right and observe a bomb technician gingerly removing the vest from a very relieved Turner. The tech's nose wrinkles in distaste. I am wondering if Turner lost his bowels too. That's confirmed when he gets up and a medic walks him to the back of the ambulance. I want to laugh but manage to keep a straight face.

Captain Thompson follows my gaze and says. "Turner's an ass and a disgrace to the uniform. Not because he shit and peed on himself. I can't say that under a similar situation I wouldn't do the same. He's a disgrace for the way he treats his fellow officers and he's been badge heavy with citizens on more than one occasion. He gave a civilian a severe head trauma injury two years ago. Cost the city millions and he's still on the force. I don't understand how."

I have always liked Captain Thompson. I lean over and whisper. "He's got a connection on the city council. But don't worry. He's bugging Edison for a job as head of his security. You can join our 'Pray for Turner' group if you want."

Thompson lets out a bark of laughter. "Boomer, you always make me laugh. Now, seriously, let's talk about what happened."

I spend the next ten minutes with Thompson and Bowls, the tech that took the vest off Turner. We discuss the type of explosives and the wiring job. Bowls snaps several pictures. Between the FBI and our bomb squad, there will be good information to review. Bowls carefully carries the vest to the bomb trailer and places it in a thick steel box for transportation. Dynamite is usually stable but if one of the pieces is old or damaged, it can become volatile.

Thompson scratches his head, messing up his salt-and-pepper hair as he processes everything. "Okay, the gate guard lets in a gardening truck. You and the FBI guy were five minutes behind the truck. If these are your run-of-the-mill terrorists, they would be suicide bombers. I'm surprised they didn't drive straight into the house. With all that firepower, it would have leveled the house and, most likely, the entire block. Makes me wonder if the homegrown terrorists have more of a self-preservation instinct than the foreign ones."

I'm following his train of thought. "Turner said he came outside to make a call. The perps probably saw an opportunity and went for it. Knocked him out, trussed him up in a stylish bomb vest, and handcuffed him to the flagpole. With the timer, they knew they had enough time to get away."

"The bastards' plan would have worked if you hadn't been here. Good job, Jayne."

Praise makes me blush. Fortunately, the Domino's pizza truck pulls up and cuts my blush short. I can see it at the bottom of the driveway being turned back by officers guarding the perimeter. Oh hell no.

"Captain, if you don't need anything else, I'm going to rescue the pizzas. This is literally a life-saving operation...the so-called cook here comes with a license to kill."

"Go for it, Boomer. I know from experience not to get between you and food."

Wise man. I should be insulted, but he speaks the truth. I jog down the driveway and yell, "Wait. Do not let that pizza guy out of your sight." I am so hungry, I swear I'll draw my gun if the pizza guy makes a run for it. Thankfully, he doesn't and I pull out a debit card instead. After he processes it, I run up the driveway carrying the four pizzas. I get a minuscule amount of perverse pleasure knowing we won't be sharing it with Turner.

Chapter 21

Sean scrambled to get Edison out. Turner had another uniform in the apartment above the garage. Sean grabbed it and headed down the back stairs. He saw Jayne talking to the Captain of the bomb squad. He liked her easy demeanor and noticed the relaxed body language between the two of them. He was still thinking about Jayne rushing to defuse the bomb. The woman appeared to have nerves of steel until you got too close and then she goes into panic mode.

Sean entered the back door of the house and handed the uniform to Angus who was pacing in the kitchen. "Give this to Edison. Pants will be short, but it's the best we can do. You need to get him dressed and walk him out to Jayne's car. We're going to have Hopps and Olsen follow you in a second car."

"Got it. He's downstairs with your two guys. I'll go get him ready. Do me a favor. Grab a loaf of bread and some peanut butter and jelly for me so the Quarter Pounder has food."

Sean laughed. "I can do that. We have pizza coming, I'll throw a couple boxes in for you normal eaters."

"Sounds good. You and Jayne figure this out fast. I won't last too long in tight quarters with Edison." Angus rushed down to the basement to give Edison his disguise.

***

Jayne walked into the kitchen carrying four boxes of pizza. "Where is everyone?"

Sean let out an exasperated breath. "No one knew anything was going on until they heard the sirens and saw the flashing lights at the front of the house. Hopps and Olsen herded everyone down to the basement. By the time I got to them, you'd already defused the bomb."

Angus came up the basement stairs with a subdued Edison in tow. Jayne did a double take when she saw him in Turner's uniform. "Good job with the disguise, Officer Ferguson. Mr. Edison, you're going to a safe place."

Edison gave her a wry smile. "When they try to blow up your house, I guess it's time to go."

"We'll get to the bottom of this. You'll be back home in mauve hell before you know it."

Angus snagged two boxes of pizza and the bag of PBJ makings on his way out. "Thanks for the pizza, Detective Moore."

"My pleasure. Now get out of here."

"Roger that." Angus turned and told Edison to keep his head down and follow. Olsen and Hopps were on their heels.

Jayne paused as she picked up a piece of pizza. "You know, it doesn't make sense. Why were they trying to blow him up? Before we had the kidnapping attempt and thought it was all about the money. Blowing him up won't get them any money."

"You're right." Sean thought for a moment and continued, "It makes no sense. We've got too many things in play. Possible ransom money, honor kill for the game, or bobblehead revenge. All of the scenarios are just a little off to me."

Before Jayne could reply, Mimi barged into the kitchen demanding to know Edison's whereabouts.

Jayne's voice was firm when she answered, "Mimi, I'm not in the habit of answering to the cook. It's been a long day, and frankly, I'm tired. The only thing you need to know is Mr. Edison is safe."

Alias came up the stairs from the basement, a look of amazement on his face. "Detective Moore. Is it true you disarmed a bomb on our patio tonight?"

Jayne had a large slice of pizza halfway to her mouth. "Alias, it's been an eventful evening. As I just said, Mr. Edison is safe for now. It looks like you get a few days off until we catch the bad guys. Now, if you'll excuse me, if I don't get a bite of this pizza, right now, I'm not going to be responsible for my actions."

A loud "harrumph" came from Mimi as she stomped out of the kitchen with Alias at her heels.

Jayne snapped. "God knows I tried to lasso my inner bitch when I talked to Mimi, but I'm as much of a cowgirl as she is a cook. Let's finish the pizza, pack our stuff, and get the hell out of here. We have a ton of paperwork to do, and I for one, want to sleep in my own bed tonight."

Sean leaned down and whispered, "Any room in that bed?"

Jayne's face flashed several emotions, and then a resolute look took over. Before she could speak, Sean beat her to it.

"Okay. Okay. Never mind. A woman who can defuse a bomb without missing a beat can probably kill me with a pizza box. We'll talk about it later."

He was relieved when he saw a slight smile on Jayne's face.

Chapter 22

At 2:30 in the morning, I finally walk through my front door. Max and Sophia greet me with a cacophony of displeased meows. What is it about cats that they have to let you know what a jerk you've been by leaving them? I swear some days I feel like getting a dog only because they will forgive anything and greet you with a wagging tail.

My mood is bouncing around faster than a ping-pong ball in a Chinese sports camp. When both cats finally give up the lecture and push against my legs purring, all thoughts of a dog are abandoned.

"Yes, my little monsters. I've left you too long. I'm so sorry. How about some canned cat food to make up for it?" I am babbling away to Max and Sophia when my doorbell rings. It doesn't take a genius to figure out who is here.

I look through the peephole in my door and see an exhausted Sean standing there. I open the door wide to let him enter.

"What's up, Sean? I thought you were heading over to Michael's." I am tired and in serious need of some sleep.

He looks sheepish. "Not to talk out of school, but Michael is entertaining your friend Madison. Neither of them looked like they were in the mood for company or a threesome."

I laugh. "I have to admit, they are kind of cute together. Why didn't you go to a hotel?"

Sean looks down at his hands. "When you were diffusing the bomb, I thought I would go insane. Thank God it only took about forty-five seconds, but it was the longest forty-five seconds of my life. I didn't go to a hotel because I needed to see you and do this. Strong arms encircle me and he gives me a hug so tight, it could rival the squeeze of a boa constrictor. My first reaction is to pull away, but then, I catch a whiff of his aftershave, tinged with a hint of sweat. I melt into his arms and enjoy the moment. I feel like a bear that has found its cave for winter. I snuggle into Sean, only to feel him break the embrace and ask, "Do you have a guest room? I'm dead on my feet."

I hate the sense of cold that replaces his heat. But I like the fact he makes no assumptions about us.

"Follow me." I walk down the hallway to the guest room as I point out the bathroom and where the towels are kept. Sean follows with the luggage he retrieved from his car. I watch him checking out the house and the family pictures on my wall.

"Hope you're not allergic to cats. Max and Sophie are in here a lot."

"No. I'm fine. My sisters and I had cats and dogs growing up, and even a few rabbits."

He turns and gives me a smile that...okay, I'll say it. I feel gushy. Then he gets right into my personal space.

"Jayne, if I've learned anything today, it is life can change in a New York minute. So, I'm going to kiss you. One kiss and then I'm saying goodnight."

I look up at him and can't help but smile. I try to contain the goofy grin on my face. I feel like I am fourteen years old and have lost all my verbal skills. "Umm. Okay."

Sean leans into me and I meet him halfway. He tilts my face up and lowers his head for our lips to meet. The electricity that goes through me could power up a city block. I feel like Dr. Frankenstein has just brought me back to life with the electric jolt of Sean's kiss. He starts gentle, more question than promise, but when I let out a moan, the intensity of his kiss deepens. His arms wrap around me and I affix myself to him like an appliqué on a jacket. My body is heating up, and I don't want to stop. It seems like a lifetime ago that I felt these sensations. My hands pull his shirt out and then I touch the hot flesh underneath. I want him and the realization shocks me.

Sean must feel my hesitation. He stops kissing me and rests his chin on top of my head. "When I first met you, all I could think about was getting you into bed. A quick one-night stand. But now, this thing between us? I have to admit, I haven't felt this way in a long time, and it's scaring the hell out of me. It's obvious I want you, but I want to do it right. I want what I always tell my sisters to wait for. Special. I want our first time together to be special." He leans down and kisses me gently. "You to need get out of here while I still have some self-control."

The electricity in me dims, and I know he's right. I'm all over the board with my emotions, and I agree, this isn't a one-night stand. I don't know when we crossed that line but now is not the time.

Sean spins me around and points me to the door. "Get some sleep. Wake me whenever. Tomorrow's Saturday, and I think with Edison in a safe house, we deserve a day off. Or at least a few hours off."

I nod. I don't trust myself to speak after that kiss. I float down the hallway and get ready for bed. My lips are still tingling, and I fight the urge to go back to Sean. Max and Sophia have already claimed their spots on the bed, and I gingerly lift the covers and slip between the sheets. Despite the day's drama and Sean's kiss, I am asleep in seconds.

***

My skin is melting from the heat of the blast. The sound of glass breaking and car alarms going off is deafening. I scream. I'm thrown backwards and land on broken glass from the patrol car. I'm trying to get up and run to Matthew, but something is holding my arms down. "Jayne. Wake up. You're safe. Wake up."

My eyes open. I can feel tears coming down my face. I'm disoriented, and for a moment, I don't recognize Sean.

I hear the concern in his voice. "You were screaming. You scared the hell out of me. I thought you were being attacked."

I notice his gun sitting on my bed. I don't know what to say, and I can't stop the tears. Sean sets the safety on his gun and places it on my nightstand. He climbs onto the bed, wraps his arms around me and holds me close. I know I'll have a lot of explaining to do in the morning, but for now, I just want to be held and go to sleep.

***

Bacon. The smell wafts through the house. I look at the clock by my bed; it shows nine o'clock. I put on my yoga pants and follow the smell. Sean is wearing one of my aprons as he stands at the stove cooking bacon. The cats are sitting on the high stools in front of the kitchen counter watching his every move.

"Something smells good. The pizza we had for dinner was over twelve hours ago, and I'm starving."

Sean's smile is huge. "Breakfast is my favorite meal to cook. Hope you don't mind, but I made myself at home. Found your stash of bacon in the freezer and enough eggs for an omelet. You good with that?"

"Oh yeah. I'm so hungry, I would even consider eating Mimi's food right now. Okay, maybe not quite that, but close. I'll make some toast." This little domestic scene warms my heart. It has been a long time since I've enjoyed cooking with someone in my kitchen.

Twenty minutes later, we are sitting at my kitchen table enjoying breakfast when my phone goes off. We both say "damn" at the same time, but when I look at the number, I smile. "It's my neighbor."

"Hey, Sheri. What's up?"

"I see you're home. Will you be able to come to the barbecue today? Tom, Lily and the girls are coming too."

I'd forgotten about the barbecue. "I'm not sure. The case is a bit complicated right now. What time and what can I bring if it works out?" I have to admit, the thought of seeing Tom and his family is pretty tempting. I miss his little girls.

"Don't worry about food. Show up any time after 1:00 pm.

I look at Sean. "Is it okay if I bring a friend?"

"Absolutely."

I can tell Sheri wants to ask for details so I cut it short. "I've got to go. I'll see you later unless something comes up with the case." I disconnect the call and casually ask Sean. "Feel like going to a barbecue today? I figure we could work the case for a bit and then take the afternoon off. What do you think?"

Sean is quick to answer. "Really? Are you okay taking me out in public? I think we're making progress."

"Oh no. We're not up to public yet. This is just going to the neighbors. It's a test run. Kind of like test-driving a car. Oh, and Tom, Lily, and the kids will be there."

Sean pushes back from the table and pulls me up into his arms. The kiss is sweet and tender. He leads me over to the sofa and pulls me onto his lap. "I am willing to go for a test-drive. And I'd love to meet your neighbors, and a huge bonus to see Tom and meet his wife and kids." He pauses.

I wait for the other shoe to drop and it does.

"That was a pretty bad dream you had last night. Can you tell me about it?" His voice is so gentle, I can feel my heart squeeze.

I take a deep breath and start talking. It's like I'm vomiting words. I want to get it out, all of it. I talk and talk, and tell him almost everything. I can't let him know the blast that killed Matthew shook me deep down to my core. It will remain my secret. Who wants to work with a cop who has issues? Telling him about Matthew completely drains me, but strangely, I feel free.

I stop for a moment and wrap up my story. "I had taken the detective test a few weeks before it happened. I passed and it seemed like a good time to leave the bomb squad. I couldn't think about diffusing bombs when I could still see Matthew getting blown up before my eyes."

Sean hugs me to him. "You're an amazing woman, Jayne Moore. You're strong and brave, and I'm proud to work with you. I'm very sorry for your loss."

His words don't make everything okay because it will never be okay that Matthew was killed. But his words give me insight into him as a man. I hug him back and say, "Thank you" into his neck.

The moment is broken when my phone rings. I pull myself off his lap and look at the number. It's DL.

"Hey DL. What's up?"

"First. Are you okay? I heard about the bombing attempt."

"I'm fine. Not a saddle I wanted to be back in, but it worked." I sigh to myself. If I ever see a bomb again, it will be too soon.

"Looks like your Billy McHendricks has been a very busy boy. We've set up a fake character in the game chat room. Billy is the only one that's taken the bait."

"We'll be in your office in thirty minutes. I knew the little piggy would come to market." I can't keep the glee out of my voice.

I hang up the phone and turn to Sean. "Let's go. DL has new information. Follow me in your car, and I'll return my loaner. I'm willing to bet that, one way or another, we'll be seeing Angus and my car soon."

***

I pull into a spot in the parking garage and watch Sean park three spots down. We are in the elevator when Sean slaps himself on the forehead. "In all the excitement, I never asked you where you had Angus take the Quarter Pounder. All I heard you say was 'Trout, Carpet.'"

I chuckle. "When Angus and I worked together we developed kind of a shorthand code for emergency situations. You know, the kind where you don't have time for a lot of words. I just said the two words that would get him up to my family's secluded lake cabin. It's fifty miles from Seattle, and there's no way anyone could track Edison to it. In fact, right now I bet he's driving your guys and Angus nuts. He's completely off the grid. I saw Angus snag Edison's phone and leave it on the kitchen counter. There are no computers or electronic devices at the cabin. I feel sorry for the guys. I'll bet Edison is climbing the walls." I could see the wheels spinning in Sean's head.

"Okay, I get the word trout, but carpet? What's that about?"

"My dad and mom own a carpet installation business. When I was a rookie, Dad was a little overprotective and insisted on meeting my new partner. I took Angus out to the cabin for a day of fishing. He and my dad got along great, and we usually fish together on opening day and once or twice during the summer."

"You fish? This just keeps getting better and better. You're the stuff that fantasies are made of." Sean waggled his eyebrows.

I can't stop the giggle. "Next, you're going to want to show me your rod."

"I've been dying to, but we're taking it slow, so just hold onto that thought."

Sean looks over and laughs when he catches me blushing. "Okay, back to work, Detective Moore. I would appreciate it if you would keep your lusty thoughts to yourself."

Chapter 23

Alias knew it was time to face the music. He grabbed Brian's phone off the kitchen counter and headed into his office. He should have called Brian's mother the night of the attempted kidnapping. Even though Brian Edison paid his salary, Momma Bear Edison owned him, and no matter how you spun it, he was nothing more than a glorified babysitter. He pulled out his cell phone and sat down at Brian's desk.

As he started to scroll through his auto-dial, Brian's phone vibrated. He looked down and saw eighteen missed calls. His palms were sweaty and his hands had a slight tremor as he answered Brian's phone.

"Brian, why haven't you answered my calls?" Barbara Edison's voice was shrill.

Alias took a deep breath. "It's me, John." Barbara Edison had always refused to call him by his nickname.

"John. What's going on? Where's Brian?"

"Barbara, you need to sit down. He's okay but there was a kidnapping attempt, and he's been moved into protective custody. They couldn't tell me where they were taking him, but I do know he's in good hands. The FBI is guarding him." Alias waited for the explosion. Talking to his second cousin--once or twice removed, he could never keep track--always terrified him. It was like watching a volcano blow, and just as frightening. He held the phone away from his ear when the screaming started.

"YOU lost my son?" Barbara Edison screamed into the phone. "Your only purpose as his 'personal assistant' is to know where he is at all times and report back to me. You imbecile, how could you let this happen?"

Alias started spewing excuses, finally ending with, "And after they diffused the bomb, they took Brian out dressed as a policeman in case anyone was watching."

In a voice so cold it could freeze beef, she asked, "When was this, John?"

    Alias was busted. This sweet gig was probably going to end, but then inspiration hit. In a voice he hoped exuded confidence and authority he said, "Last night. For Brian's protection, they ordered me not to make any phone calls until they were safely away. In fact, they confiscated both of our cell phones. I just got them back, and only after I reminded them of the prominence of the Edison family in this city." Alias hoped the last ego-stroking comment would calm her down.

    He heard a whoosh of air, like a house falling on the wicked witch. Her voice returned to her haughty tone, but with a lot less anger than before. "John, find me a charter jet. I'll start packing and will be at the airport in Nice in two hours. Call me when you have details. I want the people in charge to be at the house when I arrive, and you tell them, I want my son there as well. We'll discuss your handling of this situation later."

***

Alias spent the next thirty minutes on the phone and arranged to have a jet fueled and ready at the Nice Côte d'Azur International Airport. Amazing how money makes people snap to attention. He called Momma Grizzly back and gave her the information. He then called the housecleaning service and told them to be there in one hour.

    His next unpleasant task was to get Mimi out of the picture. Barbara Edison would immediately recognize Mimi's obvious lack of cooking skills and start scrutinizing the household expenses. That would put an end to the nest egg Alias had been building.

    He walked up the front stairs to Mimi's bedroom. He entered without knocking and stared at Mimi as she snored. The white drool marks on her pillow looked like a slug had trudged through in the night. Without the heavy makeup, her face was splotchy with broken veins staining her cheeks a reddish-purple color. Alias was about to shake her awake when her eyes popped open.

    "What the fuck are you staring at?" Mimi's voice was raspy.

    "You've got to leave. Brian's mother is flying in from France today. She'll figure out real fast that you're no chef." As he spoke he opened her closet and pulled her suitcase out.

    "I'll go but you're still paying me." Mimi sat up in bed and fixed a level gaze on Alias. "I'm sure Mrs. Edison would love to hear how your prison guard became a chef for her weird son."

Alias picked that moment to grow a spine. He straightened his shoulders and looked down at Mimi. "I'm sure the Walla Walla warden would love to be informed his female guard forced prisoners to perform sexual favors for her. Might jeopardize your monthly pension check. Face it, your sweet overpaid gig is over. Pack your bags. I need you out of here in exactly one hour."

Mimi kicked out with her foot, scoring a direct hit to Alias' groin. When he doubled over in pain, she laughed and said, "I saved you from being someone's bitch. That's a little love tap to remember me by."

One hour later Alias watched Mimi strut down the stairs looking like a sausage stuffed into a low-cut top, several sizes too small. The morning light was unkind to the layers of heavy makeup on her sagging face. Alias opened the front door as she waltzed by and did a bow at the waist with his arm gesturing out the door. She exited and he slammed it behind her.

Alias brushed his hands together and said out loud, "My days of servicing that bitch are over. Now I need to come up with a strategy to outmaneuver Momma Grizzly."

Chapter 24

Diane stares at her computer monitor as Sean and I stand over her shoulder and watch her type. She stops abruptly and turns around.

"Well, that was certainly interesting. Did you see all the white supremacy ideology 'The Viking,' was spouting? We've got to get these guys. I've been on with Big Mac and a few others that fly above the radar. Sean, as I told you yesterday, your FBI guys are working the same angle. I'm hoping the profiler can make something out of all this gibberish. I swear the trademark of all these guys is they can't spell, and their grammar is atrocious. Talk about the dumbing of America. Even the terrorist's English is better."

I focus on the monitor. "Quick, how do I screen-print?"

DL reaches over and pushes a button. The printer started up immediately. "What did you get?"

"The little piggy just said to your screen persona, the Prophet, 'Dude, if you don't like the game, don't threaten me, go after the billionaire that makes money every time we put one of your heads in our baskets.' Sounds like Billy is trying to keep the pot stirred."

DL shoves me out of the way and starts typing. "You are the one. You claim you wrote this game. You and everyone else will die. I will find all of you that have disrespected Allah."

The three of us wait for Big Mac's reply. After ten minutes, DL said, "Damn, I think we scared him off. I thought he would try and throw Edison under the bus. Let's peek into some of the other chat rooms."

After two hours and no luck in the other chat rooms, my eyes are starting to cross. Finally, DL calls an end to it.

"We've got four FBI guys who are going to monitor this all weekend. You two have been working nonstop since this case started. I say we call it a day." DL sounds as tired as I am.

"Works for me." Sean sounds a little too eager with his reply, and I elbow him in the ribs when DL looks away.

I try to sound like staring at a screen is fascinating. "Are you sure the four of them can handle it? I don't mind staying." As the words come out of my mouth, I almost laugh at Sean's stricken look and DL's triumphant one. Damn, that woman is too perceptive. She gives me a "yeah right" look, and I have to laugh.

"Okay, I admit, I'm lying."

DL laughs and Sean looks relieved.

"Okay, we're out of here. DL, see you Monday unless all hell breaks loose."

Never ever tempt fate or hell. Immediately, my cell phone rings, and I don't recognize the number. "Moore."

"Detective Moore, this is Alias. In two hours, Brian's mother is catching a charter jet to Seattle. She will be arriving at Boeing Field at nine tomorrow morning. She has requested, make that demanded, her son be at the house when she gets there. She wants you and Agent Lindstrom there as well, and I think maybe the mayor and chief of police."

"Seriously? The mayor and the chief of police?" Who does this woman think she is? I am pissed.

Alias sighs. "I'm sorry, Detective. She's always been this way. Her dad was Herman Parker. The family goes way back in this town and are very influential."

I do some quick mental calculations. She won't be here for fifteen hours. A lot can happen in that time. However, cover your ass is a cop motto. "Thanks for the heads up, Alias. I'll get back to you."

I disconnect the call and turn to Sean and DL. After I finish relaying the information, they both frown.

DL is the first to speak. "Does she even realize how she could be jeopardizing her son by bringing him to the house?"

Sean pulls out his phone. "No way is this going to happen. I'm calling my boss." Sean walks to the corner of the room, and I watch as he speaks animatedly. He stops and listens intently for what seems like forever but is only three or four minutes. His face is stony and his ears are bright red. A sure sign that he is getting chewed out. He ends with a "Yes sir. I understand, sir. No, I promise, this will work." He shoves his phone into his pocket and walks back to us. "I have a plan."

I look at Sean and DL. "Let's hear it."

Sean closes the door. "Jayne, don't say where the Quarter

Pounder is. I don't want to put DL in a bad position. I talked to my boss. We're going to grab Mrs. Edison and put her in protective custody until we can get this chat room sting going. We've got to find out who are the serious threats, and so far, the only place we have to look is online."

I mull everything over. The biggest problem is that we'll be stuck at my family cabin with all these people.

Sean is watching me. I see the look of concern on his face and smile at how perceptive he is becoming to my moods. "What's wrong?"

I shrug. "Nothing. I'm just thinking that watching the Quarter Pounder and his mother together might be kind of entertaining. Beats the hell out of waiting to see who Mimi kills off with her food."

They both laugh. I realize we have fifteen hours before we have to worry about this case. "Sean, let's get out of here."

Sean nods and we say our goodbyes to a grinning DL. I ignore her knowing look. Our steps are a lot lighter than when we walked in two hours before. We get in the car and I turn to Sean. "Let's stop at the grocery store. I want to pick up some things for the cabin. Looks like we'll have a bunch of people to feed."

"Sounds good. Hey, do we need to pick up anything for the barbecue?"

I think for a moment and smile. "Oh yeah. This is a perfect day for my chocolate Kahlua cake, and we have just enough time to make it. In fact, I'll make one for the guys, too."

Sean and I spend thirty-five minutes in the store. I get the ingredients for the dessert, and we both pick out food to take to the cabin. I figure since Angus and the two FBI agents have been stuck with Edison for a day and a half, red meat will be a nice peace offering. I am bringing chocolate candy for me, hoping it will take the edge off when I'm with her highness. I hate to prejudge someone I haven't met, but all indicators are that this woman is not going to be easy.

***

I put the finishing touches on my cake. I look up and can see Sean watching me with a smile creasing his face. "What? What are you smiling about?"

"You're like an onion. You have layers and layers of surprises.

I like seeing the domestic side of you. Your house is homey, you can cook, and you FISH!"

"Whoa cowboy, don't get ahead of yourself. I have layers and layers of faults and eccentricities too." He is starting to make me nervous.

Sean gets up off my sofa and walks toward me. Somehow the image of a lion approaching his meal goes through my head. I hold up a spoon covered in chocolate frosting as my weapon. I watch his eyes glaze over. Whatever he is intending to do is sending shivers down my spine. His hands reach out, and I think he's going to grab me. Instead, I feel the spoon being jerked out of my hand.

"Is this chocolate fudge frosting?" Sean's tongue is already working on the spoon. "It's my favorite."

I didn't think it was possible to be jealous of an inanimate object, but he is doing some serious tongue action and I have been alone too long. Whoa, where did that come from? I need to get out of this house. I look at my kitchen clock. "Time to go. You ready for the barbecue?"

"You mean my test-drive? Yeah, I'm ready." Sean's smile is wicked, as he pulls me to him and gives me a chocolaty kiss. "I think I just found a new favorite. You taste way better than the chocolate."

"You've got a pretty good repertoire of B.S. going on."

Sean laughs and hugs me. "Sorry. I know I'm freaking you out. I'm happy that I get to spend time with you like a normal guy, not FBI guy."

"Hmmm, normal. Let me think about that for a bit. I don't want to make any hasty conclusions. Cops like to weigh all the evidence." I try to keep a straight face, but the look on his face is priceless. I melt into him for a moment and then force myself to pull away. "Come on, Sean, we have people waiting. I'm sure word's already gone out that there was a car in front of my house all night. We might as well go face the music."

Sean grabs my hand as we walk out the door. He has a bottle of wine, and I'm carrying the cake. It is so freaking normal, and it kind of feels good.

***

The first person I see is Tom's wife, Lily. She lets out a squeal and rushes over. Tom must not have told her about Sean because the first thing she says is, "Jayne, I wasn't sure if we'd see you today. Did the library close early?" Then the evilest giggle I've ever heard comes out of her mouth.

I try to frown at her. "Okay, Lily. No chocolate cake for you!"

She looks over at Sean and bats her eyes at him. "I bet Sean here will bail me out on this one. Right, Sean? From what I hear, Tom did save your life a time or two, so you owe me."

Sean laughs and walks over to shake her hand. "Lily, it is a pleasure to meet you. That husband of yours did save my life more than a time or two. I'll plead your case and try and get you an extra big piece."

Lily looks at me and sticks out her tongue. Then she calls in the big guns. "Girls, your Auntie Jayne is here."

I manage to put the cake down before I am almost mowed over by two short little humans. I lean over and start smothering them in kisses. God, I have missed these girls.

"Allison, you've grown! Look at you, you're almost as tall as me!" Allison at seven is the oldest of the three girls. When she looks up at me and smiles, I see that two of her baby teeth have fallen out. "Sweetie, you've lost teeth!"

"I know, Auntie Jayne. The tooth fairy came and I got two dollars!" She squeals and I love the way she says "toof" fairy. I squat down to her level and give her a big hug. Her five-year-old sister Carrie latches on, too. For the first time in a long time, I can actually imagine having my own kids.

The moment is broken when Tom yells out, "Boomer, get over here. I want to know if I need to kick Lindstrom's ass."

Both girls say in unison, "Daddy said a bad word!"

Smothering my laughter, I stand up and walk over to my partner. "Why do you need to kick his..." I look over at the girls, "bottom?"

Tom and Sean both laugh. "Gee, Moore, funny question from someone who was ready to shoot him only four days ago!"

I look at Sean and smile. "Feels like a lot longer." Before I can continue, our hosts appear.

Sheri McLellon moved to Seattle from Minnesota to attend college at the University of Washington and never left. After living here eleven years, she's almost a native. Her fiancé, Ice Zamboni, moved to Seattle a year ago. They had been best friends as children, and when Sheri was targeted by a serial killer last year, Ice rushed to her side. The rest, as they say, is history. They both finally acknowledged their feelings ran way deeper than just friendship. And now, a wedding is in the works.

Sheri gives me a quick hug and whispers in my ear, "Who's the eye candy?"

I snort a laugh and look at Sean. Okay, I can't argue with her assessment. Seeing him out of his *Men in Black* FBI uniform, wearing jeans and a tee shirt, I have to admit she is right.

"Sheri, meet my new temporary work partner, Special Agent Sean Lindstrom."

I watch how natural Sean is. His smile is sincere as he shakes Sheri's hand. "It's nice to meet you. I've heard a lot of great things about you and your fiancé."

As he says the word fiancé, Ice sticks out his hand. "That would be me. Ice Zamboni. Nice to meet you, Sean."

I can see Sean's eyes widen as he says with reverence. "*The* Ice Zamboni? NHL superstar?"

Ice laughs. "I don't know that I'd say, superstar. Oh, what the heck, sure, superstar sounds nice."

Sheri elbows him in the ribs. "Jocks and their egos!"

Sean laughs. "You were great. I always enjoyed watching you play. We used to watch your team play when I was in Iraq. Somehow watching ice hockey in one hundred and twenty degree heat helped to cool us down a little."

Before Ice can respond, Sheri jumps in. "So Sean, you're from Portland. Is this a temporary assignment, or are you transferring to Seattle?"

I try to look elsewhere as he answers. I've been told more than once, I have a very readable face. For some reason, when I'm doing cop work, I can keep it under wraps. In my personal life, my face is as readable as a Kindle.

Sean's answer makes my day. "I'm moving back to Seattle.

My transfer was in progress when I was ordered up here a week ago to assess a terrorist threat."

Sheri smiles at me with a glint in her eye, followed by a giggle. What is up with her and Lily? It's as if Dr. Evil has invaded their bodies.

I can tell Sheri isn't through with her subtle interrogation when she asks, "Do you have family in the area?"

Sean looks over at me, watching my face as he says. "My mom lives about twenty miles away, in Redmond. And I have three sisters who all live in the area."

Before I can digest the fact that his family lives so close, Tom jumps into the conversation and tells everyone he needs to catch me up on some work things. We walk over to a corner of the yard, and he takes a sip of his beer before he starts talking.

The thing I love, and sometimes hate, about Tom is he's very astute. He wastes no time gloating. "Okay, Boomer, let's get this over with. Tell me I was right, and I won't make it too hard on you. Like your dad says, when I'm right, I'm right."

I try to play dumb. "Right about what?" I look at his face and give it up. "All right. I give. He's a good guy, and I like him. I can't believe I was fooled by that used-car salesman thing he was doing."

Tom takes pity on me. "Jayne, you haven't had anyone in your life since Matthew was killed. I know you're scared. You've got a right to be. You lost Matthew under the worst conditions possible. But he wouldn't want you to duck out on life because of him. It's time to jump back in. And I have to admit, you two look good together."

I laugh. "Okay Oprah, do you want me to add him to my vision board?"

Tom starts to chuckle and then gets serious. "You know when I said I'd kick his ass if he hurts you? He's a good guy. Don't make me kick your ass either."

I nod.

"Good. Now let me catch you up-to-date on our cases so I'm not a liar in front of my wife and kids."

Tom takes a few minutes talking about what has transpired in my absence. Then I give him a heads-up on the latest developments in the Edison case, concluding with, "Edison's mother is expected in town tomorrow morning. She's flying in on a private jet from France."

Detective Jayne and the Dangerous Game

Tom lets out a low whistle. "Welcome to the lives of the rich and famous. Sounds like she's a real piece of work."

I shrug my shoulders. "That's an understatement. But I have to say, I can't wait to see her interaction with her son. I've never seen a bigger wimp."

"Well, Jayne. One of the things I love about being your partner is you always call it like you see it. Glad you didn't have blinders on for this one." Tom claps me on the shoulder.

"I'm starting to worry about my judgment. I was ready to brand Sean as the world's biggest jerk, and I thought Edison was...Well, I don't know what I thought he was, but he's not half the man Sean is." I can't resist adding, "Make that the Quarter Pounder isn't even a quarter of the man Sean is."

Tom laughs. "At least you admit your mistakes. You'll be fine."

Like I said, Tom is a genius at getting people to confess. I blurt out, "I'd rather face a terrorist than try and have a relationship. I'm not good at it."

I watch Tom's eyes as he glances over to where Sean is standing and chatting with Lily. The concerned look on Sean's face tells me his "Jayne radar" has gone off.

"Jayne, look at that guy. I can tell from here he'd put his life on the line for you. Man up and stop trying to analyze this to death. You are a decent human being. I see how you love my girls, and I know you loved Matthew. It's time to make a life for yourself. You deserve it. Okay, that's the end of my lecture. Now, come on. Let's enjoy a night away from murder and mayhem."

Tom's youngest daughter, Andrea, toddles over. At two and a half, she is starting to put short sentences together. She motions for me to pick her up, and she covers me in baby kisses. Then she takes my face into her little chubby fingers, and says, "I kiss it all better, Aunt Jayne."

I think I turned to mush. Nothing like a kid telling it like it is. Truth is, for the first time in a long time, I do feel "all better."

I put her in her father's arms and head to the other side of the yard to reclaim Sean.

***

Sean watches me approach. I can tell he is wondering what Tom and

I talked about, but I don't feel the urge to share. It is time for showing, not telling. I walk to his side, grab his hand, and hold it. I like the look of shock on his face at my public display of affection.

"Wow, PDA? You always surprise me, Jayne. Does this mean the test-drive is over? I guess this means I passed?" Sean's voice is teasing, but his eyes hold questions.

"Yeah. You passed this portion, but I still need to check out your fishing skills. Hopefully, you know your way around a bait box." I smile up at him and wonder when I had fallen into the abyss. Then, I add, for his ears only, "And I still want to check out your rod."

Sean's hoot of laughter has all eyes on us, and my face turns a guilty bright red.

I look at him and waggle my eyebrows, then stand on my tiptoes, and whisper, "Tom gave me some advice I can't ignore. I've got big plans for you after the barbecue."

Sean leans down and plants a sweet kiss on my lips with enough heat in it that I can't wait for the barbecue to end.

Chapter 25

Sean took a sip of his beer and observed Jayne as she ate her barbecue ribs. She was an unrepentant voracious eater. She was literally sucking the meat off the bone and just watching her was getting him aroused.

He caught her eye and laughed--she knew exactly how she was affecting him. When he felt her foot go up his leg, he almost moaned out loud. He glanced at his watch, trying to figure out when they could make a polite escape. He was enjoying the people and the conversation, but it was getting harder to concentrate.

His mind kept drifting to what Jayne had said earlier. After his colossal screw over by Daphne, he'd steered clear of any sort of relationship. He'd had a few dates here and there and some gratuitous sex, but nothing with anyone that mattered. Now, he could actually visualize a future with Jayne. She was intelligent, beautiful, and brave. He knew she was brave because even though he saw something in her eyes that mirrored the pain in his own, she charged in anyway.

Finally, Jayne stood up and gave him a look. Heat shot to an area that was going to be noticeable if he didn't get out of there soon.

Jayne hugged their hosts, and said, "Sheri and Ice, thanks for inviting us, but we've got an early day tomorrow, so I think we'll head back to my place. We still have some leads we need to follow up on."

Sean watched Tom give her a knowing look which she studiously ignored.

"Come on, Lindstrom. We've got stuff to do." She flashed him a smile and started walking out the gate.

***

They barely made it through the back door when Jayne launched herself at Sean. She pressed herself against him, and their lips sealed together like an envelope. Jayne tugged at his T-shirt and ran her hands down his back, the heat searing him like he was being branded.

"Wait." Sean caught his breath and slowly undid the buttons of her shirt. As he progressed button by button, more of her red lacy camisole was uncovered. "God, red is your color. That red dress you had on the other night almost did me in. Now, this." He pulled her shirt off and his hands brushed over her nipples. He felt her back arch and an intake of breath as she gasped. He lifted the camisole, and his mouth alternated paying homage to each hard nipple. Gently nipping and sucking, he could hear her moan with pleasure.

Before she could wiggle out of her pants, he picked her up and carried her to the bedroom. "I've been undressing you with my eyes for days, now I get to actually peel off your layers."

Jayne pulled his head down for a searing kiss. "You'd better hurry."

He made it to the guest room where he had stashed condoms on the nightstand before he left.

As he laid her on the bed, Jayne spotted the condoms. "Figured you were getting lucky today, Lindstrom?"

He froze, worried she was going to be pissed, and then he heard her laugh. "I put some by my bed, too."

Sean gently tugged at her jeans. When they were off, he gazed down at her body. Her red thong, long legs, and milky skin begged to be explored. Sean's lips and tongue started at the back of her calf and worked his way up, tasting and nibbling every sensual spot. He stopped at her center, pressing his tongue into her, feasting on her wetness. When she moaned, he could feel the pulsing of her clitoris.

Jayne's voice was raspy, as she begged, "Oh my God. Don't stop." Her hands grabbed his hair, and she moved into him as she climaxed.

He stopped when he felt her last shudder and pulled himself up to her lips. As he kissed her, he felt her hand on his erection--light as feathers and then firm. He was struggling to hold on when she slipped out of his embrace and took him in her mouth. He felt her tease him, taking him in halfway, and then using her tongue on his tip.

His voice was raw. "Jayne, I want to be inside you."

She raised her head as he grabbed a condom off the nightstand, covering himself and pulling her on top of him.

He watched as she rode him, like a jockey heading for the

winner's circle. He had never been as turned on in his life as he was by watching the expressions on her face. He felt her orgasm and held off. When it subsided, she leaned down and gave him a scorching kiss.

"Don't stop. Keep riding me."

Jayne kept up the rhythm and had another orgasm. He felt like he was going to lose it and tried to hold on. Jayne continued and he could feel her tightening around him again. She looked down at him. "Now, Sean. Come with me now."

Their joint orgasm left them sweaty and breathless. Jayne was the first one to recover. "You must be a great fisherman."

Sean was falling back down to earth and could only manage to say, "Huh?"

"Because you have one amazing rod." She giggled at her own joke and Sean laughed.

He kissed her temple and snuggled in, naked body to naked body. It felt so natural, he let out a contented sigh.

"Why are you sighing? Is everything okay?" Concern shadowed her voice.

"It's a good sigh. I haven't felt this way in a really long time." Sean realized he'd just opened himself up for questions and waited for Jayne to process the comment.

Jayne cuddled in farther, and her fingers started to work their magic. "Sean, don't think you're off the hook, but right now, I don't want another woman in our bed. We'll talk when you're ready."

Jayne started to play Dora the Explorer on Sean's body, finding hidden treasures along the way and hearing a new language of ecstatic moans that were matched by her own.

***

At two in the morning, Sean and Jayne came up for air and were in the kitchen foraging for food. Sean was shirtless, wearing only his boxers, and Jayne had on her red camisole and thong.

"You're killing me but what a way to go." Sean gave her his patented good-natured leer.

"When we pick up Mrs. Edison, I'm going to walk like I've been breaking broncos." Jayne's smile lit up the room. "Okay, Lindstrom, you know my story, are you ready to spill yours?"

Sean put two plates of scrambled eggs on the counter and sat at one of the stools.

Jayne sat next to him and waited for him to start. She leaned over and kissed his cheek. "It's okay if you aren't ready to talk. I get it. Some things are hard to talk about."

"No. I need to tell you. Maybe it will explain what a jaded asshole I was to you and everyone else for the last eight years."

Sean got a forkful of eggs, chewed, swallowed, and went for it. "Daphne and I dated in high school, and it didn't go anywhere. But we would hook up sometimes when I was home on leave. It wasn't serious, but it was comfortable, and when you're making sure you don't get your ass shot off day after day, a little escape is good. Then I got discharged and this time, when we got together, it seemed to work.

"I'd only been back a month when the FBI started recruiting me, and we were both pretty excited about the future. Then Daphne announces she's pregnant. She claimed she was six weeks along, and it actually corresponded with when I got home. I was stunned but once I wrapped my head around it, I was excited. I hadn't thought of a future with Daphne before she told me about the baby, but then I was fully committed. Thankfully, she kept saying she didn't want to get married until after the baby was born. She wanted a dream wedding, and a pregnant bride didn't fit into the picture. I didn't know where I would land with the FBI, so we rented a place near my mom and started getting ready for the baby.

"Training at Quantico is for twenty weeks. I figured it would be fine--I'd be back by the time she was seven months pregnant. Daphne seemed okay with that. We skyped every day, and she would send ultrasound pictures of the baby. I was getting pretty excited and anxious to get home. When I graduated from Quantico, I had a week off to get us ready to move to my assignment in Portland, Oregon."

Sean paused, took another bite of eggs, and watched the expression on Jayne's face. He could tell she was already connecting the dots.

"Whose baby was it?" Jayne's expression was sympathetic.

"Lester Reed was the father. A guy we both went to high

school with. They were actually together, and she broke it off when I came back from Iraq. I guess she was looking for an upgrade. The minute I left for Quantico, they started up again. Les convinced her to give him a chance, and moved everything--and I mean every single thing--out of the house we had rented. He decided it was payback for sleeping with his woman."

Jayne digested everything, and then asked, "What about the ultrasound pictures?"

Sean let out a rueful laugh. "For being an astute FBI agent, I'm an idiot. She was sending me old ultrasound pics that would correspond with how far along she would have been with my baby. I went back and looked at my email, and the pictures all have a date in the corner. In my excitement, I missed that clue."

"Easy to do when you trust someone and are blinded by love."

Sean shrugged his shoulders. "I wasn't blinded by love. I cared about her, but I didn't love her. My dad left when I was ten, and I really missed having him around. I didn't want any child of mine to grow up without a dad who was fully engaged in his or her life."

"How did your mom take it?"

This time there was humor in his voice. "Turns out my mom had better instincts than I did. She suspected something wasn't right when Daphne kept refusing her offers to go to the doctor with her. She kept an eye on Daphne and planned on having a chat with me when I got back from Quantico. Plus, she said Daphne was huge for only having one baby and for as far along as she was. She was two months pregnant when we got together. I'm not sure how she was planning on pulling off the rest of her charade."

Jayne stood up, wrapped her arms around him, and molded herself to Sean. "You're a good guy, Special Agent Lindstrom."

He found her lips, and then whispered, "Hey, cowgirl. Ready to saddle up again?"

Chapter 26

Barbara Edison was a very well-preserved fifty-year-old, and oblivious when male heads turned as she hurried through the airport. Her blonde hair was pulled back in a chignon, exposing a fine-boned face with a strong jaw. Her face was void of wrinkles, attesting to a surgeon's skill. Her body was toned, and her clothes were custom made. When she walked across the tarmac to the plane, her stiletto heels were tapping out her annoyance. As she boarded the plane, the flight attendant approached her.

"Madame Edison, I am Michelle. I will be attending to you on your trip to Seattle. Let me take your wrap. May I bring you a beverage and a snack?"

Barbara Edison gave her a cool glance. "Bring me a glass of Bordeaux. Nothing to eat right now. I assume lunch will be served soon?"

Michelle nodded. "Oui, Madame. We will take off in a few minutes, and lunch will be served within the hour." Michelle smiled and walked to the forward galley.

Barbara Edison stretched out. Her cell phone rang, and she glanced at the screen. "About time you called. Your son's life has been threatened, and you don't bother to call me back until now?"

She heard Randall take a deep breath. "Barbara, you called me exactly ninety minutes ago. I was playing tennis. You do remember I'm in a tournament, right?" She could hear the exaggerated patience in his voice and knew he was mocking her.

"How could I forget? The 'Seniors Tournament,' which you have been gallivanting all over Europe for. Our son's life is in danger. There was an attempted kidnapping and a bomb at the house. I'm flying home. What are you going to do?"

"Well then, the situation is under control. I'm sure I would just be in the way. And as I said, I'm in a tournament. When are you coming back?"

Her irritation meter went off the scale when she heard the

smugness in Randall's voice. "I don't know. A better question is when are YOU coming back?"

"There's a tournament in Baden-Baden Germany next week." He said it as if it were explanation enough.

Her cell phone denied her the satisfaction of slamming the phone in his ear. Instead, she threw the phone across the aisle of the jet and heard a distinct crack as it landed. She picked up her wine and drank it down. The long flight would give her too much time to think about the past and her situation.

Her dark thoughts were interrupted when Michelle appeared with the fifteen-hundred-dollar bottle of Chateau Lafite Rothschild Bordeaux, waiting to refill her glass. Barbara straightened her shoulders and decided another glass of Bordeaux would be preferable to her overflowing glass of self-pity.

She had had no illusions when she married Randall. It was obvious he didn't love her, but she had believed he would come around. The fact that he hadn't after more than thirty-four years made her all the more determined to hold on to him, more as punishment than anything else. She would contemplate what to do later. For now, she needed to focus on Brian.

The attendant interrupted her thoughts. "Madame, the massage room is ready. Would you like a massage before dinner or after?"

Barbara smiled for the first time in days. "A massage? What a pleasant surprise."

"Oui, Madame. Monsieur Smith requested a masseuse for Madame."

Barbara chuckled and thought it a wise move on John's part. "I will be ready for a massage after my meal."

"Oui, Madame."

Chapter 27

Melanie Page Azzanni watched Randall as he talked to his wife on the phone. She was naked, laying under the thick European comforter at a quaint bed-and-breakfast in Munich, Germany. She marveled to herself how little he had changed in thirty-four years. His face was still boyish with creases around his eyes from years of squinting in the sun. His full head of light brown hair was sun-kissed from hours of outdoor tennis, and the gray sprinkled throughout made him even more handsome in her eyes.

His brown eyes were now watching her as he talked to his wife. He was caressing her foot, which protruded from under the covers. It gave her a perverse thrill that after all these years, she was finally able to turn the tables on his wife. Barbara was in for a rude awakening, and Melanie was delighted. The woman had ruined both their lives years before, and now it was almost over. Melanie's life, in particular, had taken a dark turn after Barbara had pushed them apart.

***

Randall Edison ended the phone conversation with his wife. He had been watching Melanie while he spoke to Barbara. Even after the weeks they had spent together, she still shrank into herself at any show of anger. The self-assured girl he had fallen in love with in high school was still in there, he could tell. Her green eyes were beginning to sparkle again, and her mood was lighter than when she had first come to him.

When he thought of all the things Melanie had endured because of Barbara, fury coursed through him. Barbara's selfishness and her deception had been the first domino to fall, the one that cascaded into a long line of repercussions for not only him, but Melanie, too. He was glad Barbara was going to finally pay for what she had done. He couldn't wait.

He shook off his mood and grinned at the woman in his bed. His handsome face creased with smile wrinkles. He turned to his lover and said, "She's on her way. Come on. We need to pack and head back to the states."

"I can be ready in an hour. Do you want me to make reservations?"

Randall's smile vanished. "Unlike my spoiled, elitist wife, we won't be chartering a private jet." He paused and opened his wallet. "Here, use this credit card. By the time the bill comes due, I won't have to beg for an allowance from that bitch anymore."

His smile returned when she grabbed his hand. "Randall, you're almost home free. Just hang on a little longer. We can finally live our dream." She pulled him down for a kiss, and whispered, "Do you ever wonder?"

He didn't even need to ask what. "You mean if we hadn't argued that day?" He sat on the bed and looked into her eyes. His hand sought hers, and he squeezed it. "Melanie, you were, and still are, the love of my life. And all it took was one bad decision to screw it all up. I wanted to leave her so many times, but Parker had me by the balls and I couldn't leave Brian. I had nothing to offer you. Eventually, I just gave up. But now, everything has changed, and we're going to live the life we deserve. The life that Herman Parker screwed us out of."

"Baby, stop beating yourself up," Melanie said, "No one realized she was so young. Who sends a sixteen-year-old off to college by herself? The rich little genius girl set her sights on you, and you found out the hard way that Barbara Parker always got what she wanted." Her eyes narrowed. "I wanted to kill her for taking you away from me."

"I'm so sorry for all the pain I caused you. Once Barbara found out she was pregnant, her father forced me to marry her. If I had refused, he was hell-bent on sending me to prison for statutory rape. I barely even remember the damn night. I went to a party, mad as hell at you, and I kept downing the frat boys 'special brew.' I remember Barbara flirting with me, and from there, it gets blurry. I've gone over this a thousand times in my head. Earlier that day, I saw you talking to Jack Corrison and assumed the worse. I should never have mistrusted you. I promise that will never happen again."

"Honey, we were twenty years old, and I have some

responsibility in all this, too. It was flattering that someone like Jack Corrison, the big man on campus, would be interested in me. We've both made mistakes. Let's put it behind us. We're together now, and that's all that matters." She ran her fingers through his longish hair. "Barbara is finally going to get what she deserves."

"Figures Jack Corrison would be the cause of all this. Corrison had a bigger silver spoon in his mouth than Barbara. Too bad those two didn't end up together instead of screwing up our lives." He spat out the words, and then abruptly, Randall's mood changed as he snuggled up to the woman he had wanted since he was eighteen. He gave her a hug, and asked, "Have you written a thank you note to Mark Zuckerman yet?"

As he expected, she giggled. "Can you believe that after all the years of being apart, Facebook got us back together? We're now an official cliché." Then her mood turned somber. "Eventually, he would have killed me. There is so much I need to tell you."

Randall tightened his hold on her and kissed her gently. "Honey, you're safe. He will never hurt you again." Randall's eyes got misty. "This is all my fault. My stupid decision was the fork in the road that ruined both of our lives."

Melanie shushed him with a kiss. "But you saved me."

"I'm sorry you had to leave your son. I wish we had found each other sooner before he was..." Randall fell quiet.

"Brainwashed? Is that the word you're looking for?" Randall gave a slight nod, and she continued. "When I married Mohammed Azzanni, he was just plain Mo. A nice normal guy from Saudi Arabia living the American dream. I could never have predicted that he would drag me and our son to Saudi Arabia and become radicalized. Of all the things that happened to me in the fifteen years I was virtually a prisoner, the hardest is the radicalization of my son. He is gone. The child I bore and raised is no more. Instead, a vengeful, hate-filled imposter replaced my beautiful boy. And God help me if he or his father find me."

Randall looked her in the eyes. "That won't happen. The best thing about the European Union is how easily you can travel country to country without needing your passport checked. Your husband will never be able to trace you, even if he discovers the name on your passport."

"I hope you're right." Melanie's voice shook. "I know what these people do to those who betray them, especially women." She shuddered and held him close. "Just before I left, a young, married UK woman was raped. When she went to the police, they charged her with adultery for having sex with men other than her husband and threw her in jail. In Saudi Arabia, being charged with adultery is a death sentence. Do you understand what I'm saying? If my husband or my son finds me, I'll be killed. In their country, no one goes to prison for killing a woman who has committed adultery and damaged the family's honor."

"Melanie. I swear on my own life I will protect you."

"Randall, it's not just me that I'm worried about. He'll kill you and your entire family if he finds us. You don't understand the kind of vengeance these people extract for what they consider being dishonored."

"Then let's get you back to the States where you belong. In a few days, this will all be over, and we can begin a life together. Barbara and Brian will no longer be an issue." Just then his phone beeped. He looked down and smiled. "She's in the air. Come on. Let's book our flight. I don't want her to have too much of a head start."

***

As they carried their luggage into the reception area of the bed-and-breakfast, patrons drinking coffee in the common area turned to stare. Randall and Melanie were an imposing couple. Tall and athletic, they stood almost shoulder to shoulder. Melanie's luxurious brown hair just hit her shoulders, and still had the thickness of youth. A wide smile adorned her face and charming dimples gave her an impish look.

It was the perfect picture of a confident woman until Randall opened the door and her eyes cast furtive looks in both directions before walking out. She reached into her handbag and pulled out a pair of large sunglasses. Her shoulders slumped, and she looked like someone trying to disappear. The beautiful woman of moments ago was gone, and a fearful, hesitant woman took her place.

***

Randall had his arm around Melanie's waist as he guided her through the front door. When she had stopped abruptly to put on the sunglasses, reality struck hard. She wasn't safe until they got back to the states. He had a lot to do before he could put his plan into action. Fortunately, he had the tools to always stay one step ahead of Barbara.

Chapter 28

Ten hours later, we're waiting for Barbara Edison to arrive at Boeing Field. We're standing four inches apart, and I can still feel the heat from last night. I feel good. I catch Sean's eye, and he gives me a sexy wink.

We watch the charter jet land and observe a well-dressed fiftyish woman deplane. I nudge Sean. "Look at her walk. It screams haughty."

"You can tell by her walk?"

"Oh yeah. She reminds me of the way the mean girls walked in high school, and that's not a good thing."

We stand to the side as Mrs. Edison clears customs and walks out the door.

"Okay, it's show time," I say. "You start, I can already tell she's going to piss me off."

Sean nods and takes the lead. "Mrs. Edison. I'm FBI Special Agent Sean Lindstrom, and this is Detective Jayne Moore from the Seattle Police Department. We're here to take you to your son."

Our badges are prominently displayed, and I notice Barbara Edison glances at them with a derisive look. We step toward her, and Sean deftly snags her luggage before the waiting limo driver gets to it. Sean flashes his badge at the driver and tells him he will not be needed.

I see Barbara Edison take in the situation, then stop, her stiletto heels digging into the asphalt like an oil-drilling rig. Her voice freezes us in our tracks. "I am not going with you. I am getting into this limo and going to my home. I'm meeting with the mayor and the chief of police. Get out of my way now."

I nod at Sean, and he gives me some space. I take a close look at Mrs. Edison, trying to keep my temper in check and not give our plan away. I notice mother and son have the same gray eyes, only instead of storm clouds at dusk, Mrs. Edison's eyes are like railroad spikes that are boring into me.

I take a decisive step toward her and mentally gear up for the battle. I'd like to just grab this snotty woman by the arm and kick her ass into the car. I force myself to appear calm and caring. "Mrs. Edison. Your son's life is in danger."

"I am aware of that. Why do you think I am here, Detective?" Her eyes continue to stab me.

I take a deep breath and check my inner-gag reflex. "Your home has been targeted, and your son is very worried about you. Frankly, he's been driving the officers guarding him nuts with questions about your safety. Even with his life in danger, his only concern is for you." I don't miss the look of amusement that flashes through Sean's features as I wrap up my little package of lies. I look back at Barbara Edison and figure she is trying to process everything. Best not to give her too much time to think.

I put a concerned look on my face and take Barbara Edison by the elbow and steer her to Sean's car. I decide I need to add another layer of lies to keep the woman moving. "Mr. Edison will be so relieved to see you. We'll be there soon." Taking advantage of her jet lag or her momentary confusion, I manage to get Mrs. Edison into the backseat. "One more thing Mrs. Edison. You will need to turn off your cell phone. Your son's safety depends on it."

To my amazement, without argument, she reaches into her Louis Vuitton purse and takes out the cell phone. I hold out my hand, and Mrs. Edison drops her phone in it. I notice the cracked screen but decide not to ask. I turn to Sean, and whisper, "Get us out of here now." I give him basic directions to start our journey.

***

An hour and a half later, I tell Sean to turn left into a long tree-lined driveway that leads to the cabin that has been in our family for almost seventy years. The original cabin has been added onto by each generation, and it now has three bedrooms, one bathroom, a large great room, and a decent-sized kitchen. Positioned with a good view of the lake and the mountains in the background, I feel the sense of peace that being at the cabin always gives me. It is shattered when reality hits, and I see someone peeking out from a massive tree near the house.

Sean drives in slowly, and I see him checking the rearview

mirror. He says in a low voice, "Looks like they have the house well covered."

I squint but the trees are so thick on each side of the property, it's difficult to see other homes, a feature my family loves, but not practical when you're trying to protect someone from intruders. I'm really hoping this isn't a colossal mistake, but it's a little late to second-guess myself. Sean pulls up to the door and stops the car. I jump out and am greeted by Angus.

"Jayne. You're a sight for sore eyes. What's going on? Have they figured out who's after Edison?" I can tell he is about to rant about Edison, but when he sees Sean helping Mrs. Edison out of the backseat of the car, his jaw clamps shut. He gives me a look I can't decipher. I want to hug him. He looks totally dejected and frustrated. He lets out a small sigh, takes a step closer to me, and whispers, "Is that the mother?" When I nod, he mumbles, "God help us if she's as annoying as her son."

It's hard not to laugh, but my cop face stays firmly in place. Mrs. Edison glares at me, and I involuntarily take a step back. Like a cobra, Mrs. Edison strikes, her voice dripping venom.

"Where are we? And I'm certainly hoping you do not expect me to stay in this..." She pauses and looks around in disgust. "Shack. Where is my son, and why is he in this hellhole?"

My hands clench into fists, and I am about to go off on Mrs. Edison when Sean steps in. "Mrs. Edison. As we told you, your son is in danger. This is a safe house, and we will all be staying here until we apprehend the people responsible. Now, please, you need to go inside. The officers and I will be right outside the door. I need to bring everyone up to speed on the case."

I see her patented scathing look appear. "I trust that Brian and I will be brought up to speed as well?"

"Yes, ma'am. I'm sure you're anxious to reunite with your son. Officer Ferguson, will you please take Mrs. Edison inside?" I give Angus a pleading look.

I see Angus nod, and he even manages to smile at the dragon lady. "This way, Mrs. Edison. Watch your step, the path is a little uneven."

The minute she is out of earshot, I let loose. "Oh. My. God.

Can you believe that woman? Where does she get off insulting my family's cabin? It's a *cabin*, for God's sake." As I vent, I walk to the trunk of the car and start pulling out the cooler and bags of groceries.

Angus comes back with Hopps and Olsen. All three of the men look exhausted, with dark circles around their eyes as a testament to their ordeal. Hopps shakes our hands, obviously grateful to see us.

Angus speaks for the three of them. "We hoped you were here to tell us that you two caught the bad guys, but since Momma Bear has arrived, I guess we're stuck here indefinitely."

I can't help myself. "Aww Angus, you're cute when you pout."

Angus has the grace to chuckle. "You just wait until you spend forty-eight hours with Edison. Plus, we had to help him through his electronic withdrawal. Thank God your family keeps a lot of games. Do you know he's never played Monopoly or Hearts or even Poker? What kind of life is that?"

I really feel their pain. "Hey, I understand it's been tough, but I brought peace offerings. Big thick steaks and dessert."

Hopps smiles and licks his lips. "Dessert? What'd you bring?"

"I brought you my homemade Kahlua cake." I hand Hopps the Tupperware container. "I also brought some bacon and eggs for breakfast. Life is always better with bacon."

Sean pipes in, "Okay guys, time for us to pass on our intel." We spend the next fifteen minutes outside of the cabin telling them of the few updates we'd had with the online chat rooms.

When we finish, Hopps goes back out to the woods, and Angus resumes his post behind the tree by the front door. They both snicker as they pass by us and Hopps mumbles, "Good luck. You're going to need it."

I know they speak the truth, and I whisper to Sean, "Please stop me if I try to shoot her."

Chapter 29

We leave Hopps and Angus outside and walk into the cabin. The layout of the cabin is a little complicated due to the numerous remodels in the past sixty-eight years. The large living room is L-shaped, and I notice the Edisons have placed themselves in the farthest corner. I peer around the corner and see the scowl on Mrs. Edison's face and the look of dejection on her son's. I think it will be best if we give them some alone time.

"Sean, let me give you a quick tour of the cabin." I spend the next few minutes giving Sean the history of the cabin, its original size, and the remodels over the years. When my grandparents first built the cabin, it was two bedrooms with a tiny kitchen and a small living room. No bathrooms or running water. With it situated on the Olympic Peninsula, we get a fair amount of rain, and the living room can get pretty crowded on a rainy day. As their family grew, my grandparents added one more bedroom and enlarged the living room. They finally added running water and a bathroom about thirty years ago. My sisters and I always share one bedroom--it has two sets of bunk beds and is the largest of the bedrooms.

"This cabin is awesome. Lots of great history." Sean is clearly impressed.

"We've had some great times here. My family usually comes up every weekend in the summer." I pause and get back to cop mode. "Okay, back to work for us. Looks like Edison has one of the bedrooms, and the guys have been using the bunk beds. We can put Mrs. Edison in my parents' room, and you and I will make do with the sofas in the living room."

Sean nods and then asks, "Do you need any help with dinner?"

"Not right now. You might want to walk around the outside to get the lay of the land."

I watch Sean exit and make myself busy in the kitchen. I can't hear the words, but I can tell from the tone that Mrs. Edison is lecturing her son. I notice Olsen has placed himself in an inconspicuous corner to keep an eye on both of them, but far enough to stay out of the fray. I catch his eye, and we both do a slight eye roll at the mother-son interaction.

I continue unloading groceries. Normally, when cops are stuck on a stake-out or guarding a witness, we just order fast food. Now, in the middle of the Olympic Peninsula, someone has to cook, and if it helps me avoid Mrs. Edison, I'm up for the job. As I put items away, I check the cupboards to see what else is on hand. My eyes hit on the peanut butter and jelly in the fridge, and inwardly, I groan. I can't believe Mrs. Edison puts up with her son's eating disorder. It is, after all, a sign of an imperfection. If I were to play shrink, my guess would be he needs at least one thing in his life he can control.

"What can I do to help?" Sean is by my side again, and the heat I am feeling is not from the oven. It's like I can't get enough of him. My cop face is getting harder to wear.

"I think you should go interact with the Edisons. You know, some PR work on how great the FBI is and how safe they are." I manage to keep a straight face as I watch Sean process what I said.

"I'll pay you back for that one, Boomer. You're toast." His hazel eyes crinkle and I get all gooey again. Then he returns to FBI mode. "I talked to Hopps and Angus. They haven't had much sleep in the last couple of days. If you and I take the midnight-to-six shift, it will give them a chance to catch some shut-eye."

I shrug. "I'm good with that. I'll start dinner. Fortunately, my dad taught us girls his mad-grilling skills, but you can make the salad if you want."

I leave Sean in the kitchen chopping lettuce and go out to start the grill.

When I come back inside, Sean has finished the salad and is staring out the window at the lake. "This place is great. A nice mix of old and new. I can imagine your family creating some great memories here." Sean's voice sounds a little wistful, and I give his hand a quick squeeze.

"You would need hours and hours to hear some of the crazy adventures we've had here."

Sean's voice is close to my ear. "I'll hold you to it."

A delicious shiver goes through me as I start to pull out plates and utensils. The kitchen is large enough for two people to work comfortably in it. A counter with four stools separates the kitchen from the living room. Sean and I continue to covertly watch Edison interacting with his mother. All of a sudden, he turns to me and grabs my arm.

"Pictures." He spins around and looks at various framed family shots decorating the cabin.

I'm not following his train of thought. "Pictures? What about them? These are all family pictures from the last sixty years."

Sean stands close and says in a low voice, "No. Not your pictures, they're great. You have family pictures in your home and here. I just realized there is not a single picture of any of the Edisons at their house. Not one."

I feel like a lightbulb just clicked on, and Dr. Freud is standing in the incandescent glow. "Wow. That sure screams unhappy family. Everyone displays family pictures."

"Yeah. You're right, it's odd. Think there's any way you can buddy up to Mrs. Edison and figure out the family dynamics?"

I grimace. "My dad keeps a bottle of good Scotch for company. Nothing loosens people up like a dram or two. I'll approach her after dinner. Keep everyone away if you can."

Sean nods. "I'm going to go check out the bathroom. FBI code for, I have to pee."

I chuckle as Sean walks away. I can tell that the voices in the living room are getting heated. I hear, "Mother, enough. I'm staying until the FBI says it is safe to go home. You're not the one that they tried to blow up." Brian Edison gets up and storms into the kitchen.

His troubled expression disappears when he sees me. I can tell he's nervous as he glances around, before saying, "Hello, Detective Moore. Nice to see you."

"Mr. Edison. I hope you've been comfortable here." I peek at his mother to make sure her bat ears are not picking up our conversation.

"It's been pretty hard without the internet."

I glance at the man-boy and give him a sympathetic look. "Hopefully, it won't be for too much longer."

It is obvious he has something on his mind. When he speaks,

his voice is tentative and unsure. "Did you give any thought to being my new head of security? I could use someone like you on my side."

"Mr. Edison, I'm sure you'll understand my reason for refusing your generous offer. I love being a cop. I need to serve and to help people. I would not get that level of job satisfaction from guarding you. I'm sorry. Thank you for your offer, but I respectfully decline." I pause. Even though my conscience will bother me later, I'm unwilling to miss an opportunity to offload Turner. I add, "Officer Turner is a tenacious cop. He could be an asset to you and your company."

As I say the last few words, Sean comes around the corner, and I can tell by his quick smile, he heard my answer. He raises his eyebrows slightly at the last part.

Edison gives me a sad smile and says in a low voice, "I don't have a chance in hell with you, do I, Jayne?"

I muster up a smile and try to soften my words. "I'm sorry, Brian, it's not in the cards."

He gives me a half smile. I'm embarrassed he has picked this moment to make his declaration of interest. Luckily, Mrs. Edison didn't hear him or a cat fight would have started. I do feel sorry for him, I think of my supportive parents and then look at Mrs. Edison. Poor guy. He definitely did not win the parent lottery.

Sean stands close to me. I love the way his face breaks into a big, sexy grin. Oh. Yeah. I've got it bad.

Chapter 30

I spend the next hour and a half feeding the crew and waiting on the Queen and her son. I finish cleaning the kitchen and give Sean a nod. Time to put my evil plan into action. Brian has already beat a hasty retreat to his bedroom. Mama Edison is alone in the living room. I grab a glass and a bottle of Scotch. "Mrs. Edison. Can I offer you a nightcap?"

"Shurrree. Is it going to be as cheap as the wine?" Her words are slurred, and she is sporting her usual scowl.

"This is probably not up to the quality you're used to, but it's a nice night and a beautiful sunset. You might enjoy it." I hold in my inner bitch and manage a smile.

"Go ahead. Not like I have a choice."

I pour her a healthy shot of Scotch and sit down.

She raises an eyebrow. "You're joining me?"

"No, ma'am. I'm part of your protection detail. I just thought you might want some company."

I can see her trying to think of something snotty to say. For once she holds her caustic comments in. She shrugs her shoulders and says, "Why not?"

She takes a big slug of the Scotch, and I wait a couple minutes. But I figure I better start talking before she passes out.

"Is Mr. Edison still in Europe?" I try to make my tone casual, but I notice her jaw clench.

"Yes. He plays the Senior Tennis Tour and has tournaments scheduled."

Even with a slight slur, I can hear the bite in her words.

I decide to try another tactic. "How did you two meet?"

Another big gulp of Scotch and she goes silent. Her eyes have a faraway look, and she almost smiles. "College. We met at the University of Washington my freshman year. He was a junior on a tennis scholarship. I had never seen a more beautiful boy, and for me, it was love at first sight."

Another big swallow of her drink empties her glass. I quickly refill it.

I try to think of something to say. I manage something lame. "I bet you were a beautiful couple."

Her face crumbles. It is like watching a wax painting of the Mona Lisa melt in the sun. Her façade of superiority and composure collapse. She puts her drink down and pulls a lacy handkerchief out of her pocket. "I loved him the minute I saw him. I was only sixteen and scared to death to be in college. I didn't tell a soul my age."

I try not to show any expression.

Sean walks in the door, and I give him a death stare to keep him out of the living room. Thank God he takes the hint.

"That must have been very hard for you," I say. "Did you live at home or on campus?"

"I wanted to get away from my overbearing father. I lived on campus, joined a sorority, and just tried to blend in."

"Was Mr. Edison in a fraternity?" I'm not sure why I'm asking that question, but it seems like it would have been important to someone like her.

"Yes, but he hated it. Randall didn't come from money." She paused, and a tear rolled down her cheek. "He had such plans until I ruined his life."

My eyebrows shoot up to my hairline at her admission. "I'm sure you didn't ruin his life. You've been married for many years. People don't stay together that long unless they're happy."

She doesn't respond with words. Her sobs echo in the small living room.

I do the only thing I can think of--I refill her glass. Booze wins over tears.

She takes a deep drink and continues. "I seduced him. I wanted him to be mine. He had a girlfriend, and they'd been together since high school. Melanie Page was beautiful, and Jack Corrison--you probably recognize his name--kept chasing after her. Randall got jealous, and they broke up. I saw him at a party and flirted with him until he finally noticed me. He'd had a lot to drink, but I didn't care. The only thing that mattered was that Randall was finally paying attention to me."

I'm trying to process everything. I still need to figure out why the elusive Mr. Edison is not at his wife's side. Before I can ask, Mrs. Edison continues, still lost in the past.

"I lost my virginity to him, and he was mortified. The minute we finished, he rushed out of the room." Her voice choked, and the tears were flowing. "That's when it happened, and my life changed forever."

I shamelessly refill her glass. If plying her with liquor is the only way to get information, so be it. I try to ask my next question gently, but I still have so much dislike for this woman.

"What happened after Randall Edison left the room?"

"His fraternity brother, Jack Corrison came in. I was crying, nearly hysterical, and he pretended to comfort me. He had been shut down by Melanie. She wanted nothing to do with him, so he raped me."

Jack Corrison is our senator. Oh. My. God. The penny just dropped. Since I first met Brian Edison, he has reminded me of someone, but I couldn't put a finger on it. His beautiful Hollywood cleft chin. Now I realize, he looks almost exactly like Jack Corrison. I understand why Randall Edison isn't coming to help his only son. He isn't the father.

"Why didn't you press charges against Corrison?" I am incredulous. Her father was a prominent man in Seattle. Surely, he could have taken on the Corrison family.

"When I went back to my sorority house, some of the girls were talking. Turns out Jack Corrison was known for getting girls drunk and then having sex with them, with or without their consent. One girl had tried to press charges a few months earlier and ended up leaving school in disgrace. Jack's family hired lawyers, and they got him off. I refused to go through that, so I never told my father about Jack.

"When I discovered I was pregnant, I confronted Randall. When he found out I was only sixteen, and my father threatened to send him to prison for statutory rape, he agreed to marry me. Do you know what it's like to be married to a man for thirty-four years and never once has he said he loves me? I ruined Randall's life, and he has hated me every single day of our marriage."

I watch her stare down at her watch. It is, of course, a Cartier. She keeps turning it around her wrist. I decide to give her a break from her memories for a moment. "That's a beautiful watch."

Her eyes well up in tears. "My husband gave it to me for my birthday last month. Even though he hates me, he still buys me birthday presents."

"If he is so miserable, why doesn't he divorce you?"

"He can't. When we married, Randall had a year of school left. After he graduated, my father hired Randall to work at his investment firm. My father discovered Randall embezzled money. Randall was faced with prison or staying married to me." She let out a harsh, mirthless laugh. "He should have picked prison. He would be out by now. He's never really held a job after my father fired him. He just plays tennis and golf, and I pay for everything. My clever father wrote into his will that I would lose my inheritance if we ever divorced. Money is a great motivator."

Hmmm. Interesting. I have one more important question. "Does Mr. Edison know he is not Brian's father?"

Her face drains of all color. She grips the arms of her chair and tries to stand. "How dare you." She manages to get up and then leans down and gets in my face. "You shut your mouth. I'll have your badge if you utter another word." It's like water has been thrown on her, but instead of melting, the wicked witch sobers up. No longer slurring, her voice is firm. The secret she has held for years is leaking out, slowly, like air out of an old inner tube, and there is no way to stop it.

Never one to be intimidated, I tempt her wrath and continue. "From your reaction, I'll take that as a no. You do realize that this adds a whole new element to our investigation. Someone is trying to kill your son, and money is a big motivator. You and your husband would inherit all of Brian's money, correct?"

She gives me a smug smile. "I'm the only one in Brian's will. I inherit everything. I was the one who paid for everything all those years while Brian was working on his game. Randall gave him absolutely no support, emotionally or financially. It was all me."

The words deflate her. She sits down hard in her chair, and from the set of her mouth, I know she won't be providing any more information.

I stand up and say, "Let me show you where you'll be sleeping."

She manages to get out of her chair and follows me down the hall. I can feel her eyes boring into the back of my head. As she walks through the bedroom door, she grabs my wrist in a vise-like grip and hisses. "I mean it. One word about what I told you, and I'll have your badge."

I pry her fingers off me. Then I look down at her, and say, "So far tonight, you've threatened me, and now you're trying to break my wrist. That's assaulting a police officer. I'm going to take your emotional instability into consideration and overlook it this one time. I suggest you go to sleep. Tomorrow, Agent Lindstrom and I will be exploring this new information and see if that leads us any closer to who's trying to kill your son. Oh, and by the way, you probably have a target on your back, too."

The look on her face is priceless. As I expect, she slams the bedroom door in my face. For some reason, it makes me smile. Oh, yes. The plot is getting thicker by the minute, and pieces are beginning to fall into place.

I walk away from her bedroom door and look at my watch. I have only a few minutes before we need to relieve Hopps, Olsen, and Angus. I'll fill Sean in later.

Chapter 31

Billy McHendricks was passed out on his bed. He and his friends had started partying at noon with generous doses of Tequila and marijuana. A persistent ringing pulled him out of his party coma. His cell phone was on the nightstand, and he picked it up, mumbling, "Who is this?" Confused that the ringing continued, it finally occurred to him that the burner phone was making the intrusive noise. He dug under his mattress and grabbed the phone. When he answered, a computerized voice spoke.

"There is a package on your front step. The coordinates and instructions are written on the box. Follow them exactly. Do not open the box."

Billy shook himself awake. The voice sounded a lot like Darth Vader, and he wondered if he was dreaming. "Dude, what are coordinates?"

"Look at your phone, you cretin. Enter the numbers written on the box into your GPS application. You must leave immediately."

The disembodied voice gave Billy the chills. He looked at the clock next to his bed. Two in the morning and he was still stoned and very hung over. "Can't I go in the morning?" Billy whined.

"If you want your share of Edison's money, you will go now, you lazy useless piece of human waste. You are the one who is so anxious for revenge because of Edison's betrayal. You must dirty your hands like the rest of us."

Billy sat up and tried to think of what to say when the line went dead. "Shit. Now I've pissed off Darth Vader." He stashed the burner phone back under his bed, pulled on a pair of stained, rumpled jeans, and headed downstairs. He decided to wake up Zeas and Ronds, who had passed out on his couch.

"Wake up. We gotta go on a road trip." He kicked at their feet as he walked to the front door. A shoe box wrapped in brown paper sat on his porch. He bent down and picked it up. He noticed the writing on the outside of the package and numbers that must be the coordinates the Darth Vader voice had ordered him to put into his phone. He shut the front door and walked into the kitchen, put the box down on the table, and searched his phone for the app. Once found, he followed the instructions to enter the coordinates.

Billy had just finished when Eric came into the kitchen rubbing his eyes. "What's going on? What road trip? Where are we going?"

Billy stared at the phone. "Looks like we're going someplace fifty miles away on a lake. This app has GPS, so I guess we'll just follow the directions."

"Why do me and Steve have to go?"

Billy wasn't in the mood to explain himself. "Because I said so. Go wake up Zeas. We leave in five minutes."

He watched Eric shrug and shuffle into the living room to roust Zeas and heard him say, "Dude, wake up. Road trip."

Billy and Eric headed to the front door with Zeas trailing behind him.

***

The three men got into Billy's Camaro. Ronds called shotgun and pushed Zeas into the back and then flipped the seat up. Billy roared off as Eric lit up the bong and took a hit. At the first red light, he offered it to Billy while he waited for the traffic light to change. Eric turned to give Zeas a hit and noticed him holding the shoebox. He asked Billy, "Dude, what's in the box?"

"Yeah, what you got?" Zeas started to give the box a shake when Billy spotted him in the rearview mirror.

"Fuck. Put that down. I have no idea what's in it, so don't mess with the box." A light sheen of perspiration glistened on his forehead.

Billy was regretting his decision to make Eric and Steve go on the road trip. They wouldn't get off Billy's case. Both kept sucking on the bong and then asking, "Dude, what's in the box? Why are we on a road trip?"

Billy's slim hold on having any kind of patience finally snapped. "I'm trying to get the money Baby Brian owes us. Now shut up and let me drive."

Both Ronds and Zeas shut up, either from amazement or from taking so many hits on the bong. Billy didn't care which; he welcomed the silence.

The hour drive became two hours before the Camaro finally turned into a dark tree-lined driveway. Billy stopped the car and blinked. "Shit. I'm too fucked up to do this."

He heard his passengers laugh like two hyenas that have just taken down a wildebeest.

Billy decided to just sit and think for a moment. His eyes were drooping, and he held the package on his lap. Squinting, he tried to make out the writing on the top of the box. He used his phone as a flashlight and deciphered the typed instructions.

Chapter 32

Sean, dressed in all black, sat on a stump in the woods to the side of the house. The driveway led to a large open area. Jayne had informed him earlier that the grass volleyball court was dual purpose. The septic tank lay under the grass, and on big holiday weekends, it turned into a tent city with all the relatives and friends gathering. Sean could imagine Jayne playing volleyball, and he looked forward to being invited.

His mind was filled with images of him and Jayne when a flash of headlights caught his eye. He started to radio Jayne, stationed at the front of the house on the lake side, but she beat him to it.

The minute the car turned into the driveway, he heard her whisper into the radio, "Did you hear that?"

Sean answered quickly. "Affirmative. I have eyes on a vehicle stopped about seventy feet from the cabin. Hopps, do you copy?"

Hopps replied immediately, "Affirmative."

Jayne said, "I'm going to circle around through the woods and get on the other side of the cabin."

"Copy that. Hopps, leave Angus and Olsen inside. Post yourself outside the door and shoot anyone that gets close."

***

Billy blinked three times and tried to clear his head. The instructions said to deliver the package and call the number on the box to confirm. He had nothing to write the phone number on so he punched it into his phone and figured he would hit send when he dropped the box on the porch. The minute he stepped out of the car a beam of light hit him in the eyes.

"FBI. Place the package on the ground in front of you and put your hands in the air."

He could barely make out someone walking toward the car, keeping a distance between him and the package.

"Hey, FBI Dude. I'm just dropping off a package. No big deal." He squinted at the dark frame. "Are you the guy that came to my house with the hot chick cop?"

The voice yelled, "You heard me, put the package down, and your hands in the air."

Billy started to speak again. "But…"

"Do it now before I shoot you."

His hands shook as he leaned over and put the package on the ground in front of him. He was still holding his phone as he raised his hands in the air.

He heard the man yell to someone else. "It's McHendricks."

Billy looked down and saw a red dot on his chest, and the beam of a flashlight coming from the woods. He heard a woman's voice yell out, "McHendricks, it's Detective Moore SPD. I see two men in your car. Who are they?

Billy was sweating bullets but finally answered. "My friends, Eric Ronds and Steve Zeas." Shit. It was those cops that had come to his house.

He heard the lady cop yell, "Zeas and Ronds, out of the car, hands in the air." Billy froze in place as Eric Ronds got out of the car and Steve Zeas pushed the seat forward and climbed out of the backseat. Billy heard them both giggle as they exited the car. Fuck. The idiots were too stoned to be scared.

Billy's whiny voice pierced the night. "What's the problem? I'm delivering a package, and my friends are along for the ride. Here, I've got a phone number you can call."

He heard the FBI guy yell out, "You're not calling anyone. Drop the phone. You three just stay where you are."

Billy figured he'd do better with the hot lady cop, so he turned in her direction and said, "I'm going to call Darth Vader. He'll explain everything. I don't know why you people are freaking out."

He heard her start to yell something as he pressed the send button.

***

The noise is deafening. The three men had been standing close together, and the bomb in the box vaporizes them like a puff of smoke from a giant bong. I feel like it is Deja vu of Matthew's death. The bomb blows me backward over a fallen tree. A huge fireball lights up the driveway.

Afterward, the Camaro continues to burn, but everything else has gone out. My head throbs, and it is so quiet, I fear permanent deafness.

When I actually hear Angus yelling for me, tears of relief run down my face. I roll over, onto my knees, and push myself up to a standing position. Angus reaches me just as I start to sway on my feet.

I feel Angus grab me and hear him say, "Are you hurt?"

I shake my head. My voice is scratchy when I ask, "Where's Sean? Is he okay? How about everyone else?"

"Hopps is getting Sean. We've got Olsen watching the Edisons. Come on. Let's get you into the cabin."

He half carries me back to the cabin. The blast slammed my hip into the ground so hard, I felt like a pile driver. I can already feel myself stiffening up.

***

Sean's ears were still ringing. He'd been blown back into a tree, his head split open, and he felt blood running down the back of his neck. He tried to spot Jayne as he forced himself to his feet. He started running in the general direction, and relief flooded through every pore when he saw Angus coming toward him with Jayne. As he staggered toward Jayne, Hopps ran up to him. He put an arm around Sean's shoulder, and, as Angus was doing for Jayne, half carried him back to the cabin. Sean stopped at the entrance and refused to move until Angus got Jayne to the door. The door to the cabin was shut, and he didn't give a damn what Angus and Hopps saw. He grabbed Jayne and hugged her to him.

"You okay?"

"Yeah. You?" He watched her eyes widen when she spotted the blood on his shirt. "What's hit?"

"My head got slammed into a tree." Sean grimaced as he touched the injury.

Sean felt Angus push them along as he opened the cabin door. "Let's get you two into the house, and I'll take a look at your head, Sean."

Sean and Jayne limped into the cabin and sat on opposite ends of the sofa. The other sofa was occupied by Mrs. Edison and

Brian. Olsen sat in a chair in the corner, his weapon drawn. Hopps stayed by the door, gun out, and ready.

Angus took charge. "I'll go get a bag of ice for Sean." He came back moments later with a first aid kit, a towel, and a plastic bag filled with ice. "Let me take a quick look at it. Head wounds always bleed a lot."

Sean could feel Angus gently prodding his scalp, before he proclaimed, "I can see the cut. It's a couple inches long but, fortunately, doesn't look very deep. I'll clean it, and then you can press the towel and ice into it. The bleeding should stop soon."

Sean held the bag to his head and watched Jayne. Now that he knew about Matthew's death, he was worried she would be having flashbacks. Her face was deathly white, and her eyes looked haunted. He'd seen guys in Iraq with that look and it was not good.

Before he could try to get her alone, Mrs. Edison chose that moment to start in. "We were almost killed tonight. I told you staying at this dump of a cabin was a mistake."

Sean started to answer, but he was caught off guard when Jayne got up abruptly and announced she was going to the bathroom. When he tried to get up to follow her, she shook her head no and left the room.

He looked at Mrs. Edison and her son. "We need to curtail this conversation until Detective Moore returns." He saw Mrs. Edison's eyes harden and could swear she looked like she was going to come after him, but he didn't give a damn. Something was up with Jayne, and his gut said he wasn't going to like it.

***

I have to get out of the living room. I can feel Sean's eyes on me, and I know that Angus is also watching me closely. I manage to hobble into the bathroom, lock the door, and sit down on top of the toilet lid before the shakes start. Tears complete the breakdown as they stream down my face. I muffle my sobs by biting on a towel. I can't believe this is happening to me again. I lost Matthew, and now, when I am finally opening up again, I almost lose Sean. I keep replaying the bomb going off and not knowing what happened to Sean. I can't do this. I can't go through it again. I'd rather be alone. The future I've envisioned with Sean is over. I am not going to watch another man I love die.

I push my fear down to the place where I keep my secrets. I take deep breaths until my hands stop shaking and then take a cold washcloth and hold it against my eyes. I shed a final tear, square my shoulders, and put on my cop face. I grab some Advil from the medicine cabinet and leave the bathroom.

When I limp back into the living room, I hear Hopps ask, "How did they track us?"

My eyes zero in on Mrs. Edison, who is wearing silk pajamas and nervously twisting the expensive gold watch on her wrist. I notice the older woman's face is drained of all color, and for the moment, she is subdued.

And then I have an epiphany. "Mrs. Edison, I need to see your watch."

Barbara Edison frowns and shakes her head like she doesn't understand the question. Then true to form, she lashes out. "We've almost been blown to bits, and you want to talk about my watch? You incompetent fool."

"I need to see your watch. Please take it off."

I am surprised when Mrs. Edison complies without further complaint. Sometimes shock works in your favor.

She takes it off and hands it to me. "As I told you, my husband gave it to me last month for my birthday."

I walk into the kitchen and open a drawer where my dad keeps his "inside" tools. Selecting a small screwdriver, I pry the back off. A tiny device falls out. Sean and I exchange looks.

Luckily, my phone escaped damage and I focus the phone's camera on the small device. I use a screwdriver to flip it over and photograph the other side. I make sure the magnification of the lens catches the serial number. Then, I pick up a hammer from the drawer and, using the anxiety of the evening, smash the tracking device to smithereens.

Brian Edison walks in just then, looking like dingy chalk. "What happened? What was that?"

I stare at him, surprised he hasn't connected the dots. "You've been at this cabin for three days without issue. Your mom shows up, and within hours, your friends try to deliver a bomb. She had a tracking device in the fancy watch your father gave her."

Brian Edison's confused expression changes, and his face flushes with anger. "You're saying my friends were involved in a plot to kill me?"

I look at Brian and try to soften my tone. "Brian, we don't know if Billy knew what was in the box. He said he was delivering it for Darth Vader. He was obviously very high. We know he's been in some chat rooms with people we believe are ISIS supporters. I'm sorry." I watch Brian Edison deflate and note that his mother doesn't spare him an ounce of empathy. Before I can say anything else, I hear the sound of sirens on the highway that circles the other side of the lake.

I see Sean cock his head toward the sound and hear him say, "Well people, I guess this answers the age-old question, 'If a bomb goes off in the woods, does anyone hear it?'"

Chapter 33

Every part of my body hurts. Sitting on the sofa, I can hear cars and large vehicles outside the cabin. The three F.B.I. agents jumped into action when the local law enforcement showed up. Sean manages to go outside even with his head still bleeding. I figure Angus and I are way out of our jurisdiction, and let's be real, I am in no hurry to get off the couch. I need space from Sean, and I have to figure out how to tell him I just can't even think about starting a relationship with him.

Business first, I need to call my Lieutenant and give him an update.

I limp out of the room to place the call. I don't want the Edisons listening. The phone rings three times before he picks up. His voice is groggy, and I notice it's five in the morning. My bad.

"LT., Moore here. Sorry to disturb you so early. We're at the safe house, a.k.a., my family cabin, with Brian Edison and his mother, Barbara Edison."

Lieutenant Johns cuts to the chase. "You don't sound good, Moore. Get to it. What warrants a call so early?"

I spend the next seven minutes telling him about the bomb and the tracking device. I finally finish with the story of Mr. Randall Edison.

"Jesus, Moore, you've had a hell of a night. You okay? When can you get in here to go over this in more detail with the task force? We're meeting this morning at eleven o'clock."

"I can be there. I need to get the Edisons settled into another safe house. I'll let Agent Lindstrom know about the meeting."

In typical fashion, LT hangs up without saying good-bye. Damn, that's annoying.

***

I go back to the living room and sit on the sofa. Angus has made coffee, and he brings me a cup. I'm touched that he remembered to put in my standard splash of milk and two sugars. I give him my best smile, but I can see lines of worry etched into his face. My thoughts are racing, and I have to force myself to stay in cop mode.

Angus sits by me, and I wait for my lecture. It's tough when you know someone so well. His body language is screaming concern.

He keeps his voice low and takes my hand. "Jayne. I know you, and I know you're a tough cop. You just went through a horrific experience, very reminiscent of a painful time in your life, and now, I see you already trying to push Sean away."

Damn. Angus has always been too perceptive. I pull my hand back and tersely whisper, "Don't. Just don't. You don't know what it's like, and I'm not going to discuss it here. You know how much I care about you, but this is none of your business."

Angus looks at me like I've just killed his kitten. My heart now adds another hurt to the growing list. Fortunately, I'm distracted by the whispering going on between Brian and his mother. My hearing has come back, but I'm not able to catch the conversation. Finally, Brian approaches me.

"We're not safe here. What are your plans?"

I'm grateful to end my conversation with Angus and respond to Brian. "Right now, whoever had Billy McHendricks deliver the bomb probably thinks we're all dead. The tracking device has gone silent for them. They will surmise it's the result of the explosion. We will be moving you and your mother, but not until we announce your unfortunate deaths. I need to discuss some things with Agent Lindstrom, and then we'll fill you in."

A few minutes later Sean walks in the door and sits down. Positioned on opposite ends of the sofa, we are bookends of exhaustion. Brian comes back to our side of the room and immediately starts peppering him with questions.

I hear Sean trying to placate Brian, and then he asks me to go with him to the kitchen. I manage to pull myself off the couch and follow. Sean looks around and tries to give my hand a quick squeeze, but I pull it away and shake my head. I'm not ready to talk about anything, so instead, I ask the million-dollar question. "How did those three morons manage to get their hands on a bomb?"

He keeps his voice low. "I seriously doubt they had the brain power to create a bomb. Honestly, my money says he was told to deliver it by 'Darth Vader' and probably didn't think about asking what was in the box. Billy sure as hell wasn't planning on blowing himself up or killing Brian, not the way he's been fighting for more money. He said he had to call Darth Vader. He must have been stoned out of his mind."

As much as I don't want to think about seeing three people being vaporized in front of me, it keeps popping into my head. It's so hard to keep up my façade of calm with Sean. I'm surprised he bought my lie when I said I was okay. I keep seeing the bomb go off. It was like watching Matthew die all over again. Even taking into account that those were three of the most worthless individuals I've ever come across, they were still human beings and had mothers that may, or may not, have loved them. Someone will mourn their deaths, even if it's just their local marijuana store.

Sean, oblivious to my thoughts, continues. "We need to figure out who he connected with in the chat room. He probably had instructions to call a number when the package was delivered. When the car door opened, I could smell the marijuana from fifty feet away. Those idiots. Who doesn't figure out they're being used to transport a bomb?"

He stops for a minute and looks into my eyes. "Are you sure you're okay?" I nod and he continues. "They weren't the brightest bulbs on the tree, but what a pathetic way to die. Unfortunately, all of the evidence was incinerated, too. The phone and the package were blown to bits. The FBI will continue to comb through the crime scene area, but it doesn't look good. For now, we're going to follow the plan. The sheriff wrote up the report that Brian and Barbara Edison died in the explosion. We'll leak that news to the media, and worry about the details later. That should flush out Randall Edison, the grieving widower, and father. Now we have to figure out where to take these two."

I manage to pull my shit together and respond. "I have some thoughts on that. Belfair is a small town about twenty minutes away. I'm thinking we need to book them a motel room. Mrs. Edison will stand out like a sore thumb in her haute couture, so I'm going to dress her in some of the old clothes Mom leaves out here for when we do yard work. Though my mom may kill me."

I see Sean's eyes light up in merriment.

"You are a very brave woman. My phone will be ready for the

photo shoot."

***

I spend the next thirty minutes booking adjoining rooms at a motel in Belfair. I anticipate Momma Edison pitching a fit, but I am way past caring. This is what happens when you piss me off and treat me like something on the bottom of your shoe. Despite the awful things that have occurred, cops always manage to find some bright spots. I pull out a pair of my mom's old jeans, a t-shirt, and her old tennis shoes, and lay them on the bed. I then rally the troops, partly for support, but mainly so they can enjoy watching Queen Momma Bear Edison lose it. Who doesn't love a good show?

Three FBI agents and Angus stand in strategic locations in the living room. I'm sitting across from Brian and his mother. I look from one to the other and tell them, "This is what we're going to do. We are leaking a report to the press that you were both killed by a car bomb. We're moving you to a motel in Belfair, which is about twenty minutes from here. Officer Ferguson and Agents Hopps and Olsen will continue to guard you."

As expected, the Queen starts in.

"Did you just say a *motel*? Don't be ridiculous. Frankly, I'd rather die than go stay in some dingy little motel that doesn't even have room service."

I try to count to ten, really, I do. I make it to four. "Mrs. Edison, let's be real here. You will die if you don't follow our instructions. You and your son were almost killed last night." I am quickly losing enthusiasm for this game of wills. "Mrs. Edison. Your son's face, and your own, are well known. We couldn't smuggle you into a four-star hotel even if we wanted to, and there isn't one within two hours of here."

"I'll hire a jet and take Brian somewhere safe." Her voice is almost pleading, and it sets my teeth on edge even more than her bitch voice.

I pull out my last ounce of patience and continue. "Mrs. Edison, you fail to understand the severity of this situation. There are people who are trying to steal your son's money. Besides your own husband being a suspect, we also believe terrorists are in the picture. They will stop at nothing, and waving a red flag by using your platinum or gold or whatever kind of charge card, is announcing to the world that you are alive. So please, go into the bedroom, change into the clothes I put out for you, and prepare to go slumming in a motel because that is what's going to happen."

I pause for breath and continue. "Brian, you can wear my dad's fishing hat, and I'm sure one of the FBI guys will loan you a pair of their cool, intimidating sunglasses. These gentlemen will get you settled into the motel. Agent Lindstrom and I will go back to Seattle and work with the task force. Do I make myself clear?"

Mrs. Edison stands and stares down at me. I swear the temperature in the room drops when her icy voice states, "When this is all over, I'm going to have a long conversation with the mayor and the chief of police. You, young lady, will regret the way you have treated me." She addresses her son. "Hurry up, Brian. We need to leave this hellhole and move on to the next one." She turns and walks out of the room, dragging her son behind her.

"That went well." I am so tired, I can barely muster a snicker. Fortunately, I have witnesses to our interaction, so it shouldn't go down with the brass the way Momma Edison hopes. Even if she tries, my union representative will be all over it.

We rehash the plan for a few more minutes, making sure everyone is on the same page. I hear the bedroom door open, and Mrs. Edison walks into the room. Her hair is no longer in the smooth sophisticated chignon--it is loose, hanging on her shoulders in soft waves--and she is virtually unrecognizable as the rich, snooty bitch from earlier. With the clothes and hair, she looks like a different person. She appears younger and softer around the edges. Then her eyes meet mine, and the hate glare zaps me from across the room. She looks at the others, and it is clear she is just spoiling for a fight.

No one says a word until Angus, bless his heart, says, "Mrs. Edison, I know this is very difficult for you. Please understand, we all have your safety as our main concern. Now, if you'll allow me, I'll take you out to the car, and we'll be on our way." He looks at her with such kindness, she is at a loss for words. Mrs. Edison shakes her head yes, and follows him out to the car without sparing us a backward glance. Hopps and Olsen stay at a respectful distance behind them. Neither of them wants to break the spell, in case Momma Bear Edison snaps out of her submissive moment.

I want to celebrate my victory, but in my current state, putting one foot in front of the other is all I can manage. Sean stands in front of me, looking just as exhausted. It is now eight a.m. "I talked to my lieutenant. We need to be in Seattle by eleven to meet with the task force. Normally, I always hate to leave the lake, but now, I can't wait to head back to Seattle and try and put this out of my mind. I should never have used my family's cabin as a safe house."

Sean's voice sounds tired. "Jayne, there was no way any of us could have predicted this. Don't beat yourself up. Let's get out of here. FBI will haul the burned car out. Is your dad going to be mad about the grass?"

I sigh. "No. My dad is going to be furious about the fact that I was almost blown up. He takes umbrage when people try to kill his daughter. The grass will be no big deal."

Sean chuckles. "I knew I liked your dad. I'll be happy to help him with the grass." Sean grabs my hand, and I see confusion on his face as I jerk it away.

"Sean. No. I can't. This won't work. I thought I was ready but I'm not. We need to just go back to a few days ago." A sob escapes. "I can't. I just can't." But it is ripping me apart to see the look on his face.

"Jayne. Stop. I know you lost Matthew, and tonight was a close call for both of us. I know you're afraid, but don't ruin our chance. We can face all of this together. If nothing else, tonight shows how tenuous life is, and we should live now, and not hold back."

I just stare at him. I feel the pressure of tears and force them back.

Sean watches me, his face a mixture of compassion and anger. Finally, he just sighs. "I can't do this now. You're not off the hook, but you have a reprieve until we finish the case."

All sorts of arguments go through my mind, but I hold my tongue and just nod. My heart feels like its fractured, and it is just too damn much to process right now.

***

Sean goes back to FBI asshole mode. He shuts down in front of me and reverts to the guy I started working with five days ago. It is kind of disconcerting, but I have to respect his professionalism. The drive to the ferry gives me enough time to fill Sean in on the revelations Barbara Edison made last night.

Sean is quiet until I finish. Then he takes a moment to process it all.

"So, Barbara Edison's father forced her to marry at sixteen, and even when Randall Edison embezzled money from his firm, he still kept him around?"

I, too, have similar thoughts. "I don't think divorce was an option. Despite it all, I honestly believe she loves her husband. No father is going to force his daughter to leave the man she loves unless that man is violent toward her. Randall Edison was a prize for her, and she was going to make sure she kept him. Even if she had to have her father's help. What kind of woman does that?"

Sean's forehead wrinkles as he says, "She sounds like a spoiled little princess that always got whatever she wanted. I agree. How could you live with a man who isn't with you by choice?'

After volleying questions back and forth, we realize we are stuck until DL and the Feds run a background check on Randall Edison. I fire off a text to DL and ask her to work with the Feds on getting information on both Randall Edison and, on a hunch, Melanie Page. I am anxious to see what will shake out of this dysfunctional family tree.

We drive onto the ferry, and Sean turns the motor off. We are the first car in line and have a view of Puget Sound. Instead of ogling the scenery, we both recline our seats and fall into a deep sleep for the hour ride.

The next thing I know, a ferry attendant knocks on our window. I am disoriented, and my hand immediately goes for my gun. I see the look of shock on the attendant's face, and my hand drops. I nudge Sean, but I grab his arm before he goes for his weapon. We've already traumatized the poor ferry worker enough.

Chapter 34

Sean pulls the car into the parking garage. While the nap on the ferry had helped, I feel like I've gone twenty rounds with Laila Ali. My headache is gone, and Sean's head seems to be fine. I make a mental note to keep checking his pupils.

We are silent as we make our way to DL's office. She looks up as we walk through her door.

"Whoa. I've seen roadkill with more life in it than you two." I hear the concern in her words. "You okay?"

I sit down in one of the two chairs by her desk; Sean takes the other one. I start the story. "I'm sure you've heard, we had quite the evening. Edison's three friends, McHendricks, Zeas, and Ronds were blown up last night. We believe Billy McHendricks was working with someone he met in the chat room who had him deliver a package to Barbara Edison."

Sean interjects, "That's the working theory for the bomb. We also have some suspicions about Randall Edison. DL, did you receive the pictures of the tracking device?"

DL nods her head and swings her chair around. "I got them and I also sent them to your guys. We've tracked the device to a manufacturer in Germany. We're working on getting a customer list."

"Great. What's the word on Randall Edison and Melanie Page?" My Spidey senses are going off. I have a gut feeling that I can't put to rest.

DL gives us a wide smile. "We got very lucky with Edison. I checked his passport, and he cleared customs in Seattle at three o'clock this morning. I handed off researching Melanie Page to the FBI guys. I was tied up finding Randall Edison and information on the tracking device. I figured we needed more hands on this."

I nod in agreement. "Do we know where he is now?"

DL answers, "We do. Randall Edison went home to what you refer to as 'mauve hell.' He didn't arrive until close to four in the morning, and as far as we know, he's still at the house. Maybe he's waiting for his next-of-kin notification."

I look at Sean, and we both shake our heads at the same time. "Interesting that he shows up now, after telling his wife he's too busy playing in a tennis tournament. Change of heart, or something more?"

"We're working on it. The FBI is rooting around." DL looks up as two men, both with thick glasses, approach. One is tall and ridiculously thin, so much so that his glasses keep slipping down his nose. The other, a polar opposite, is short and round. The one thing they share is a big smile as they walk through the office door.

"Sargent Davis, we hit the mother lode."

The tall one introduces himself as Paul Goodwin. I can tell the other tech, James Jackson, is painfully shy. He barely mumbles hello. Sean shakes hands with both of them, and then introduces me. Paul Goodwin looks so much like the character from Ichabod Crane. I have to stifle a giggle.

Paul Goodwin starts. "We ran Melanie Page. She left the University of Washington shortly after Randall Edison married Barbara Parker. Her grades went down, and she lost her scholarship. She tried to join the pro tennis circuit, but she had been picked up for two D.U.I's, and no one would give her a shot. For a while, her life went down the proverbial tubes."

Paul pauses for a drink from his water bottle. "She's been married three times. Her first husband put her in the hospital four times in two years. The second one only lasted eight months, but from the arrest reports, another round of domestic abuse. All of this happened in her twenties. After her second divorce, she ended up working as a tennis pro at fancy sports club in Redmond. At age thirty-four, she met and married Mohammed Hussain Azzanni. She has a twenty-year-old son by husband number three, who, by the way, she is still married to. Interesting, her husband is a Saudi. They got married in the U.S., and when their son was five, he moved his wife and son home to Saudi Arabia."

My brain is sluggish, but I perk up and ask, "Mohammed Azzanni?"

Goodwin nods. Before he can proceed, I turn to Sean and DL. "That's the uncle that sent his nephews to the UW. The plot thickens. So where is Melanie Page Azzanni now?"

Goodwin's thin features pinch together in a smug smile. "We came up empty on that one. No record of Melanie Page Azzanni leaving Saudi Arabia. However, I took the liberty of running Randall Edison's passport, and, of course, it confirms what Sargent Davis told you. I looked at the video of Edison clearing customs and did a facial recognition scan on the woman standing by him. You'll never guess who she is." Paul Goodwin pauses dramatically. "Wait for it...okay, anyone guessing Melanie Page Azzanni is half right. She cleared customs with an American Passport for Patricia Arnold."

We all absorb this new bit of information as we stand up to head to the task force meeting.

Paul Goodwin glances down at his stack of papers. He does a nerdy laugh and says, "But wait, there's more. I sound like one of those announcers, don't I?"

When we just stare at him, he clears his throat, and says, "One more little bomb, no pun intended. Melanie Page Azzanni's husband and son are Muslim. Well-known, off-the-scale, kill-all-the-infidels kind of Muslims. Not the nice, have some hummus and tea kind of Muslims, like my neighbors. We are working with other agencies to gather all the intel on her husband, Mohammed Azzanni. The only thing we have discovered so far is that he is on Homeland Security's watch list."

This is too neat of a package, but I've seen crazier things. And, generally speaking, crazy shit usually comes together fast once the pieces start to fit. "So Brian Edison creates a game that basically attacks and ridicules ISIS. Someone that we believe to be an ISIS supporter threatens him and also talks smack with Brian Edison's ex-best friend, Billy McHendricks. And, add to the mix, Randall Edison's old girlfriend arrives in Seattle with him this morning. Her husband sent his two nephews here to help kidnap Brian Edison. This is getting too nuts, but it feels like we're getting close to the answer."

***

We spend the next forty-five minutes alternately getting our butts chewed and then congratulated for managing to keep the royal pains in the ass safe. I have no doubt, based on the amount of flak we got, Mrs. Edison will make good on her threat to make my life miserable with the brass. It is already starting. FBI Chief Inspector Hennessey and Lieutenant Johns enjoy alternating the roles of both good cop and bad cop.

Hennessy takes a break from busting our chops and turns to the agent next to him. "Kimball, tell the group what you learned from the nephews' roommates."

A tall man with red hair stands up to address the group. He pulls out his phone and starts to read his notes. "It appears that the drivers of the van, Omar and Saad Azzanni, talked incessantly about 'Heads in a Basket.' They told their roommate it was a disgrace, and in their country, the creator of it would be killed."

Sean pipes in. "But why kidnap him? Why not kill him on sight?"

Kimball smiles. "That's where it gets a bit complicated. According to the roommate, the younger Azzanni's were both impressed and upset at how much Edison was worth. We think they went a little off from their uncle's orders. It looks like they were going to try and get his money before they killed him."

I sat there trying to put this Rubik's Cube of colorful facts together. "That may have been a goal of the drivers, and maybe their uncle, but obviously, based on the two bombs, it looks like money is no longer a factor."

The room goes silent for a moment, and then Lieutenant Johns says, "You're right, Moore. Seems like there might be more than one group of terrorist cells in our pristine town, and we're working on it. Now, tell us what you learned from Mrs. Edison."

I share the information that Mrs. Edison gave me on her marriage, and how she trapped Randall Edison. DL and her FBI counterparts go next and share their information on Melanie Page Azzanni.

A lightbulb goes off in my head, and I throw out a question for the group. "One thing we have overlooked. Randall Edison knows Billy McHendricks. Billy and Brian and the other two have been best friends since middle school. Plus, all of them were working on the game in Edison's basement. Billy had to have crossed paths with Randall Edison any number of times. Randall could have hatched a plan to kill his wife and Brian, and then settle up with McHendricks."

"Billy McHendricks was greedy, and it is no secret he hated

Barbara Edison. He blamed her for only getting a million dollars instead of more. It's not a stretch to think that Randall Edison could have planned this, and then got Billy to do his dirty work. Randall Edison was on a plane when the bomb blew, but he could have someone else involved in the plot. Someone with the brains to make a bomb and deliver it to Billy. And let's not forget the tracking device in Mrs. Edison's watch."

    The brass decides Sean and I need to go to the house for a next-of-kin notification and interview Randall Edison. Just based on the tracking device in Barbara's watch, Randall Edison is a suspect. We are to interview him and then haul him downtown if we don't get what we want.

    There are more questions than answers. And now, Melanie Page's nephews-in-law are involved in the kidnapping plot. Too many odd things going on with this case.

    I'm anxious to get answers and meet the man who has lasted over thirty-four years with Queen Edison. Even if he is at the center of the plot, he still deserves a medal. I spent less than twenty-four hours with the woman, and seriously wished I'd had a tranquilizer gun on me.

Chapter 35

Randall Edison stormed into his former prison. Barely inside the door, he saw Alias in his boxers, with a baseball bat raised and ready for action

"What the hell? Alias? What are you doing here?" Randall's last memory of his wife's cousin was a scruffy kid that Barbara had deemed "white trash."

"I thought you knew. Your wife hired me to manage the house and assist Brian." Alias' eyebrows rose in question.

"Of course, she did. That woman needs to control everyone and everything. So, essentially, you're the babysitter, and I'm sure, even though Brian pays the bill, you actually report to Barbara."

Alias' face turned red. "I'm helping to run the house for Brian. I'd hardly call myself a babysitter."

Randall looked at Alias and decided he really didn't care what the situation was. He gave him the look Barbara always used to get her way, authoritative as well as dismissive. "I don't give a damn what your 'job' is. Where is Barbara? Her phone has been off for hours, and I need to talk to her."

Alias sat down on the stairs. "Dude, they're not here. The cops have them under wraps 'cuz people are trying to kidnap Brian, and then they tried to blow us all up."

Randall sighed. Why did things never go his way? "Where are they now?"

"I don't know. The FBI took Brian away two days ago, and Barbara was supposed to arrive at Boeing field yesterday at nine in the morning. I know the FBI was meeting her plane. When she didn't show up here, I figured she went with them."

"Okay, so you don't know where your boss is. I'll worry about it later. For now, I need some sleep. Not all of us fly on chartered jets. What room is available?"

"The maid was here yesterday. I'm in the room by Brian's bedroom. You can take any room you want."

Randall almost felt sorry for Alias. He knew what it was like to be controlled by Barbara. "I'll take the guest bedroom." He picked up his bags, and as he walked past Alias, added, "I've been under her thumb for more than half my life. Leave while you can, Alias. The money's just not worth it."

***

Melanie Page was sitting in a hotel room three miles away. Randall had dropped her off and gone home to, as he said, "drop the bomb on Barbara." She laughed at his choice of words. She'd wanted to pay Barbara back for stealing Randall and ruining her life. Well, now it was the little rich bitch's turn to experience the anguish of losing someone you love.

Melanie hit the mini bar for another bottle of wine. She thought to herself, the cheaper the hotel, the smaller the bottles, but at least I won't have to put up with this for much longer. She refilled her glass and then rifled through her suitcase.

She pulled out the gun that Randall had purchased for her in Germany and smuggled into his checked luggage. The shiny nine-millimeter pistol winked up at her from its box. He'd bought it for her so she would feel safe whenever he had to leave her to go back to San Tropez and be with Barbara.

Melanie put the gun on the nightstand by her bed. Even with more than seven thousand miles between her and her husband, she was still fearful.

***

DL was monitoring the chat room as well as multi-tasking on her assignments from the task force meeting. She almost missed it when the Avenger posted, "I avenged the wrongs done to my mother by spilling the blood of those who hurt her. Now I will hurt the infidels who mock our beliefs."

"Crap." DL reached for her cell phone and called Jayne, simultaneously doing a search on her computer. Jayne answered on the first ring. DL skipped the preliminaries. "Where are you? Put me on speaker. I have information you both need to hear."

Jayne answered, "On our way to Edison's. We're about five minutes out. What's up?"

"The Avenger just posted in the chat room. He says he

avenged the wrongs done to his mother."

"Mother?" DL heard Jayne and Sean say together.

DL glanced at her screen; the information she sought popped up. "You're not going to believe this. Melanie Page Azzanni's son came to the United States three months ago. He has American citizenship, and the name on his passport is Adam Azzanni."

Sean reacted first. "Send us his passport picture."

DL pushed a button on her computer. "Done."

Jayne interjected. "The cadence of the Avenger's words always struck us as foreign. This kid left the states at age five, so he would probably have more of a European cadence. This also validates Sharon Gibbs' theory that the Avenger is stateside. Now, the million-dollar question. Where is he?"

DL repeated the chat room text. "Now I will hurt the infidels who mock our beliefs."

Sean added, "He would assume that the bomb delivered by Billy took out Mrs. Edison. We announced that Barbara and Brian Edison died in an explosion. What if he hasn't seen the news? His next logical step would be to go after Brian Edison at his home. Or, Billy McHendricks. There's no way he knows that McHendricks died in the explosion. He could consider him a loose end."

Jayne said, "Billy McHendricks would be on my hit list, but Adam has made this personal by avenging the wrongs done to his mother. It's obvious that he's obsessed with the Edisons. DL, the timing pattern Sharon Gibbs recognized in the chat room made her suspect the person worked during the day. Can you check if Adam Azzanni has a job?"

DL hit some keys. "He might have a social security card. Give me a few minutes."

***

Sean pulled the car over to the curb and picked up his phone to look at the picture. Adam Azzanni looked like any other twenty-year-old kid. Brown curly hair and blue eyes. His expression was serious, but a small grin played on his face. "I hope he doesn't blow himself up before we figure out how he managed to persuade that idiot Billy McHendricks to do his dirty work."

Jayne looked over at him. "More importantly, what does he

know about his mother and Randall Edison?" She stopped for a minute. "He wants to kill off Barbara Edison so she's out of the picture, and Mom can now live happily ever after with her first love? That's a pretty devoted son, and it stinks to high heaven. No way would a radical Muslim let a woman leave without punishment."

Sean pulled the car out and hit the lights and siren. "We've got to get to Randall Edison. He'll tell us where Adam's mom is."

Three minutes later, he shut off the siren but left the lights. The guard stepped out from the shack and waved him through.

They parked in front of the house, walked up to the front door, and rang the bell. Alias answered within seconds.

"Agent Lindstrom, Detective Moore, what can I do for you?"

Sean spoke. "We need to see Randall Edison immediately."

Alias smiled and said, "Of course. Let me go see if he's available."

"No Alias. We'll just follow you to him, and if I were you, I'd start moving." Jayne said as she entered the front door.

Alias turned and walked down the hallway to Brian Edison's office. Sean saw an older man look up, obviously startled at the intrusion.

Alias made introductions, and Sean thanked him and told him he was no longer needed. Alias left the room as Edison started in. "Are you the officers who have been working on Brian's case? Where are they? Where are Brian and Barbara?"

Sean and Jayne had already agreed their priority was getting to Melanie Page Azzanni. Jayne nodded at Sean to take the lead.

Sean paused for a moment. "Mr. Edison, we're not here about your wife and son. It is imperative we find your companion, Melanie Page Azzanni."

"What are you talking about? What do you need with Melanie?"

Sean noted he didn't deny knowing her whereabouts, and continued. "It is not something we can divulge at this time. We need her location. We know you two are together, and we know you flew into SeaTac on the same flight last night."

"She's at the Marriott over on Broadway. What's this all about?"

Sean played bad cop. "We are not at liberty to say. Mr. Edison, we need to talk to her. We'll have an officer pick her up and take her downtown."

In a flash of rage, Randall Edison swept his arm across the desk, and everything flew to the floor. "I'm leaving my wife. Do you hear me? I'm leaving her. And now you're after Melanie? Even from the grave, her father continues to screw up my life."

Jaws dropped and two sets of eyes stared at Edison.

"Well, not this time. I'm finished. I'm done. All the wasted years I stayed for the benefit of my son. Recently, I found out the precious grandson of Herman Parker is not my son. Where's my wife? Answer that, because I can't wait to tell her about the interviews I plan on doing. I'll expose all the dirty laundry they've tucked away throughout the years. They've lied to me, blackmailed me, framed me for supposedly embezzling from clients, and kept me on a puppet string for over thirty years. And I put up with it all because they threatened I would never see him again. And they KNEW he wasn't mine." Edison paused and shouted, "ENOUGH."

Chapter 36

Randall Edison does a total meltdown. I can't figure him out. He is a dichotomy--wimp one minute and a man of steel the next. I try to imagine the horror of living with Barbara Parker Edison for more than three decades. My gut says he's not the one trying to kill her. He doesn't have the balls, or he would have stood up to the old man years ago.

I decide to take over the bad-cop role. "Mr. Edison, we know that you and Melanie Page Azzanni are together. How did you reconnect?"

He sits down hard in the desk chair. "Just like everyone does at this age, Facebook."

I almost chuckle. "Are you telling us you haven't had contact with Melanie Page for over thirty years?"

His shoulders slump. "We had loved each other since we were seventeen. We both got a tennis scholarship to the UW. We had a stupid fight our junior year, and I got drunk at a frat party. Barbara flirted with me, and I was really pissed at Melanie. Barbara and I ended up having sex, and she got pregnant. I had no idea she was sixteen. When Barbara's father forced me to marry her or go to jail for statutory rape, he watched me like a hawk. Ironically, if he had looked after his sixteen-year-old daughter with half the intensity he focused on me, this never would have happened. I barely even remember the night that caused the shit storm that became my life.

"Once Barbara announced she was pregnant, I never saw Melanie again until four months ago." Randall Edison stopped for a moment. "Melanie's life spiraled out of control, too. She lost her scholarship, and years of bad choices followed. She had every right to hate me. I ruined her life, just like Barbara and her father ruined mine. It's a miracle she still loves me. I love her and I want happiness in my life. This"--he pauses and gestures at the house--"has never been a happy place."

I glance at Sean and raise my eyebrows in question. Sean

catches my drift and starts in.

"Mr. Edison. What is your relationship with Billy McHendricks?"

"Billy McHendricks? One of the three morons that hung out with Brian? I'm not sure what you mean. I didn't have a relationship with any of them. Hell, I barely had a relationship with my own son. What has this got to do with Barbara and Brian?"

I give Edison a hard look. "We can check your phone and computer. Are you sure you have not been in contact with McHendricks?"

"Why in the hell would I be in contact with him? What is going on here? You can check anything you want. I want to know where Barbara and Brian are."

Sean ignores his questions and asks, "Did you put a tracking device in your wife's watch?"

Edison's head shoots up. "Her watch? No. I don't know anything about that. I downloaded an app for her cell phone, so I could make sure she didn't show up unexpectedly at a tournament." His bark of scornful laughter fills the room. "As if the woman would ever show interest in anyone but herself. She was too busy trying to establish herself as American Royalty with San Tropez's rich and powerful."

Sean asks again, "How did a tracking device get into the watch you gave her?"

"I bought the watch a couple months ago in Germany. Herman Parker probably despised *his* wife as much as I do mine, but he always acknowledged any gift-giving occasion with a piece of jewelry." He stops and a sardonic grin plays on his lips. "I called Brian's Admin and asked her advice on a gift. Sharon suggested a watch and Melanie helped me pick it out. We both thought it was a perfect gift...a watch, indicating that her time was running out."

Whoa. Did he just admit to something? I try to keep the hardness out of my voice and remain neutral. "Her time was running out? Is that when you decided to kill her?"

His athletic body stiffens in his chair. "What are you talking about? Don't you understand symbolism or irony? She robbed me of thirty-four years of my time, and after Melanie told me the truth about

Brian, I finally had a reason to escape, as well as get what I was entitled to."

I am incredulous. Can this man be any more obtuse? Maybe he really is Brian's father. Slow on the uptake seems to be part of their DNA. I am going to choke to death trying to swallow my inner bitch. "Mr. Edison, how on earth did your lover learn that Brian is not your son?"

"Blood type. Melanie's sister Madeline transcribes medical records. Last year Brian was in a serious car wreck and needed a transfusion. Madeline noticed the blood type in his file. Barbara and I are both type O. Brian is type B. At the time, Barbara lied and told me she was a match for him but was too underweight to donate. Fortunately, the blood bank came through. Then, before Brian hit it big, Barbara went back to the same hospital for minor foot surgery. Madeline did her medical transcription and noticed the blood type. My medical records are at the same hospital, and she checked my blood type."

"Melanie's entire family hated Barbara. They all believed I had dumped Melanie to 'marry up.' Madeline couldn't wait to inform Melanie that Brian was not my son, and the joke was on me. Melanie got copies of the medical records to show me. It all started to make sense. I loved my son, but I'd never bonded with him. He was so different from me, and Herman Parker made sure that he was the dominant male influence in Brian's life. I was nothing more than a sperm donor, and now we know it wasn't even my sperm that made the little billionaire."

Sean and I automatically say, "Quarter of a billion."

"Regardless. He has enough money to keep his mother in the lap of luxury for the rest of her life. I'm sure as hell getting a piece of it as my severance package, for my years of servitude. What a fucking joke." His face twists in anger.

"That still doesn't explain the tracking device in your wife's watch." I'm not convinced he hadn't it put in.

"I have absolutely no idea. We selected the watch, and Melanie went back to pick it up for me. Then I left her in Germany and went to San Tropez for Barbara's birthday. I know nothing about a tracking device. Like I said, I use an app on my phone to keep track of Barbara." He reaches into his pocket, and I start to reach for my gun. He pulls out his phone and hits a few buttons. "See, here it is, here's the app."

Our conversation is interrupted by the front doorbell ringing repeatedly and frantic knocking. I look down the hall and see Alias rushing to the door. The minute he opens it, a tall brunette pushes her way through. "Where is he? Where is Randall?" Rushing past a startled Alias, a woman who I assume is Melanie Page Azzanni yells, "Randall."

Randall rushes out of the office and meets Melanie in the hallway near the music room. "Melanie, what are you doing here?" His voice is hoarse from all his revelations.

"Oh, darling. I came as soon as I heard. We're free. You're free. I'm sorry Brian is dead, but not that bitch."

I watch the color drain out of Randall's face. "Dead? What are you talking about?"

"It was on the news. They died in an explosion last night."

Randall wheels around and confronts us. "Why didn't you tell me? What the hell is going on?"

***

As if on cue, the front door is thrown open, and Barbara Edison storms down the hall. When her eyes light on Melanie, they widen in shock, and she screams, "What are you doing here? Get that whore out of my house. How dare you bring her here."

Melanie puts her hands on her hips and spits out the words. "He's leaving you. Your lies have finally caught up with you."

Barbara storms up to Melanie and stops a foot away. "So you think you're going to get him? He's stayed married to me all these years. Do you really think, if he was so anxious to be with you, he would have waited this long?" Her laugh is full of scorn. "He has a taste for the finer things in life, he likes money, and he'll never leave me for you because then he would be penniless."

Randall spoke, his tone cold as he realizes he has nothing to lose. "Why, Barbara? Why trap me into this loveless joke of a marriage? Being married to you was like being a fly that was constantly having its wings pulled off. You and your father did everything to save face at my expense. Who is Brian's real father?"

She spits out the words. "I wanted you, and you only had eyes for her. Parkers never lose. You're Brian's father."

Melanie got into Barbara's face. "So who did you really want? Him, or did you just want to ruin me because I had Randall and I also had Jack Corrison pestering me? You couldn't stand it that someone from a poor family, on the wrong side of the tracks, could have my choice of men. Randall and I loved each other. Why did you have to interfere?"

"I told you. I wanted him." Barbara's dismissive tone makes something in Melanie snap.

"And I told you, I loved him and still do. He's leaving you for me." Melanie's voice rises, and she turns to Randall.

Randall puts his arm around Melanie and glares at his wife. "Yes. I'm leaving. You'll be getting divorce papers as soon as I can get them drawn up. And unless you want all your family's dirty laundry on the front page of *The Seattle Times*, you won't fight it, and you'll pay to keep your secrets buried."

Barbara Edison raises her arm to strike Melanie.

Randall pushes Melanie behind him. "Don't even think about it, Barbara."

Before Barbara could snarl out a reply, the front door bursts open and a young man rushes in with an automatic weapon in his hands.

"Adam." Melanie takes a step away from Randall and stares at her son, her eyes wide with terror. "Why are you here? I thought you were with your father."

His eyes scan the room. "I am not Adam. I am Abdul. I have not been Adam since we left this land of infidels. As your son, I must avenge those that have hurt you." His eyes rake over Barbara and Randall Edison. "I thought his wife had died in the explosion last night. I did not realize I had failed."

***

Sean and I start to pull out our weapons. Abdul screams. "Drop your guns." To emphasize how serious he is, he points the gun at my head.

I can feel Sean's internal struggle. I try to signal him not to drop his gun, but then the barrel of Abdul's gun is rammed into the back of my head. I drop my weapon, and Sean does the same.

Abdul holds the gun on Sean and I and turns his attention back to Melanie. It is obvious he is not through berating his mother. "I told you, as your son, I tried to kill your enemy. As my father's son, I must kill you. You left us to take up with this spineless weakling. You have dishonored your family and your husband. Our laws, the laws of Islam, dictate you must die. I will kill you for our family's honor." He then spits on the floor, and screams, "Why did you do this?"

Melanie's eyes fill with tears. She ignores his question, and asks, "How did you find me?"

"Father talked to your friend that helped you escape. He was quite persuasive, and eventually, he found out about your new passport. We knew where you flew to when you left Saudi Arabia. Father sent me there to watch you."

"Adam. I love you. I'm your mother and I have always loved you. Please don't do this. We can have a life here. Do you remember how happy we were before?"

Abdul shakes his head, and for a brief moment, tears fill his eyes before he blinks them back. "No. My life is not here. I must do what I have been ordered to do. Father said you must die."

He raises his gun just as Barbara Edison picks the wrong time to put a dog in the fight. "Your mother is a useless slut. She threw herself at my husband and they both deserve to die."

The front door opens again and Sharon Gibbs rushes in with a gun in her hand.

***

I see Sharon, and for a moment, I fear for her safety. Then, I notice the gun and her cold hard eyes, minus the thick glasses. Her face is grim and her steps are determined.

She notices my look of astonishment and says, "Surprise Detective. Didn't I tell you I was working on a project that was going to make me a lot of money?" Her voice is not the same as the sweet little Admin I met last week. Her entire demeanor has changed.

The penny is starting to drop as the pieces come together in my head, but I fear it is too late.

"Sorry to barge in Detective Moore, but I'm cleaning up some loose ends before I leave the country with Brian's money". She gives Barbara Edison a hard stare. "I thought they both died in the explosion. I should never have trusted that moron Billy to do the job right."

I glance at Sean and catch his eye and quickly look down at the floor. I'm hoping that he goes for his gun, but then Barbara Edison picks this moment to butt in.

I watch her turn from Melanie to Sharon. "Who do you think you are? You...."

Sharon cuts her off and says, "I'm the genius who outwitted you and your son. Remember how you laughed at me and called me a little nothing? You said your son was a true genius destined for greatness and would never care about someone like me. Well, who's laughing now?" Sharon's face has a frightening expression as she points her gun and shoots Barbara Edison, point blank, three times. Each bullet finds its mark as Barbara's body jumps and contorts, like a puppet being controlled by a wicked puppet master. She jerks violently and falls to the floor.

Sharon Gibbs' smile is serene as she looks at me and says, "I've always hated that woman. Didn't I tell you that being short doesn't stop me from getting what I want? Like my mother always said, sometimes you just have to do a workaround." She turns back to Abdul. "Stick to the plan. Do it now."

Abdul slowly nods his head, his attention is back on his mother and Randall Edison. "You defiled my mother."

Melanie screams, "No Adam. Please. No." She pulls the gun out of her purse and points it at him, her hands shaking. "I'm begging you. Don't do this." She shoots and a chunk of plaster falls from the ceiling.

While Abdul is distracted, Sean and I drop down for our guns. Abdul turns towards us and fires. I feel the bullets slam into my stomach and I see a burst of red on Sean. Then another shot rings out. It hits Abdul with such force, he spins and gets a little air before his body slams onto the floor, landing close to Barbara.

I see Angus standing in the hallway holding his gun on Sharon Gibbs. I hear him yell, "Drop your weapon."

I want to scream out to Angus as Sharon points her gun at him. Before she can fire, Angus fires and Sharon falls by me. I can see the light going out of her eyes, replaced with a vacant stare.

I turn to Sean and try to reach out to him but nothing will move. The sounds of sirens fill the quiet that is engulfing me. What seems like only seconds later, the house is filled with paramedics and cops. I feel hands lift me onto a gurney. I try to call out for Sean, but everything fades to black.

Chapter 37

"Come on, Jer...we're going to be late."

Jayne's mom was standing on the front porch waiting for her husband when she saw a police car pull into the driveway. When a grim-faced officer got out and started walking toward her, she knew. Her knees buckled, and she grabbed the railing to stop her fall. She screamed, "Jerry." And saw the bleak look in the officer's eyes.

"Mrs. Johnson. I'm Officer Larry Pederson. I am so sorry to inform you that your daughter, Detective Jayne Moore, has been shot."

Jerry came to the door just as the officer said the word shot and started peppering him with questions. "How bad? Where is she? Where's our daughter?"

"Sir, I'm sorry. It's pretty bad. She's at Harborview. I'll drive you there. Officer Ferguson told me to tell you that he's with her." Officer Pederson turned and started walking back to the patrol car with Terra and Jerry at his heels.

Lights and siren got them to Harborview within minutes. Officer Pederson dropped them at the emergency entrance and then left to pick up Emily and Amy at the UW. Jerry had called his younger daughters on the way.

***

Jayne's parents rushed into emergency and were met by Angus. His eyes were rimmed in red, and he reached out and grabbed Jerry's arm. "Come with me, she's in surgery. I'll take you to the waiting area."

Angus set the pace as they race-walked through the hospital maze to the surgery waiting room. When they arrived, Jerry saw a wall of blue uniforms, and he knew it was bad. He barely registered a group of men in suits and knew Sean must have been shot, too. A tall man with wiry gray hair, wearing an SPD uniform, walked up to them.

"Mr. and Mrs. Johnson, I'm Lieutenant Johns. I'm so sorry. I know you have questions, and I'll tell you everything we know. Jayne is in surgery. She and Agent Lindstrom were shot by a suspect with ties to terrorism. The suspect was neutralized by Officer Ferguson. Jayne was hit twice in the gut. They wheeled her into surgery about half an hour ago. We were told to expect a long surgery."

Jerry was the first to speak. "By neutralized, do you mean killed? Because if you didn't kill the bastard, I will."

"Mr. Johnson, the suspect was killed at the scene."

"Good." Jerry's bravado failed when he looked at the stricken face of his wife. He held her close, murmuring into her ear. "She'll be okay. I know she will be. We have to have faith."

***

Terra sat in the crowded waiting room. She noticed a woman sitting by herself, twisting a tissue. She approached her and asked, "Are you Sean's mom?"

The woman nodded, and Terra reached out to hug her. "I'm Jayne's mom, Terra. My husband is Jerry. Please come sit with us. It looks like they're both going to be in surgery for a while."

"Thank you. I'm Joanna Lindstrom. My daughters are on their way, but I appreciate the company."

Terra's eyes welled up with tears, and she struggled to continue. "They are going to survive this."

Jerry grabbed his wife's hand and spoke to both women. "They will. I know they both will."

Joanna Lindstrom sat down next to Terra. "Sean called me yesterday. He said he only had a few minutes, but he wanted to tell me about his new temporary partner. He's very impressed with your daughter. He said she is intelligent, brave, compassionate, and has a wicked sense of humor. Then, almost as an after-thought said, she's beautiful, too. Actually, he added smoking hot. I would say my son is quite taken with your daughter. This is the first woman he's talked about in almost eight years."

Jerry nudged Terra. "Told you so. When I'm right, I'm right. We met Sean a few days ago, and I could tell he liked her."

Terra squeezed her husband's hand, and said, "We enjoyed meeting your son. Let's just pray that those two get a chance to see where it will go."

The soft chatter of the cops and FBI people in the room drifted past their ears as the three parents fell silent, lost in their own thoughts and prayers.

The quiet was interrupted when Amy and Emily rushed in sobbing and fell into their parents' arms.

***

Jerry saw Tom Kruze walk into the waiting area. Tom's eyes scanned the room until they finally lit on Jerry. He rushed over. "What's going on? All I know is Jayne and Sean were shot."

Jerry pulled him to the side of the room and filled him in on all the details, ending with, "It's been six hours. A nurse came out three hours ago and said the bullets have done more damage than they had originally suspected. I haven't heard anything about Sean."

"Jayne is one of the most stubborn people I know. She will pull through. She loves her family more than anything, and if I'm not mistaken, I think she's starting to have feelings for Sean." Tom looked around at the sea of blue uniforms. "Everyone in this room cares about her. She has a lot of people rooting for her. Now, what about you and Terra and the girls? Do you need anything?"

Jerry looked down, and replied, "A miracle. Can you get me a miracle?"

Tom gave him a man hug and walked over to talk to Lt. Johns.

***

Jerry was pacing the room like a caged tiger. It had been seven hours, and they hadn't had an update in four hours.

"I'm stepping out for a minute," Jerry whispered into his wife's ear.

She looked up at him with red eyes. "Do you want me to come with you?"

"No. I just need to do something." Jerry silently walked out of the waiting room area. He saw a nurse in the hallway and asked for directions to the chapel.

The small chapel was empty. Jerry looked around and took a seat. He bowed his head and alone, let the tears flow. Finally, he scrubbed the tears from his face and started talking out loud. "God, I haven't asked you for anything since my sister died and I needed your help to get Jayne. Now I need help again. Please save her. She's a good person and has had so much sorrow in her life. Please spare her and Sean. They both deserve a chance." As Jerry rose to go back to the waiting room, he heard a sob and turned to see Joanna Lindstrom sitting two rows behind him.

"Thank you for including my son in your prayer. I'm praying for Jayne, too." She managed a weak smile, and Jerry squeezed her shoulder as he walked out.

"They're going to be okay. I know it." Jerry's voice was shaky but firm.

***

When Jerry walked back into the surgery waiting room, he barely registered that there were some new cops in the waiting area. Tom was sitting by Terra and the girls. Madison had joined the group with a man he assumed was Sean's friend Michael.

Madison jumped up and hugged Jerry, wiping tears from her eyes. "I'm so sorry."

Jerry hugged the young woman who had made mud pies with his daughter when they were six. He felt her pain and tried to distract her. "Maddy, introduce me to Sean's friend."

Madison looked over at Michael who jumped up from his chair. She made the introductions, and the three of them returned to their chairs sitting quietly.

Jerry took his seat by his wife and asked, "Any word?"

Terra silently shook her head. She twisted a tissue in her hands and a sob came out. "I'm scared, Jer. It's been so long."

Jerry put his arm around his wife and pulled her in for a hug. He felt tears in his own eyes but knew his job was to be strong. He wrapped his other arm as far as he could around his youngest daughters. "She's going to be all right. I just know it and you all know…"

In unison, he heard, "Yeah, we know. When you're right, you're right."

He was relieved to hear a small giggle from all of his girls.

***

Finally, after eight hours, a weary doctor walked into the room wearing scrubs with his mask pushed to the top of his head. "Jayne Moore's family?"

Immediately Jerry, Terra, Amy, Emily, Tom, and Madison shot to their feet.

"We have a small room at the end of the hall. Let's go there to talk." The Doctor led the small procession to the end of the hall, opened the door, and ushered them in.

The room was painted a sunny yellow with two floral-patterned sofas and a small refrigerator in the corner. The cheeriness of the room was wasted on the worried family.

Leaning against the wall, the surgeon addressed the group. "I'm Doctor Hector Smith, and I was one of the three surgeons working on your daughter. She came through the surgery fine and is in ICU. After we've chatted, you can go in to see her, but no more than two at a time. You'll need to change into some fashionable hospital clothing. At this stage, we're very worried about infection."

Terra was the first to speak. "You said she's okay, right?"

Dr. Smith gave her a sympathetic look. "Let me share all the information about the surgery. Jayne had two bullets enter her abdomen, and they bounced around quite a bit. Several internal organs were hit, and at one point, we thought she was going to lose a kidney. Her bowel was hit and, unfortunately, spread fecal matter into her abdomen. We spent hours trying to get it all, but there's a good chance that infection will set in. We're being proactive with antibiotics, and we'll just have to wait and see."

Terra asked, "What about all the female stuff? Will she be okay in the future if she wants children?"

Dr. Smith smiled. "There were three doctors working on Jayne. One, Dr. Takihashi, is the best OB/GYN surgeon in the United States. He is very optimistic that whatever Jayne's future brings her, children if she desires, will be part of it."

Jerry let out the breath he had been holding. "Thank God."

"We removed a large section of her bowel, and her stomach is a little smaller where we had to patch it up. As I said, a lot of organs had damage, some just grazed, others more damaged. We just have to wait and see how the next few days go."

A phone buzzed, and Dr. Smith looked at his screen. "Okay, family, Jayne is in a room in the ICU. You can go in two at a time and spend five minutes, and that's it for today. Are there any other questions?"

Jerry held his hand out to the Doctor. "No. Just let me say, on behalf of me and my family, thank you, Dr. Smith, and all of the other people who helped Jayne."

Dr. Smith's face gave nothing away. "You're welcome. We're not out of the woods yet."

***

Jerry and Terra decided to each take in one of the girls instead of letting the two of them go in together. Dr. Smith had cautioned them that studies had proven an unconscious patient can sometimes hear, and to only say positive things.

"Jaynie, it's Dad and Emily. We love you. Everything went well with the surgery. We're here for you. Now it's Mom's and Amy's turn. We'll be right outside the door. I love you, baby girl."

Terra, Amy, Tom, and Madison all got their five minutes, and everyone, except for the stoic Tom, broke down in tears in the waiting room. Jayne--their beautiful, lively daughter, sister, and friend--looked like death.

Chapter 38

Melanie Page and Randall Edison sat in an interrogation room that smelled like sweat and stale onions. Four metal chairs and a table were the only things in the room. One wall had a large two-way mirror, and the gray walls had numerous stains whose origin Melanie didn't even want to think about.

Melanie stood up and rubbed the small of her back. "Barbara didn't deserve to die like that. I'm sorry."

Randall's head jerked up, and he met her eyes. "I know. I was just sitting here thinking about the last thirty-four years."

"Why did you stay? Brian is a grown man. You could have left."

Randall scrubbed his face with his hands. "I told you the truth when I said you're the only woman I've ever loved. I'd lost you, and there was really no point in leaving Barbara. I was miserable, but I was going to be miserable on my own, too. It was almost like Stockholm syndrome. After her father framed me for embezzlement, and then fired me, I didn't even bother to look for another job. All my needs were met, and I knew Barbara was never going to divorce me. I decided that her punishment was to support me. I'm not proud of those years. I was angry and bitter, and at one point, I thought about killing myself. I wasn't even acting like a man."

"But still you stayed." Melanie was watching his face.

"Yes. I stayed. It wasn't a marriage at all. I was just existing, no good to anyone. Then one day I read an article in the paper about inner city kids and tennis. I went to the Boys and Girls Club mentioned in the article and got involved. Those kids literally saved my life. I finally had a purpose, and even though I had to live like some sort of kept man, it gave me the time and opportunity to do something worthwhile." Randall stopped and grabbed Melanie's hand.

"Randall, we've both done things we're not proud of. But I know you, you're a good man." She gave his hand a squeeze.

"I'm hardly a saint. It gave me immense pleasure to know that

Barbara was miserable, too. She could have been the poster girl for 'Careful what you wish for.' Her father's punishment for her getting pregnant was that if we divorced, she would be cut off financially. It's kind of funny--wouldn't you think she would have done anything to make me happy? Yet she actually went out of her way to be a bitch. When Brian was little, there was no way I would have left him. Then I guess I just became complacent. I still wanted to be in Brian's life even though his grandfather did everything he could to keep him away from me."

"I felt the same about Adam. I kept hoping I could influence him and offset their brainwashing."

"I don't think he wanted to kill you. There was still a little piece of Adam left in him."

Melanie burst into tears and sobbed.

***

Director Hennessey, John Kimball, and three agents watched through the two-way mirror.

Kimball reviewed the known information one more time. "I feel sorry for those two." He noticed Hennessey checking his phone, and asked, "Any word on Lindstrom?"

Hennessey looked up. "It's not good. His heart stopped twice on the way to Harborview. They just took him into surgery. It's going to be a long one, and they didn't give good odds on the outcome."

Kimball scrunched up the papers in his hand. "Son of a bitch. I went through Quantico with Sean. He's a good man."

Director Hennessey nodded. "Get to it, Kimball. We've got a lot of shit to sort out."

"Yes. Sir." Kimball walked out of the observation room and into the interrogation room.

***

"I'm Special Agent John Kimball, Mrs. Azzanni and Mr. Edison. I'm sorry for your loss." Kimball looked into Melanie's puffy eyes and could see her anguish.

"I lost my son many, many years ago, Agent Kimball. I wish I had been strong enough to escape with him years before."

"How long had your son been radicalized?"

She sniffed and blew her nose. "Adam was five when my husband moved us to Saudi Arabia. And even at that young age, Mohammed's parents insisted that Adam enter into training to be a Wahhabi, a defender of Islam."

Kimball paused for a moment. "Let's start at the beginning. We know your husband came to the US on a student visa, and after he graduated, he went to work for Microsoft. How did you and Mr. Azzanni meet?"

"I was the tennis pro at a club that a lot of Microsoft people frequented. When I met him, we just clicked. He was living the American dream and called himself Mo, not Mohammed. He was charming, funny, and gentle. I went through a bad time after college, made a lot of bad choices." Melanie paused and took a sip of water from the bottle on the table. Fresh tears brimmed over in her eyes. "I was so stupid. I thought I knew him. I never expected my life to turn out like this."

"During the time you dated, did he express any extreme beliefs or ideology?"

Melanie shook her head. "No, he had cut ties with his family and was just a regular guy. He was sweet and attentive. We got married after six months of dating, and a year later, we were blessed with our son, Adam. The three of us were so happy."

Kimball noticed the pained expression on Edison's face but kept his focus on Melanie.

"Why did he leave a lucrative job at Microsoft and uproot you all if he had cut off ties with his family?"

Melanie wiped fresh tears. "I thought he had cut off ties with them, but it turns out they were the ones to disown him when he married me. After almost six years, Mo's parents reached out and ordered their son to come home. It was his duty to them and his country. I never understood how they had such a hold on him after no contact for so long, but he did as they demanded. He packed us all up, and we moved to Saudi Arabia."

Kimball watched Melanie's hands shake as she tried to regain her composure. "My life became a living hell. They forced me to become a Muslim and made me wear the black abaya whenever I left the house. I haven't driven a car in over fifteen years--women are forbidden to drive in Saudi Arabia. They watched my every move, and if they felt I failed to be an obedient wife, my mother-in-law or my husband would beat me. But that's not the worst thing they did. They ruined my beautiful son. When he was seven, he refused to answer to Adam. He informed me he was now Abdul, a soldier for Islam. My sweet and loving little boy became a programmed monster, just like his grandparents wanted. They needed to offer him up to the Wahhabi army."

"What is your husband's involvement with ISIS?"

"I don't know. Mohammed and Adam wouldn't speak of it in front of me. They would talk for hours behind closed doors. I do know that Adam started playing 'Heads in a Basket.' He and his father were incensed at what they perceived as disrespect to Islam."

"Did you ever hear them talk about retaliation for the game?"

"Not directly, but just before I left, I overheard Mohammed tell Adam he would get revenge for Allah."

"How did they connect you to Randall Edison?"

"When I met Mohammed, I was honest about my past. It shows how Americanized Mo had become when he accepted the fact that I had been married twice before. I told him about Randall and how my life changed after Barbara trapped him. By the time I met Mo, it had been almost fifteen years since I'd seen Randall. I thought I had put it all behind me."

Special Agent Kimball paused to phrase his next question. "If they watched you all the time and you were so isolated, how did you manage to reconnect with Randall Edison?"

"I had very few friends. Because I'm an American, many of the women ignored me. Some of the women wanted to know what life in America was like. The first time I answered and told them about my old life, I was severely beaten by both my husband and his mother. I never made that mistake again. I finally did make a real friend, Aamina. Our husbands were friends, and I was allowed to visit her unsupervised. I'm sure both men felt Aamina would report my every move. She is a wonderful friend. I'm so afraid of the problems I have caused her. Did you know Aamina means peaceful? She is one of the most peaceful Saudis I have ever met."

Kimball smiled at Melanie. "Go on. How did she help you?"

"Her husband had a computer. Aamina is very smart. She had studied abroad, and was proficient at using the computer and hiding our browsing history. I was so lonely and miserable, I just wanted to see what was going on in America. I would surf the news whenever I was visiting. When Aamina discovered Facebook, my life took a turn. Of course, neither of us could join Facebook, but when I found Randall, I sent him a message."

Edison took both her hands in his. "Best day of my life."

"How long did you message each other?"

Melanie looked at Edison and smiled. "About a month."

"Then what happened?"

Melanie and Randall spent the next twenty minutes describing the elaborate escape plan they'd put in place with Aamina's help. Kimball took notes and finally decided he had all the information that he was going to get. As he stood to wrap up the interview, Edison asked a question.

"Where is Brian? I need to be there to help him deal with Barbara's death."

Kimball sent a quick text and received a reply within seconds. "They're on their way back. ETA is one hour."

"Thank you." Edison turned to Melanie. "I need to see him and try to explain everything."

Kimball noted the defeat in Edison's voice. He paused and turned before he exited the door. "I wish you two the best. I think you've both had enough suffering."

Chapter 39

"Jaynie. Jaynie. Wake up, baby. Wake up." I can hear my dad's voice and a lot of sniffling noises.

My mom picks up my hand, and I try to give it a squeeze. "Jer, she squeezed my hand. It was faint, but I know she did."

My dad's voice chokes with emotion. "Come on, baby girl. If you want a vacation, do it somewhere other than a hospital. Wake up, Jayne."

My eyes flutter open, and I struggle to focus on faces. I can barely make out my sisters at the end of my bed. I can't see their tears, but I can feel them. Plus, Amy always hiccups when she cries.

Waking up to my entire family at my bedside gives me a scare. I look at my dad and croak out, "Sean. Did he make it?"

I watch the expression on my dad's face, as he struggles with how much to tell me.

"He's alive."

A sense of relief floods me, but it is short lived when my dad won't look me in the eyes. I want to beg him for more information, but I can't find the energy.

My mom leans over and pushes the button by my bed and then tells Emily to get a nurse.

A middle-aged woman with steel-gray hair comes into the room. She introduces herself as Nurse Watson and starts to fiddle with my IV and whatever else they have me hooked up to.

I grimace as a wave of intense pain slices through my abdomen. Nurse Watson reacts immediately and puts a small device in my hand that is connected to a machine hooked onto the IV pole.

"This is your pain medication. You can press the button as needed. It's calibrated for no more than two an hour." As the nurse speaks, she pushes the button, and the pain starts to subside. I can already tell this is a no-nonsense kind of woman.

"I'm so thirsty." I feel like I have crossed a desert and have eaten sand all along the way. My voice sounds like I've been chewing on glass.

"I'll go get some ice chips for you," Nurse Watson says. She turns to speak directly to my mom. "Just give her a little to start with."

She finishes fiddling with all my tubes and walks out of my room. Within a minute, she returns with a small glass of ice.

My mom spoons a teaspoon of ice into my mouth, and it feels like a little piece of heaven. At the thought of heaven, I have a flash of memory. When the bullets hit me, I never saw the white light, but I could feel Matthew near me. Matthew pushed me back toward life and toward Sean. I remember a warm glow and his determination for me to live.

My thoughts are interrupted when my dad hovers over me and tells my mom. "She said not to give her too much."

My eyes are back in focus, and I stare at the dark circles under his eyes. "I'm sorry. I know I must have scared you, Mom, and the girls. How long have I been asleep?" My voice is croaky and weak.

"Baby girl, I don't even know where to start. A bomb at the cabin, you being shot, and most importantly, my charred grass."

Whew. A joke. I smile, and he relaxes a little.

"Tell me about Sean." My eyes brim with tears as I say his name. I can see my dad struggling with what to tell me. I know he will tell me the truth. He always has.

"You've been out for three days. The two bullets ripped up your insides pretty good. It was a very intense surgery. You were under the knife for eight hours. I've never seen so much blue in the waiting room in my life. Cops kept coming in at the end of their shifts to give blood and just hang out. They said they didn't want one of their fellow officers to be alone. Your partner didn't leave for two days. Tom convinced me to tell the nurses he was your brother, so he could come in and see for himself that you were going to be okay. Madison has been in and out the last three days, too."

I smile. Even with all the shit-talking cops do to one another, when one of us is hit, we band together. Tom Kruze is the best partner I've ever had. I feel bad that everyone has been so worried. "Tell him and Lily I'm okay. Send my love to the girls."

My dad smiles, and I see my mom grab her phone and fire off a text. She looks sheepish. "Sorry, honey, but they made us promise to let them know the minute you woke up. I'll send Madison a text, too."

"It's okay. I'd do the same for Tom's family if this were reversed. Tell Madison I said hi." It hurts to talk, but there is so much I want to know.

I look back to my dad. He knows exactly what I am thinking. "What the hell happened?"

"I don't know all the details, Angus will have to fill you from little I've been told, Sharon Gibbs had created an online persona called the Avenger and recruited Abdul and some guy named Billy to do her bidding. Sharon's goal was to get Edison's money. From what I've heard from Angus, she had transferred millions to an offshore account. Our information is pretty sketchy, I know your lieutenant and DL will have more information."

I think for a moment and say, "I've got to say, I never in a million years suspected Sharon Gibbs. She played her part well, I was convinced she was in love with Brian Edison."

I watch as he takes a sip out of a plastic water bottle. I can tell he wants to change the subject. "We've met Sean's family. We were all in the waiting room while you two were getting patched up. Next time, skip the bullet holes, and go for matching tattoos instead."

"Dad. Another joke? We'll have to put you on stage." My mom still has my hand in a death grip. "I want to see Sean. You still haven't told me how he's doing."

Mom's hand tightens, and I can no longer feel my fingers. "Mom. I want to see Sean."

Nurse Watson comes in again, checking fluids, and typing information into my chart. I look over and see the frown on her face. "Detective Moore. You took two bullets to the stomach. One bullet nicked your bowel and fecal matter spilled into your stomach, which resulted in peritonitis. For the last three days, you've been in a coma, your temperature spiked to one hundred and four degrees, and to be honest, we didn't know if you were going to make it. So, no. You are not getting out of this bed until I tell you it is okay."

I ignore her and start to swing my feet over the edge of the bed. I feel woozy and ask, "Can someone get me a wheelchair? I'm going to see Sean."

Nurse Watson gets into my face. "Did you listen to what I just said?"

I grit my teeth. "If you don't take me to see Sean, I will rip the IV out of my arm and crawl to his room. I need to see him. Even if it's only for a minute." The tears streaming down my face derail the conviction in my voice. I add a weak, "Please."

An hour later, Nurse Watson wheels me down the hall. My parents pull the IV rack with all the bags hanging off it, making us look like a grim parade. As much as I need to see Sean, I am fearful. When we reach the door to his room, an involuntary gasp escapes my lips when I see him. He is so white, he looks like the belly of a dead fish. Oh God, why did that image have to be in my head? "Please move me to the side of his bed."

"I'm giving you ten minutes and then back to bed, Detective." Nurse Watson's voice is firm, and I already feel exhausted as I nod my head yes. She leaves the room, and I continue to stare at Sean.

Unshed tears fill my eyes as I notice the bandage on his head and the tubes coming out of his chest. I stroke the stubble on his cheek and watch his chest until I can see it gently rise and fall. I hold his hand and will him to wake up. I can't stop the tears, and they fall, unchecked, down my face. "Sean. I was so wrong. Wake up."

I feel someone enter the room. I turn my head and see an attractive woman with Sean's hazel eyes. The dark circles around her eyes rival my parent's matching set. I start to let go of Sean's hand.

"No. Please don't let go," she says quietly. "You must be Jayne. I've heard a lot about you."

I wonder when all this information was shared. We'd been together almost 24/7 for six days. "Mrs. Lindstrom. It's nice to meet you." It hurts to talk and my voice is still croaky.

"Oh honey, call me Joanna. I've spent so much time with your parents, I feel like I've known you forever. And I, of course, gave them an earful about my son here."

My parents hadn't shared any information on Sean. I look at Joanna Lindstrom and can tell she is making an effort to be cheery. "What do the doctors say?"

Her face collapses, and her raw pain terrifies me. I turn from Sean and grab his mother's hand. "Please...I need to know."

She puts a lot of effort into smiling, but it comes out more like a grimace. "He took four bullets. Three to the chest and one in the head."

I can't stop the sob that escapes.

"The one to his head isn't too bad. He now has a new part in his hair, but as far as they can tell, it didn't do any damage. The other three bullets ricocheted around his chest, barely missing his heart. With all the damage, his heart stopped twice on the way to the hospital. He was in surgery for eighteen hours. The doctors put him in a coma to ease the stress on his heart." She squeezes my hand. "He's young and he's strong. My boy will pull through because dying is not an option. There are too many good things ahead for him."

I listen to the force of her voice, and pray that on some level, Sean can hear his mother. I know Nurse Watson will soon be in to get me, but I can't stand the thought of leaving him.

"They say that even though you're in a coma, you hear things. Sean knows we are here for him. I think what he needs now is you." Joanna gives me an encouraging smile.

I smile at her and turn my attention back to Sean. I study his face, something I hadn't had the luxury of doing before. I stare with envy at his long dark eyelashes and wait for his eyes to open. I'm a mess. They say depression sets in when you are shot and stare your own mortality in the face. I have no thoughts about my own mortality, I just want Sean to fight for his.

True to her word, Nurse Watson comes in exactly ten minutes later to wheel me back to my room. My parents follow behind her, and I see them both give Joanna quick hugs, and I hear their words of encouragement.

When I get back in bed, I can't stop the sobs from escaping. It is the same feeling of hopelessness I felt when Matthew died. I look up at my parents and a stab of envy hits, almost as painful as the bullets. They have shared a good life together, and I want the same thing with Sean. My anger over the situation envelopes me, and I want to scream.

My dad, always in tune to my moods, takes my hand.

"Jayne. Stop it. He is not going to die. That boy is going to live, and you two are going to get your chance for happily ever after. Think about it, Jaynie. When have I ever been wrong? You know what I always say: when I'm right, I'm right. And I'm right about this."

My mom stands behind my dad and nods. "You have to believe it."

Nurse Watson chooses now to pop in with a tray and a little cup of pills. "Detective Moore, you need to rest. You're going to drink some broth, and as a special treat, I have orange Jell-O. Then it's back to sleep for you."

"No pills. I am not going to sleep. I'll eat and then I'll go back and sit in Sean's room." My voice is croaky but firm.

The nurse tries to intimidate me with a stare-down, but I win, or at least I think I have.

"We'll compromise. You will eat, you will take your pills, and then I will give you ten minutes at his bedside." Her voice is just as firm, and truly, I am too wiped out to take her on. I just nod my head.

Fifteen minutes later she takes me back to Sean's room. His mom is asleep in a chair, and Nurse Watson manages to wheel me to the side of Sean's bed without waking her. I hold his hand and watch his chest move up and down. The rhythmic movement is comforting.

I fall asleep at Sean's bedside and wake up when Nurse Watson is taking me back to my room. She helps me back into my bed, and I mumble to her, "No sleeping pills tomorrow. That wasn't a fair fight."

I hear her chuckle as she whispers, "Detective if I fought fair, I'd never win."

***

On the fifth day, they try to wake Sean up from the medically induced coma. Nothing. We take turns talking to him and encouraging him to wake up. Still nothing. His mom, sisters, and I stay by his bedside. Nurse Watson has long given up trying to keep me in my room and comes in with a tray of broth and more Jell-O. Apparently, I am on the bullet diet. Get shot in the gut, and this is what you get to live on for a few weeks. I'd kill for a slab of beef and some chocolate. Good thing they don't allow guns in hospitals.

Joanna looks over at me and smiles. We're sitting next to

Sean's bed, each of us holding one of his hands, and have been chatting about him as a little boy. I love watching how animated Joanna gets as she tells her stories. Then she looks at me with a quizzical look on her face. "You never told me how you met Sean."

I smile wide. It is, after all, a pretty good story. I begin to tell her about her son posing as a used-car salesman. I delete the part with all his sleazy lines. We are giggling quietly. I get teary-eyed at the memory of the vivacious man, so full of life, the man who I'm beginning to envision as a part of my life.

"Librarian." His voice is faint and raspy.

Joanna and I look at each other. His mother speaks first. "Sean. Wake up."

His eyes remain closed, and he mumbles, "No. Sleeping now."

I gently shake Sean's hand and try again. "Sean. Wake up."

Nothing but a soft snore. But it is a different sound than what I'd been hearing for the last five days. It is the same sound he made when he held me after my nightmare. For the first time since I woke up in the hospital and saw Sean looking like a dead fish, I feel hope.

***

Nurse Watson lets me go to his room if I have followed her orders about napping and taking my pills. She drives a hard bargain, but I'll do whatever it takes to see Sean. It usually works out that I nap for two hours, and visit Sean for half an hour. The short trek down the hall to his room exhausts me, and then I'm ready for another two-hour nap. Remind me not to get shot again…it really zaps my strength.

Usually, Nurse Watson digs in her heels at night. She likes to make sure I'm tucked in and knocked out for the evening before she goes off-shift. I'm surprised she hasn't come in to try and drag me back to my room. It's late, the room is dark and Joanna is asleep in her chair.

For once, my eyes are dry. I feel like I have cried buckets in the past few days. I can't believe I was almost too afraid to keep him in my life. I reach out for his hand and whisper. "I need you, Sean. Please come back. You owe me a first date." The eyes I thought were dry squeeze out a few more tears. I seem to have an unlimited supply of waterworks.

I reach for a tissue, dab at my tears, and turn back to Sean. The door is open to the hallway and a sliver of light falls across the bed. I gasp when I see Sean staring at me. I'm afraid to make a sound and break the spell.

He smiles and whispers, "Boomer."

That does it. The dam bursts, but it is happy tears. He squeezes my hand.

"Come here."

I lean over him, and he says, "Closer."

I get as close as I can, and he gives me a soft kiss on the lips. The effort exhausts him, and he falls back to sleep. I turn to wake Joanna and see the tears freely flowing down her cheeks.

"Oh Jayne, he's going to be okay." She gets up and comes over to my side of the bed and wraps me up in a huge hug. I now know where Sean gets his amazing hugging skills. I hug her back, and we both cry and laugh, resulting in a few unladylike snorts from me.

***

Nurse Watson comes in as Joanna and I are having our cry-laugh-snort festival. The smile on her face belies her stern tone. "It's time for bed, Detective."

Joanna says, "You go, honey. I promise if he wakes up again, I'll send for you. You need your rest, too."

"Thank you." She gives me a quizzical look, and I continue. "Thank you for raising such a strong stubborn son."

Her smile is the last thing I see as Nurse Watson wheels me back to my room.

Chapter 40

I'm holding court in my hospital room. Lieutenant Johns, DL, and Angus are sitting around my bed, and I'm peppering them with questions. There are still so many gaps in the information I have about everything that went down.

"How did Abdul Azzanni get into the country? I thought he was on a no-fly list?"

DL answers. "His father is on a no-fly list. Abdul has a US passport with the name Adam Azzanni. He wasn't flagged."

"Okay. How did he connect with Sharon Gibbs and Billy McHendricks?"

Lieutenant Johns jumps in, "Gibbs befriended Abdul in a chat room and presented herself as thirty year old radicalized *male* American Muslim who wanted to avenge Allah and kill Edison for creating "Heads in a Basket." It looks like, by the emails we recovered, he fell for it. She really egged him on talking about how the game laughed at ISIS and how rich it had made Brian Edison. Once she had him hooked in, she started working on her plan to get rid of Brian and his parents."

DL adds, "She also reeled in Billy McHendricks, which is why we couldn't get him to take our bait. We've combed through McHendricks' laptop. Talk about disgusting. He had a lot of violent video games and an unbelievable amount of porn on his computer. We went through his trash bin and found a plethora of deleted emails between him and an email address we've traced back to Gibbs."

I'm trying to process everything and interject. "The true surprise was that Sharon Gibbs was actually the wizard behind the curtain. Interesting how she was giving us screen prints of the chats. It obviously took attention away from her. She wasn't even close to being on my radar. What an actress."

DL shrugs her shoulders. "You're not the only one that was fooled. We discovered she was seeing a psychiatrist and he diagnosed her as a total sociopath. Sharon Gibbs was extremely manipulative, had no remorse, and had a grandiose sense of self. True traits of a sociopath. She managed to get both Billy and Abdul to do her bidding. When Sharon suggested that Edison buy a watch for his wife, she had Abdul put the tracking device in"

Lt. Johns looks at his notes and adds, "When the kidnapping attempt of Edison failed, we think Abdul connected with Sharon in the chat room while he was following his mother in Germany. Since the Avenger was broadcasting that Edison should be killed, Abdul, knowing his father's wish, joined in the plot. With his American passport, he managed to make his way here. He was a very busy boy. We found evidence Abdul was also working with a terrorist cell. Looks like some really bad guys are going down. His computer is in the possession of the FBI. We also have his smart phone, and the FBI labs are working on getting the information off of it. We have evidence he made the bomb that was strapped to Turner but, unfortunately, the FBI forensics team couldn't recover any evidence from the bomb at your cabin."

A thought hits me. "So Sharon had Abdul build the bomb and take it to McHendricks?"

Lt. Johns answers. "That's what we think happened. You mentioned McHendricks kept saying Darth Vader sent him. We found a voice machine hidden at Gibbs' apartment, it was set on the Darth Vader voice. Also, when we found the burner phone under McHendricks bed and hit redial, Gibbs' phone lit up like a winning slot machine."

"I feel sad for Melanie, and can only imagine the terror she felt toward the husband she once trusted, and the son she loved." I look at DL. "It's tragic. But the good part is, Abdul was unable to complete any other terrorist missions."

LT graces me with a rare smile. "Good job, Jayne. Once you requested the info on Melanie Page, the dots started to connect. We traced her to Saudi Arabia and her husband Mohammed's family.

My brain is still a little scrambled trying to put all the pieces together, but one thought surfaces. "I'm glad Randall Edison and Melanie Page finally get their chance."

He gives me a blank look and Diane intercedes. "Yeah. Me too. They both have been trapped in bad situations for far too long.

Special Agent Kimball interviewed them, and he thought their story was pretty sad. Looks like those two are going to disappear together. They're both looking over their shoulder waiting for Mohammed Azzanni to reappear to get revenge for the death of his son."

Lieutenant Johns stands up abruptly. "Boomer. I've got to get back. You get better. I've been told you won't be able to work for at least eight weeks, if not more. Let me know when you're cleared to come back." He pauses and, in a rare moment of affection, gives my hand a squeeze. "You did good, Detective."

Angus rises at the same time, but I can tell he has more to say. "Hey DL. Can you give us a moment?"

"No problem. I've got to get back anyway. I'll check in with you tomorrow." As she and Lt. Johns walk out of the room, Angus comes up to the side of my bed.

"Jayne. This is all my fault." His voice sounds so dejected, it tears right into my heart. I start to protest, and he shuts me down with a stern look and continues. "I was so damn rummy, running on little-to-no sleep. I didn't even see Sean's car parked in front of the house. Plus, Mrs. Edison insisted I drive to the back of the house. She told me she would walk through the front door, and I could go in through the kitchen. God. I'm such an idiot. I was getting her luggage when the shots started. If she hadn't been such a snooty bitch, I might have come in the front door with her. Thankfully, walking in through the back gave me a clear shot at Azzanni and Gibbs. I just wish I had gotten there sooner."

I grab his hand. "Angus, you're one of the finest cops I know. Almost everything I have learned is from you. Please, don't beat yourself up. This wasn't your fault. They got the drop on both Sean and I. We were all running on empty. If you hadn't been there, Sean and I would both be dead."

He leans over and kisses my forehead. "You're like a daughter to me, Jayne. Plus you are one hell of a cop. You do us all proud."

I can't let him go without a confession of my own. "You were right about me pushing Sean away. I was scared. I'm still scared, but I'm tired of only being half alive. I need him."

"Jayne, I knew you'd figure it out. You're a brilliant cop and one hell of a smart woman. You just needed a wake-up call."

He smiles and turns to leave before I can reply. I think I saw some tears in his eyes, and my own start to tear up. There really is no such thing as a hard-as-nails cop.

***

I walk down the hall and enter Sean's room. He is still making his way back to the land of the living. His sisters have finally convinced their mother she needs to go home for a few hours. Poor Joanna has been at her son's side since he got out of surgery. We are now on day ten, and she needs a break.

I stand in the doorway, and Julie, Sean's oldest sister, gives me a big smile. In such a short time, I have become so attached to these new people in my life.

"Any change?"

Julie shakes her head. "No. The nurse just said she thinks he's getting close."

I lean over and kiss him lightly on the cheek. "Sean. I had some visitors today. There's so much to tell you."

His response is a soft snore.

"I'm going to go down to the cafeteria," Julie says, as she stands up and stretches. "Do you want anything?"

"Chocolate. And a huge steak." The thought of it brings a big smile to my face.

"I heard that. No chocolate. No steak." Nurse Watson has entered the room as silently as rolling fog. It's a nurse ninja skill she has down pat.

Julie laughs, and says as she leaves the room, "I'll be back in a few minutes. If he wakes up, tell him I love him and to get his lazy ass out of bed."

"Will do." I watch as Nurse Watson fiddles with his IV and all the other miscellaneous wires he is hooked up to.

She gives me a worried look and sits down in Julie's vacated chair. "You know Detective, there is not a magic formula for when people recover from a gunshot wound. It takes time for the body to heal from the inside. Agent Lindstrom is healing. His vitals are good, and in my opinion, he'll wake up when he's ready."

I nod my head, and mumble, "You're right."

Then she brings out the big guns. "You need to use this time to heal yourself. Doctor Smith told me this morning, you'll be out of here in a week to ten days. Now the real work begins. I've had a lot of police officers come through my ward, and the physical injury is only part of it. Anger or fear are common feelings after being shot. You're channeling all of your energy into sitting by this man's bedside. You need to think of yourself first, or you'll be no good to him when he wakes up."

My partner, Tom, picks that moment to walk into the room. Nurse Watson stands up to shoo him out, but he beats her to the punch. "I'm here to drag Jayne back to her room. Oh, and I agree with everything you just told her. Come on, Jayne, time for a partner-to-partner facts-of-life chat."

I know from experience that Tom is like a dog with a bone. If he has something to say, I might as well get it now, because he will never give up. I see Nurse Watson give him a smile and a thumbs-up. Jeez, now those two are in cahoots? I get up and start my slow shuffle back to my room. I'm dragging my feet, feeling like a kid, on my way to the principal's office.

Tom loops his arm through mine and gives me a little squeeze as he walks beside me. "Good to see you up and around, Boomer. I have to admit, I was getting a little nervous when it took you three days to wake up from surgery."

"How do you think I feel when it's been ten days for Sean? This is killing me." My voice is small, and I fight another rash of tears. All these waterworks must be a side effect from the shooting. Maybe Nurse Watson is right.

"I'm telling you, Sean is as strong as a horse. He took three to the chest, and he's here. He's going to make it. What about you? You took two bullets to the gut. How are you doing?"

I mumble, "Okay."

We arrive at my room, and Tom takes me over to my bed. He helps me back into it like he's been doing it all his life. He pulls a chair up to the side of the bed and takes my hand into his big mitts. "I'm worried about you. I talked to your dad, and he says you refuse to talk about the shooting. And Angus is beating himself up about it."

"There's nothing to talk about. Angus and I already had a

conversation. It's not his fault. It could have been worse--Azzanni could have killed Sean."

"Or you. Why are you being all tough-girl about this? Your life matters, too. You need to recognize the fact that you were almost killed. You have to deal with the emotions, or you're no good to yourself or your partner, and I have a vested interest in this." Tom's voice is firm.

"Are you worried about me being your partner?" I feel like I've been slapped.

"Never." He pauses, and then in a gentler voice, says, "I got shot just after Allison was born. I remember looking down at the blood and thinking I'd never get to see my baby grow up. I was lucky, it was a through-and-through shot and didn't hit any organs, but it still hurt like hell, and for a moment, I thought I was dying. Before Lily and the kids, I never thought about dying on the job. But being shot affected my performance for the first few months I was back to work. I finally had to go talk to a shrink. You've been through a lot, and while Sean is down for the count, you need to deal with your own shit."

I can't look at him. "I know."

He laughs. "See. Was that so hard to admit? Jayne, you're the best partner I've ever had. You are my family. I don't want you to go through what I went through before I reached out for help. Lily, me, and the kids, all love you. That big FBI guy loves you, too. Promise me you'll see the department shrink and talk about anything that is bothering you." He pauses to make sure I'm looking at him. "Promise?"

I nod and give his hand a squeeze. "I have always felt invincible. I know that's stupid and also wrong, but this may have punched a hole in my confidence."

"Yeah. Been there, done that. You'll get past it. I promise." Tom stands up, then leans down and gives me a sweet brotherly kiss on the forehead. "Don't ever scare me like that again. And when Lindstrom wakes up, I'm going to kick his ass. You never got shot on my watch."

I am about to reply when Nurse Watson rushes in. "Agent Lindstrom is wide awake and asking for you."

"Tom, help me get out of this bed." If happiness is a drug, then

I am higher than a kite.

With Tom by my side, we shuffle as fast as I can to Sean's room. Tom delivers me to the door, tells me I don't need him hanging around right now, and leaves for the cop shop.

I stop at the door to catch my breath and look at Sean. He is still pale, but the dead fish look is gone.

He looks up, catches my eye, and smiles. It is the most beautiful thing I've ever seen. The tears come, and I don't care who sees. Happy tears are the best kind. I make my way to the side of his bed and look at him. His eyes are alert, and I can see him looking at me, really looking at me. I am mentally rejoicing until I see the concern on his face.

"Jayne. You look tired. Nurse Watson says she had to fight with you every day to get you to rest." His voice is raspy from lack of use.

I shoot the tattletale nurse a look. She smiles back at me and counters with a smug, 'I told you so' look of her own.

"I'm fine."

Sean's eyebrows rise up a bit.

What's with everyone and their penetrating looks? "Honest." I change the subject. "I met your mom. She's great."

"I knew you'd like her. Lean over here for a minute." He pulls at my hand.

I lean in and hear the sweetest words. "I don't know where I've been, but I know I missed you. Are you over the crazy notion that you can live without me?"

Tears well up in my eyes. Damn waterworks. "I've had a lot of time to think while you were having your nice long nap. I'm terrified of being in a relationship but I'm more terrified of being without you."

"Good. Maybe being asleep while you figured that out was for the best. Now come closer." He kisses me, and I hear his sister laugh as she walks into the room,

"Now I know you're going to be okay. Only my brother would wake up from a coma and be making out within minutes." Her giggle makes us both laugh.

"Hey, this is my girl. And if you think that was making out, you've been dateless too long." Even with the raspiness, Sean's teasing voice is music to my ears.

"What was it you said about a first date?" Sean asks.

I grin from ear to ear. He'd heard me. "You owe me one."

"Yes, I do." Seeing his smile lifts my heart.

My parents pick that moment to stick their heads into the room. My mom is the first one to speak. "Honey, I don't want you to tire yourself out." I can hear the worry in her voice.

My dad walks up to the side of the bed and smiles at Sean. "You owe me some grass, and I intend to collect. Oh, and while we're at it, we'll do some fishing."

Sean manages to croak out, "Looking forward to it. Sir."

Dad smiles and says, "Jayne. You need your rest."

I reluctantly let go of Sean's hand. "I'll see you later."

I lean down to kiss him. I hear him croak in my ear, "Come back soon."

I laugh and whisper. "Just try and keep me away."

Chapter 41

By the end of the week, the doctors allow Sean to have more visitors. We are both told we will be released in another five or six days. At least we are finally up and moving. Sean can now walk to the end of the hall unaided but needs the wheelchair to come back. We spend our days together, and most of our visitors are people we both know, so they get a two-for- the-price-of-one visit.

When Angus comes for another visit, he fills Sean in on what he'd told me earlier, complete with another heartfelt apology. Sean, like me, reassures him it wasn't his fault.

Angus tells us about Barbara Edison's escape from, as she put it, "red neck hell." She had made good on her threat to call the mayor. She gave him an earful and then told Angus to pick up the phone. The mayor had caved under her tirade, and he ordered Angus to take her back home, but to leave Brian with the FBI. A wise move that saved Brian's life.

"That was one strong-willed woman." Angus gives a rueful smile. "She reamed me a new one all the way back to the house. I hope wherever she is, she has finally found some peace."

I've never been known for having a streak of forgiveness, and tell him, "From everything we learned, she's probably in hell, shoveling coal with her father."

Angus slaps his knee. "Speaking of hell. I forgot to update you on Turner."

Sean and I both perk up.

Angus has a wide smile on his face and can't contain his glee. "Now, mind you, I always look out for my fellow cops, but Turner is a rotten apple, and he was bringing the department down. DL should probably be the one to give you the news."

"Oh hell no. Angus, you started this, you have to finish." I grab his hand and squeeze it.

He pauses dramatically, savoring the moment. Angus loves telling a good story. "DL traced that picture of you back to his phone.

It was pretty easy. If we hadn't had all this other drama going on, she would have nailed him within minutes. But, that's not what brought him down. He got caught taking some drugs out of the evidence room. He's got a girlfriend on the side, who convinced him they could make a fortune, and he could leave his wife. He figured he could pull it off and then leave the department to take that lucrative job with Edison."

I am incredulous. "Seriously? He was dumb enough to try and steal drugs out of the evidence room?"

Angus smiles, but then his expression turns serious. "A cop like Turner gets away with enough stuff, he starts to feel invincible. We're lucky he was caught before he got someone killed. He's in jail right now, awaiting trial on the drug charges. Even though it won't matter, you'll be happy to know that Lieutenant Johns added a sexual harassment complaint into his file, too. Lieutenant Johns made it clear that no one messes with one of his officers."

Lieutenant Johns support makes me happy. Turner was a thorn in my side but manageable. Angus was right--a cop like that would eventually get one of us killed, and prison was a good place for him.

***

Brian Edison shows up toward the end of our hospital stay. He came to see me, but there was no way Sean is leaving my side.

He looks uncomfortable as he shakes my hand and sneaks in a quick kiss on my cheek. "Detective Moore. You're looking better than I expected."

"Thanks. You can dispense with the Detective Moore. I'm off your case, and after everything that's happened, you can call me Jayne."

"Jayne and Agent Lindstrom, I just want to thank you for everything you did for my family. I'm still in shock that she's gone."

I manage to say, "I'm sorry for your loss."

Edison continues, "My mom had a safety deposit box. I found a stack of her journals going back to her years at the University of Washington. It explains so much about their acrimonious marriage. I think deep down, I always suspected he wasn't my father, but now I know he tried to do the right thing. My grandfather always pushed him away from me, and I guess I just got into the habit of doing the same thing. When I look back, I know he was trying to be a dad to me, and that counts for something."

Even though his mother was an absolute witch, I am still sorry for his loss but can't seem to come up with anything nice to say. Instead, I ask the burning question. "So what happens with your dad now?"

"He came over the day I got back and tried to explain everything. It was before I got my mom's journals so a lot of what he said was pretty hard to accept. When I read the journals, it all made sense. After all the things my grandfather and my mother did to him, I understand his bitterness. I'm trying to make it up to him. My mom's will cut him out of any money, but I gave him the money I inherited from her." He laughs. "That would be the money that was my money, to begin with. It's all good. And with the money that should have gone to my friends, I also started a foundation for teenagers struggling to pay for college."

My mind is reeling with all this information. I wonder if he has connected the dots that if he had given his friends the original money promised, so much of this wouldn't have happened. I decide to keep my mouth shut. Instead, I address the elephant in the room. "I have to admit, I was completely caught off guard that Sharon Gibbs was behind the plot to kill you."

I watch his face drain of color and he finally replies. "I don't think anyone was as shocked as me. The FBI told me she was a sociopath. Sharon was a little quirky at times and now that I look back on it, she did manipulate quite a few things. Once she got my mom off to France, she also, unbeknownst to me, set herself up as the Chief Financial Officer of my company and transferred millions to an offshore account. I'm lucky I was able to recover the money."

"She seemed so nice, and I honestly thought she was in love with you." I watch his face as he processes my comment.

"I guess I just didn't notice. I think that might have been what pushed her over the edge. I didn't ignore her but I didn't give her a lot of attention either. Probably the worst thing you can do with a sociopath."

I can sense his discomfort. He gets a sheepish look on his face and abruptly changes the subject. "You told me you weren't interested in being my head of security. Does that still stand?"

I nod and he continues. "I figured as much. Officer Turner was going to take the job, but I've been told there have been some unexpected career changes for him."

Leave it to Turner to lie about his reasons. I decide to speak freely. "Brian, it turned out for the best. Turner would have been a bad fit for you. Sean and I will see if we can come up with a few people that will be good for the job."

Sean says, "I know a lot of Iraq Vets who would love a chance to work for you. And you'll be in good hands."

Brian sighs and looks at me. "Guess you can't always get what you want. Too bad my mother didn't learn that lesson years ago." He turns his attention back to Sean. "Here's my card. Tell them to call me directly. I'll be happy to meet with any candidates you send."

We had nothing more to talk about, so I faked a yawn. "Oh, sorry. I'm still getting my strength back."

Edison takes the hint and stands up.

He laughs and adds, "I forgot to tell you the other big news. I'm selling my house, and as you suggested, I'm buying a McMansion on Lake Washington. Too many bad memories in that house and I want to start fresh."

"Please tell me that you are banning all things mauve in your new house," I say.

He chuckles as he walks out the door. "No more mauve hell, Detective. I promise."

**

Two hours later Sean comes into my room. "Come on. We're going on a date."

"What are you talking about?"

He's brought in the big guns. My BFF Madison is holding a pretty robe and some fancy slippers, and Michael is at her heels. I notice Sean has ditched the flimsy hospital robe for a black terry cloth with plaid pajamas. I start to giggle. "Last time the four of us were together, we ended up in a shootout. Do you really want to risk a repeat?"

Sean gives me a wicked grin. "You're worth the risk. Besides, there's no one else I'd rather be in a shootout with."

It's pretty weird that I have already fallen in love with a guy that I haven't even had a first date with, but I don't care. I realize now that life is full of uncertainties, and I can't think of anyone else I'd rather face them with than Sean Lindstrom.

"Come on, Boomer." Sean reaches for my hand. "I have a feeling we're going on one hell of a ride."

Chapter 42

"Wow. That was some first date. Think you'll want another one?" Sean's eyes crinkle at me, and of course, I melt.

"I'd say you got off pretty cheap on this date. Just wait until I'm cleared to eat solid food again. If you can keep up with my appetite, we'll see."

The truth is, I had a great date with Sean. Madison and Michael faded out of the picture as soon as they got us down to the cafeteria. Sean and I sat and talked for four straight hours. That we do basically the same thing for a living doesn't matter. There are so many other topics to discuss. Lucky for him, he's both a Mariner and a Seahawks fan. I couldn't be with a man who doesn't love my teams. We disagree on movies…he's more of a chick than me and defends all the romantic comedies his mom and sisters forced on him. I'm a sci-fi geek. At least we both absolutely hate cop or spy shows. Movies are supposed to let you escape reality, not remind you of it. I'd say we have some Netflix in our future.

Whenever I think of the future, I know Sean will be right there next to me. I can't believe how this all happened so fast, but I'm through questioning it. My fear of relationships is over, and for once, my heart is optimistic and open.

***

Dr. Smith walks in with a stern look on his face. They had run blood tests on me yesterday, and I didn't like his expression. "Nurse Watson says you've been a difficult patient."

What the heck? Did she rat me out? "I don't think I've been that bad."

"According to her, you talk nonstop about food, and she can never get you to stay in your room." A slight smile plays on his face. "You haven't been a very easy patient."

My face is turning red, and before I can open my mouth to defend myself, Nurse Watson waltzes into my room, a chocolate cupcake on a tray and a smile on her face.

"Detective Moore, while it has not always been a pleasure to be your nurse, it has been my honor to have you as a patient. Knowing that someone like you is watching over our city will help me sleep nights. You are the most stubborn woman I have ever met, but that just adds to your strength and personality. I have to admit, I will miss you."

My mouth can probably catch flies right now as it hangs open. Then, of course, the waterworks threaten to start up, as my eyes mist over. "Nurse Watson, thank you for your care and your diligence in watching over me." I see her chuckle at that comment. "No offense, but I hope our paths don't cross again anytime soon."

"Duly noted, Detective." She puts the cupcake on the tray in front of me. "Congratulations on being discharged."

Dr. Smith finally chimes in with the medical info. "Your blood work is good. We beat the infection, but I'm still going to keep you on antibiotics for another week. We'll also send you home with some pain pills. I want you to start physical therapy. You're going to need to rebuild a lot of abdominal muscles. Other than that, you're good to go."

I take a big bite out of my cupcake. I savor the taste of chocolate and swallow. "Thank you both for everything. Nurse Watson, you are one tough lady, and I know I owe a lot of my recovery to you. Thank you for kicking my butt when you needed to."

I think they both sense that I need a moment alone. I am trying to process what comes next. Home? I'm finally going home? Wait. What about Sean?

It takes me five minutes of debating with myself on what to do. I've heard of rushing things but I don't care. As I am getting out of bed to go to Sean's room, my parents come in.

"Jayne, we heard the good news. We're here to take you home." Dad pauses and takes my hand. "Okay, baby girl, why am I not seeing a big smile on your face. Have you developed a fondness for hospital food?"

"Dad. Mom. I want Sean to move in with me. Is it crazy to want that so fast?"

I look from his face to my mom's and back again. So far, the smiles remain intact.

"Jayne. You are a grown woman, and we are certainly not going to tell you how to live your life. Besides, we've already had a chat about this with Joanna, and we all agree it would be best for you two to be in the same place. We plan on taking turns on doing food and stuff. Your mom made up a schedule."

My mom looks positively sheepish. "Now honey, I know you don't like to be told what to do, but we figure you'd come to the same conclusion as the rest of us. You two belong together."

I couldn't help but laugh. Why is everything always so obvious to everyone but me? "I was only a few hours behind you on this one. Can you and Dad pack my stuff? I need to go see Sean."

I watch the two of them share a knowing look. I hope someday, if I have kids, I can be as smart as those two.

***

I walk down the hall to Sean's room, trying to think about how to broach the subject of living together. Sean looks up as I enter his room.

I jump right in. "Dr. Smith just told me I'm clear to go home. What have your doctors said?"

"They said probably in two days. Are you going to your place or your parents'?"

"My place." I decide to just go for it. "But I was wondering if you would like it to be our place?"

The look on his face is priceless. I swear I even see tears in his eyes. He gets out of bed and grabs me in one of his boa constrictor hugs.

"I thought you'd never ask. I was trying to figure out how to tell you I love you. I do, you know. I love you, and I can't imagine a day of waking up without you next to me."

Okay. Cue the waterworks.

"I love you, too, Sean Lindstrom. My only regret is we wasted so much time being a car salesman and a librarian. We have a lot of time to make up for."

Sean kisses me until my toes curl. Then he whispers, "And the rest of our life to do it."

EPILOGUE

Six Months Later

I dab at the tears in my eyes.

"Jayne. You've got to stop crying." My mom holds both of my hands and looks up at me.

"I can't help it. I never thought this would actually happen." I look at myself in the full-length mirror. A bride stares back at me. Simple. Elegant. Perfect. Everything is just perfect. I dry my happy tears.

"Honey, bend down a little, so I can help you with your veil."

My sisters say in unison. "We'll do it, Mom. We don't want her dress to wrinkle from bending so far over to reach you." They both giggle.

The room is full of giggling women.

Sean and I planned a very small wedding, but we ended up with a huge wedding party--Sean's three sisters, Julie, Anna, and Jackie; my two sisters, Amy, and Emily; friend Lily and neighbor Sheri; and, of course, my maid of honor, BFF Madison. According to my dad, the wedding party will outnumber the guests. Sean has his eight groomsmen; he calls them his squad--his best man, Michael; my partner Tom; neighbor Ice; Cousin Mark; and four of his Marine buddies, Austin, Conner, Steve, and Mike. The last four are now employed by Brian Edison.

There's a knock at the door. It's time. The girls all line up, just like we did in rehearsal, and we walk out the door. A handsome groomsman takes my mom's arm and escorts her to her front-row seat. My bridesmaids and maid of honor are ready to walk down the aisle. Three of the cutest little flower girls are giggling and have handfuls of rose petals to throw.

My dad takes my hand and kisses it. "I don't want to mess up your makeup." He laughs and then looks into my eyes. "It's not every day your baby girl gets married. Jayne, I have loved you like my own for your entire life. I know your mom and dad are smiling down on this day."

"I know. And I know they are so proud of you. You are the best dad I could ever have wished for. I love you. Thank you for my mom and my sisters." Tears are threatening again.

"You're welcome. Oh, by the way. You forgot something."

I panic and glance around me. "What? What did I forget?"

My dad laughs, squeezes my hand again, and says, "You forgot to tell me I was right. I told you that you would get your happily-ever-after."

I look up at him and then down the aisle at the man waiting for me. Sean's smile is just for me, and I can see happily-ever-after right in front of me. It might be bumpy with our two careers, but if I've learned anything, it's that some things are worth fighting for and Sean and I will be there for each other.

I step on my tiptoes and give my dad a kiss on the cheek. "What can I say? When you're right, you're right." And then, I take my first step toward the rest of my life.

THE END

From the Author:

Thank you to my husband Gary Arnold, and to family and friends who always support and encourage me in my writing. Your continued support means everything to me.

Thank you to my writing group: Mark Bowman, Ed Nichols, Kathleen Lawrence, Bart Bardeleben, and Dave Smith. Your critique of this book along the way helped immensely. I honestly couldn't have done it without you. It takes a village…

Sincere thanks to Diane and Steve Davis for their help with the cop talk. Thank you both for your years of service to your community. Diane, thank you for sharing your moniker "Dickless Tracy" with me. Terra and Jerry Vietzke, you inspired me to write Jayne's parents as loving and supportive and maybe just a little sarcastic! (The sarcastic was for you Jer!)

Thank you to my readers Kitty Burnett, Ro Burnham, Sally Deines, Suzan Berard, Julie Wasson, Val Walser and Lynne Milnor for your input and support. I appreciate you reading the multiple versions while this book transitioned to what it is.

Thank you to Christina Haines, my pretend daughter, and personal geek. You always figure out what buttons I've pushed that have blown up a page and fix it. Your help in creating the cover and formatting were invaluable!

A huge thank-you to my editor Janice Hussein. Your attention to detail and suggestions were spot on. Thank you for making this book so much better.

To all the people that buy this book and write a review, thank you. Your input is so appreciated and it keeps me inspired. Oh, and everyone, please, please, please write a review. Good or bad, it helps me to develop as a writer.

Other Books Available By This Author:

Historical fiction:
- "The Good Deed"
- "The Misdeed"

Romantic, Comedy, Thriller
- "Ice"

Made in United States
Orlando, FL
14 December 2021

11763932R00137